GROOMING LUCY

'I've been bad,' replied Kelly in a broken, barely audible sniffle.

'Yes, you have been. Tell me what you did,' said Lucy as she allowed her hand to slide a little further down on to the girl's skirt.

'Please Miss, I can't,' cried Kelly, her head bowing, her whole body racked with juddering sobs.

'I won't ask you again,' hissed Lucy, her left fist reclaiming the pigtail as her other hand swept down to the hemline of the skirt and raised it up easily. A quick twist and the hem was safely tucked into the waistband, and Kelly's magnificently tight young arse was free, with only the thin band of white cotton keeping her sex from view. Lucy placed her open palm on the downy warmth of the plump, tight cheeks, and sized up where to administer the first of the slaps as the confession began.

'Please Miss, it was him. He made me do it,' cried Kelly.

Lucy raised her palm to shoulder height, aimed carefully, and brought it down on the girl's left buttock with an echoing crack which frightened them both.

'That's what they all say!' Lucy shouted as she landed a second slap on the other cheek.

GROOMING LUCY

Yvonne Marshall

This book is a work of fiction.
In real life, make sure you practise safe sex.

First published in 2000 by
Nexus
Thames Wharf Studios
Rainville Road
London W6 9HA

www.nexus-books.co.uk

Typeset by TW Typesetting, Plymouth, Devon

Printed and bound by
Cox & Wyman Ltd, Reading, Berks

ISBN 0 352 33529 7

Prologue

Minami-san didn't know what age she was. Mid-sixties at least, maybe seventy at most. Her parents had died somewhere in the firestorm which raged through Tokyo under American bombing at the close of the war, and she had no memory whatsoever, either of them or the home she had fled.

Osaka had been her home ever since, and she had stayed in the same apartment for fifty years, a two-roomed mat-floored wooden house with – unusual for the city centre – generous gardens to front and rear.

She had been alone since her husband's passing some ten years previously. He had founded the Kirishima electronics company, and sold it just before his death – Minami-san would never have to worry about cash, and her only son was well-established in California.

Minami was waiting for death. It might be another twenty years, it might be tomorrow. It didn't matter to her. Not that she had no will to live – she took loving care of her garden, and still worked every day, but she had simply seen enough of the world, and would move on as and when her time came with no great regret.

In the small pool at the bottom of the rear garden, the fish circled endlessly, and she fed them every morning at dawn, sitting on the low wooden bench, watching as they weaved among one another, liquid bands of gold and bronze snouting the surface, the circling ripples disturbing the old, fat toad who always sat in the same cluster of reeds, watching her.

It was a cold morning. Autumn was peaking, and the chill of the morning told her that the coming winter would be harsh. No matter. The spring would, as always, be clear and mild, her favourite season.

She finished the plain breakfast of rice and pickles, then prayed awhile before the tiny shrine which was usually concealed behind one of the sliding panel doors in the twelve-by-twelve living room. The Buddha figure was solid gold, very small, and even now, after thirty or more years of daily meditation, she could not gaze upon it for long without finding some new aspect to it, some fresh arrangement of light and shade. In the reflections she saw her own past, faces and incidents from half a century ago melding with those of yesterday.

But sometimes, at moments she could neither predict nor control, Minami would see new faces, scenarios, and they would be just as clear as the memories. Sometimes these new faces would subsequently appear in the course of her work, or she would see them in the newspapers, or on a television screen. She didn't worry about these snippets of the future, because they seemed to her to be as natural as those from the past, but on this morning, with the cold air of the garden still fresh on her neck, and the light tinkling of the wind chimes at the window indicating a stiffening breeze, she saw three, four faces in quick succession, and they were all foreigners.

Minami had met very few foreigners in her life. She did not purposely avoid them, but they frightened and unsettled her with their strange manners, their loud voices and jerky, brash movements.

The faces she saw, although blue-hazed and distant, were sad and full of confusion: a young woman, beautiful, with the eyes of a mountain deer, long dark hair and a smile, slightly crooked, which seemed loaded with melancholy; two young men, one taller, both dark-haired, the smaller of the two stocky, with pale blue eyes which made her spine feel cold; and an older man, very tall and with a mass of bright white hair, eyes grey.

And, about them all, the almost palpable aura of wealth and power. So much power, so much wealth, and so much sadness.

Minami-san closed the shrine and headed to work. The forty-minute walk was becoming more arduous, but she hated the overcrowding of the subway and insolent jostling of the school-bound young on the bus.

Inside the restaurant, the cleaners were drinking tea, their work completed. They all said good morning to Minami, and she smiled and bowed to them and went downstairs. The lock was becoming stiff, and she made a mental note to have it oiled later.

The girls were also finishing their breakfast, and rose when Minami entered. She knelt on her cushion, and tea was poured for her. She took a tiny wafer from the plate and snapped it in two, then listened as Naomi, her head girl, related her report of the night's work – five clients, three of whom had left before dawn. All regulars. Yamamoto and Izumi were still in their rooms. Minami nodded. A normal night.

The girls excused themselves and left to change, and Minami heard them chatter low, giggling with the girls who had just arrived for the day shift.

Minami finished her tea, ate another small wafer, then prepared to check on the clients. She put on her white, thick socks, and pulled the thin grey kimono on over her clothes, then took her birch-rod from its hook, and checked first on Yamamoto.

The handwritten docket on the frame of the door stated that he had arrived at three-thirty that morning. Minami could imagine him staggering in, aflop with drink and fatigue. She had never understood why these silly men insisted on drinking themselves to death. Her husband had done it. Yamamoto was in his early fifties, but looked older. He was a typical customer – the head of a publishing firm, he was moderately wealthy, well-regarded by his peers, and nurtured political ambitions. But he was, like all the others, little more than a child, and came here to be treated like one.

She went in, and he was there, as usual, on all fours, his ankles and wrists bound with the finger-thick rough white rope, staring at the edging of the mat below him. He

3

always wore his thick spectacles, but otherwise he was completely naked.

He did not register her entrance, nor did she greet him in any way. She shuffled across the mats, checked the knots visible between his ankles and wrists. The ropework at the ankles was a little shoddy. It was probably Tomoko – she still wasn't good at finishing them off properly – Naomi would have to reprimand her.

A series of circular stains on the rug below Yamamoto indicated that he had lost control at some point. Perhaps the girls had overdone it, and it was clear from the raised welts on the man's buttocks and back that he had indeed been severely flogged. His scrotum, which had been pulled up between his arse cheeks, was swollen and almost purple.

Minami moved in front of the man and tapped the right side of his face with the fine, pencil-thick end of the rod. He bowed his head, touching his forehead to the mat. She moved beside him, a yard away, her feet together, and picked the spot. She would be careful not to touch his testes, as they had already received enough attention, and several of the more prominent welts were also to be avoided; fresh pain would not register on damaged flesh.

She touched the rod-tip to his knee, and he immediately shufffled his legs back, straining himself as far upright as the tight bindings would allow. There was a band of white, unscathed skin which straddled both thighs, just above the rope which bound his knees. That would do.

She raised the birch and waited. He drew in his breath, and she watched the muscles on his back tense and solidify in readiness for the blow. Somewhere in the garden to the rear of the house, a bird was singing.

The finely grained hardwood cracked across his skin with the sound of a snapping branch, and he emitted a howl which, although little louder than a squeal, seemed to be coming from his very pores. His body began to shake violently, as it always did, and Minami moved quietly from the room, carefully closing the door behind her. The new shift would get him bathed and dressed, and he would head off, hobbling slightly, for his office.

4

She had just checked the docket for Izumi, and was about to slide the door open when the faces came back, appearing on the thick paper screen in front of her like ghosts.

Minami shivered. The faces merged and warped, became one, then shifted again and it was the face of the girl she could see again, the sad, dark eyes, the half-smile. Seldom was she given names for the faces, but a name came now, clear and insistent, echoing about her mind as the image became clearer, the colours more natural, the smell and texture of the woman's hair within reach, and the name repeating itself, in a man's voice.

She formed her tongue to repeat the sound she was hearing, and it was a strange name, awkward, but as clear as if it were being said directly into her ear.

'Loo-see,' said Minami quietly. 'Loo-see,' she said again, acquainting herself with the sound and feel of the name.

The image disappeared, the voice faded. Minami committed the sound of the name to memory, then dismissed it from her thoughts and got on with her work.

One

Lucy checked her lipstick one last time. It was cleanly applied, the darkness of the plum colour sharp against her lightly foundationed complexion. Just a little bit heavy with the eye make-up, and a slight tousle to her shoulder-length auburn hair.

In the dimness of the basement car park, her natural colouring was diffused, replaced by a mannequinish plasticity which always unnerved her – it was like looking at someone else's eyes, someone else's face.

She got out of the car. The coolness of the autumn air smarted her thighs beneath the knee-length rubber coat. She raised the collar slightly, for all the good it would do on the fifty-yard walk to the elevator. The hold-up stockings were requisite, if impractical. Her heels echoed about the vast, low-ceilinged cement oblong. An expensive car door slammed somewhere far behind her, but she didn't look over her shoulder. No point.

Coming here virtually naked beneath her coat was par for the course of late. If she ended up raped, she could almost imagine the defence case, the slavering acquiescence of the judge, her public shaming as a prick-teaser.

She punched the 'up' button and waited, studying her reflection in the slightly warped steel doors. The distortion made her appear taller than her five foot six, and she briefly enjoyed the sensation of seeing herself in super-model mode – with a slight movement of her hips, and by pointing her right leg forward just so, she could half close

6

her eyes and imagine herself with legs to grace any catwalk. Stocking-sheathed, foot absurdly arched to show the fineness of her ankle, the reflection was the outline of a designer's sketch. The rubber coat was a favourite, and she was pleased with its deceptively flounced appearance on the steel mirror. He was in for a treat.

A shuffle behind, still distant, but close enough to make her start and turn. The car park was always eerie: too many vehicles, not enough people, as if perhaps the cars themselves were watching her. Maybe it was a cat, or even a fox. It wasn't unknown for them to make their way this far into London. But no sign of any movement, no shadows disturbing those already cast by the neatly lined-up vehicles under the ugly tangerine lighting.

Despite her self-assurance, the sudden clanking grind of the elevator still gave her something of a fright, and she shifted quickly inside when the shutters did part. The stark blue lighting within the box did nothing to dispel her tartish appearance, and she used the fifty-second ascent to quickly smooth a line of make-up at her jaw. But the make-up couldn't disguise the fact that she was tired – dog-tired.

Bloody work, non-stop, and even when you thought you'd finished, you found that you'd really just started another shift. Swapping one outfit for another, day-in, day-out, until it got to the point when you had to check you were wearing the right one at the right time. But she knew this was the right one. She bowed her head before her, shook her hair out lightly, then threw it back to fall upon her shoulders the way she knew it would – dishevelled, as if she'd just emerged from a windswept walk in the park. She pouted, blew herself a half-hearted, exaggeratedly sexy kiss into the mirror, then frowned. Perhaps it would do it for him. Then again, it might not. Problem was, Lucy knew she was getting to the point where she really didn't care much either way.

It was pleasant enough for the first hour or so. The meal had been superb, if perfunctory. No messing about with starters and sweets, no lingering looks over the single fat candle flickering in the centre of the glass-topped round table by the windowed wall.

The food was Thai, fine and hot and, usually, satisfying, but she fiddled with it, chewing carefully and swallowing reluctantly. He'd offered small-talk, mostly to do with his work, but Lucy had felt her gaze drawn to the cityscape's horizon, where darkness and streetlights fought with each other, where she imagined quiet places to be. And he'd laughed at some work-related incident and asked her how her own business was going. As if he gave a shit. She just wanted to get it over with, and was pleased when he suggested that she make herself comfortable while he visited the boys' room. Even that one, infuriatingly juvenile phrase was almost enough to send her back to the car park. She watched the distant throb of red lights as a plane made a slow ascent far to the south, and decided not to leave just yet. Perhaps, just perhaps, she could get some pleasure from it.

Lucy was sitting, legs crossed, on the sofa when he came back in. He had untucked his shirt and wet his hair. At least some of that gel had been rinsed out. The slacks looked new, but he'd obviously been wearing them that day and hadn't bothered to change for her. The shirt, likewise, showed signs of having had a tie aboard at one point, but that had also been ditched in an effort to make him more casual. Lucy slowed the sigh by way of concealment: why didn't men realise how obvious they were, how bloody predictable? Now he'd probably put on some sexy music and offer her a refill before sitting beside her. She watched him as he crossed to the hi-fi, and waited for her prediction to become reality.

But it didn't.

He strolled back towards her as he used the remote to flick on the widescreen.

'Thought you might like to see this,' he said, and she felt a shiver of apprehension.

'If it's what I think it is, I doubt it,' she said, and she knew there was enough annoyance in her voice to forewarn him.

He sat along from her on the broad-based sofa, arched his arm behind the back, his fingers inches from her left shoulder. Lucy slowly, but deliberately, crossed her arms. This was just spinning it all out, making it more of an ordeal than it had to be. Unless, of course, he needed it. That would explain a lot. He needed the visuals to get him going. The screen continued to flicker annoyingly, and he repeatedly thumbed the button to bring the scene he wanted.

'If you look really closely, I think you might see someone you know,' he said, and Lucy's heart skipped a beat. She hadn't had anywhere near enough wine to blur her senses, but, when he said that, the images onscreen seemed to fuse into an anonymous blob of shifting pinkness. Was she supposed to be in there? If so, when, where, and with whom? She sat forward and silently cursed herself for ditching the contact lenses that morning.

The soundtrack was muted and unhelpful, a predictable sequence of gasps, grunts and throaty exhortations. Lucy leaned forward and squinted, aware that he was quietly sniggering beside her.

'Well?' he asked as he reached forward for his glass.

Lucy sat back as the configuration of the dark and light-skinned flesh became clearer, and she could make out the limbs, the sides of faces – a manic jerk of the hand-held camera brought a fuzzy close-up, then sharpened to the features of a man she knew. Martin.

Lucy slumped back in the sofa, closed her eyes, and raised an open palm to Don.

'Turn it off,' she said, quietly but firmly.

Don laughed.

'What ?! Come on Luce, it's only a bit of fun. Old Martin thought he'd impress the lads with his Jamaica exploits, only he didn't know we managed to get a copy of it when he crashed out. Come on!'

Lucy stood up, and watched as Don deliberately forwarded the tape to the point where Martin found noisy relief at the hands of the larger of the two girls present, the image shaking and shifting in tandem with the man's ever-deepening and lengthening grunts.

'And you thought you'd impress me with this?' Lucy asked, her eyes riveted on the screen as the tumbling confusion of images suddenly became more controlled, steady, and soon Martin, poor old office buffoon Martin, was being captured in all his corpulent glory, half-smashed across an unmade and not-very-clean bed, one of the girls laughing and grimacing at the camera as her giggling friend experimented with the focus, closing in now on Martin's podgy, bliss-ridden face, then his wilting, leaking cock.

She looked down at Don. His gaze was somewhere between the table-top and the screen, and she realised that he was watching the reflection of it all on the coffee table, surreptitiously relishing every moment.

'I'll bet you've tossed off to this, haven't you?' Lucy asked, and Don's eyes flashed angrily to meet hers.

'I was only trying to spice things up a little. It's a bit different isn't it?' he retorted, but the colour on his cheeks betrayed his embarrassment.

'Yes, it's different all right,' Lucy replied as she crossed to the alcove beside the kitchen and unhitched her coat from the hook, 'different enough that I can't stand staying under the same roof as you tonight. I'm going to Phillipa's. Call me when you grow up. If you ever do.'

They'd already been married for almost five years. It was close to collapse, and she knew it, and knew that he knew it too. In his own way, he was trying, but his efforts were so typically laddish, so predictable, so very Don. The set-up of her as tart had worked years ago, when they'd been engaged. His family had been particularly insistent that co-habitation was not an option until she had a ring on her finger, so they'd enjoyed the enforced postponement of living together by enacting such scenarios. It had always been pretty much the same: Don would call her, pretending to be a client, and Lucy would fit him in – if she could – take his instructions, then follow them to the letter. It had been fun. Had been.

The two-mile drive to Phillipa's flat became twenty, then thirty minutes. It seemed impossible that there could still be so much traffic at ten on a Thursday evening, but Lucy knew that it probably wasn't any heavier than usual. It just felt worse.

It was like everything lately – work was going so well that she really didn't need to be in the office every day, and how those days dragged. Seemingly interminable meetings to update her on the progress and success she already knew about; endless lunches with bores who always insisted on paying, desperate to impress, ingratiate. And even at home, the hours seemed to heave from one to the next with glacial grimness. And she knew why. She knew exactly why, but had no one to talk to about it.

She checked herself briefly in the mirror at the next set of reds. WORKS AHEAD. EXPECT DELAYS. Phillipa would be ready to go out, as she always did on Thursdays. The Hellhole. Lucy had only ever been there the once, and had thoroughly hated every minute of it. The masks, the absurdness of the posturing, the whole debauchery of it was nauseating. And that, to Phillipa, was it's attraction: the perfectly groomed television presenter by day, demure and conservative in dress and tone, could become a wanton vamp by night.

The snaking line of taillights wound as far as Lucy could see. Her thoughts turned to the business. Perhaps it was time for a break. She had managed, through seven years of fourteen-hour days, to assemble a workforce second to none. The recruitment agency had snowballed as soon as she opened the first offices outside the capital, and since the move to the European capitals three years ago, it seemed to have developed a momentum and power which needed little more than careful monitoring. She had recently employed the services of a third accountancy firm, solely to examine the practices of the other two. Money had become more meaningless than ever. She could float the company now, walk out with somewhere between ten and fifteen million, and never ever have to work again. But she knew she couldn't – then, with nothing to occupy her days, the awful chasm which had widened and deepened between her and Don would be her only focus, and she knew she couldn't bear it.

11

She flipped the CD player on, mad that she'd allowed her thoughts to return to the problem, to him. Yes, she loved him. There couldn't be any doubt about it, otherwise she would have been long gone by now. He'd given her so many reasons, so many times.

He still hadn't given up his 'others' as he called them – the girls he used to satisfy those urges he considered too base, too primitive for Lucy to be subjected to. He'd always been open about it, and it hadn't always been the bugbear that it had now become. Lucy had, as a twenty-year-old, been impressed and somewhat awed by what she consider-ed his sophisticated sexual tastes – she'd often quizzed him on what exactly happened during the expensive sessions with the 'others', but his unease had always stopped her digging too deeply. He needed it, was all he would say. He needed it to maintain an even keel, a balanced outlook. Martin, his long-suffering deputy, had once confided to Lucy that Don was certainly specific enough in his requirements of the 'others', and that those specifics were really not for discussion in polite company. Lucy had plied him with more of the single malt he preferred, and eventually wrung some of the more impolite details from him: Don was, it seemed, well known to several of the more illustrious escort agencies, and was indeed a valued cus-tomer. He liked them young, and he liked them submissive – the more submissive, the better, and the better, the more expensive. But money wasn't really an obstacle – the hefty hospitality expense account operated by Martin ensured that Don, Martin himself, and several other senior man-agers could indulge their preferences on a fairly regular basis, especially if it could be arranged that favoured clients or potential partners would also benefit.

A distant set of lights beamed green. At last.

Phillipa was as welcoming as ever, but seemed strangely agitated, almost frantic with excitement.

'Wait till you hear this,' she gushed as she virtually dragged Lucy through the door into her typically untidy lounge.

'Trevor's lined up to take that new chat show, and guess who's a shoe-in for the nine o'clock?' she said in one breath.

Lucy stared blankly at her friend. Phillipa's eyes were wide and waiting.

'You?' Lucy said, plainly underawed.

Phillipa's face assumed an expression of wounded exasperation.

'Yes. Me. Yours truly. Well?' Phillipa said, as she sarcastically waved her fingers in front of Lucy's eyes to check if anyone was at home.

'That's great news. It really is. I'm sorry. I'm a bit fazed right now. Any chance of a drink?' Lucy replied, and she could hear the fatigue in her own voice.

Phillipa's shoulders slumped, she closed her eyes, shook her head, then clasped Lucy close and cuddled her.

'Oh God, I'm so sorry, darling. Here you are, not even in the door, and I'm boring you with the latest instalment of my wonderful life. Come on, let's have a good stiff one.'

Phillipa beckoned Lucy to the sofa in front of the imitation coal fire, turned up the heat so that the blue flames licked higher about the everlasting logs, then heaved a pile of magazines and newspapers off the sofa with one smooth movement and bid Lucy sit.

'Spill it then,' Phillipa called over from the section of the bookcase which held the drinks.

Lucy unbuckled her coat and slipped it off, allowing it to lie behind her. She arched her neck back as far as was comfortable, then twisted it sharply. She could feel the tension snap in her tendons, the familiar dull ache of stress washing down through her neck and across her shoulders.

'What can I tell you?' Lucy thought out loud.

'Don?' asked Phillipa as she returned with a three-quarters full bottle of tequila and two shot glasses.

Lucy nodded wearily as she watched Phillipa sweep the remining detritus from the other side of the two-seater. She looked fantastic, even though she hadn't yet changed for her weekly trip to The Hellhole. Lucy always wondered why Phillipa felt she had to be clad in leather and rubber to feel 'dressed'. What she wore for work was, as far as Lucy was concerned, ever so much more attractive if only because it was so understated, so clean. The burgundy crushed velvet two-piece was not the type of outfit the trendy twenty-somethings of the city were wearing that season – if anything, it would be more commonly seen on a forty- or fifty-year-old. The length of the skirt alone gave the game away as far as fashion-awareness was concerned – Lucy knew from experience that the tight-waisted skirt concealed taut, finely muscled thighs, but Phillipa never showed them off at work. She was happier to stick with the calf-length concealment which, she maintained, gave the 'old grey-heads' so much more to think about. And her dark hair was still puffed and set as it would have been for that day's broadcasts, expertly coiffured so many times per hour, her make-up now gone to show the natural sallowness of her partly Mediterranean complexion. Even her lipstick, usually ruby, was barely detectable now.

Lucy was aware of her mind wandering yet again as Phillipa slid the little glass towards her along the low walnut table.

'Go on then. That'll help.' Phillipa smiled as she raised her own glass and waited.

Lucy sat forward, raised the little blue-tinted receptacle, and allowed the flames of the fire to dance through the liquid before her.

'Cheers,' said Lucy.

'Bottoms up, dear,' replied Phillipa, and the two threw the shots down in silence.

The dull throb of dance music pulsed through from the bedroom. Phillipa must have been just about to get ready. It wasn't fair to disrupt her evening like this. On the other hand, Lucy really couldn't face The Hellhole. Not tonight. It would be worth it if she knew there might be a chance to get a proper chat with Phillipa, but once inside the club the whole prospect of conversation with anyone was a non-starter.

'Phillipa,' Lucy said, and she felt herself uncharacteristically hesitant with her friend. 'You'd tell me something honestly wouldn't you?'

14

Phillipa nodded gravely, frowning as she replenished the glasses, then looked up to catch Lucy's eye.

Lucy summoned the tiniest of smiles as she put the question, but made sure she maintained eye contact as she delivered it.

'Do I look like a tart?' Lucy asked.

There was a three-second silence during which Lucy's guts flipped – Phillipa's expression was grim, unmoving as she looked deep into Lucy's eyes. And then her eyes moved to Lucy's neck, bare, the sheer neckline of the cream thin silk blouse and the merest suggestion of cleavage it allowed, down further to Lucy's leather mini-skirt beneath which the lower rims of the dark lace hold-up hems were only just visible, then further down her crossed legs to the stab-point stilletos.

'You look fucking brilliant darling,' Phillipa replied quietly, her expression still serious, her voice low, quavering.

'I don't mean, do I look –' Lucy tried, too late, to rephrase the question, but when Phillipa's eyes came back to meet hers she knew she'd given the wrong signal altogether.

'What do you want me to tell you, Lucy?' Phillipa said, lifting the second glass to her lips, peering at Lucy as she pouted her lips carefully to the rim.

'I just don't know what I'm . . . I don't know why it's so fucking difficult to –' Lucy allowed her head to flop back on the sofa. It just wasn't working. It seemed impossible to crystallise her feelings into easily communicable sentences. Phillipa was waiting, and Lucy was suddenly aware of her friend's breathing.

Lucy picked up her own glass and threw the tequila down her throat, then returned the glass silently to the table-top, all in one swift, smooth movement. The drink burned its way down her chest. She closed her eyes and heard Phillipa down her measure.

'He doesn't know what he's got, the bastard,' Lucy heard Phillipa say, 'and he never has. I've never been one to say I told you so, but Jesus, Lucy, you must have known this might happen. The guy's a shit. OK, drop-dead gorgeous, I'll grant you that. But there is one overriding priority in Don Langford's life, and that is, Don Langford. You always knew that.'

Lucy nodded, eyes still shut.

'Yeah. You're right. I know you're right. But it should be so simple. I mean, I love him, I still fancy him to bits. He would be a great dad. I just wish he would realise that I, if he would only just open his eyes and see that I –' Lucy stopped, snapped her eyes open, and reached for the tequila bottle.

'When was the last time you two had a decent fuck?' asked Phillipa, and Lucy felt a spark of annoyance at the crudeness of the enquiry, annoyance which must have registered in her eyes as she glanced at her friend.

'Excuse me for asking,' Phillipa continued, 'but I think it's pretty relevant. Well?'

'Relevant, maybe,' replied Lucy as she topped up the two tiny glasses, 'but it depends on how you define "decent". If you're talking about a candlelit squirm in front of the fire, three, maybe four months ago. If you're talking about a ten-minute blow job followed by a half-hearted emptying over my back, the weekend. Of course, if you want to talk about the last time I've had a decent orgasm, try about three months ago, and then again, if you want to talk about his last decent orgasm, try last night, or maybe this afternoon. I don't know. You'd really have to ask him.'

Phillipa declined the glass Lucy raised to her, and leaned forward to gently restrain Lucy from lifting hers.

'Come here,' Phillipa said, and Lucy recoiled slightly as Phillipa's fingers slid behind her head, gently gripping the hair at the nape of her neck.

Lucy closed her eyes, and felt her breath suspend as her friend shifted across, and suddenly Phillipa's voice was close, soft but stern in her ear.

'You need to be fucked young lady. That's why you're here isn't it?' Phillipa whispered harshly.

Lucy's thighs tightened instinctively as Phillipa's other palm fell upon her thigh, gently squeezing as she leaned further across and took Lucy's earlobe between her teeth, nipping hard before the fingers twisted tighter and turned Lucy's face towards her.

'Don't tell me you don't want it, darling,' gasped Phillipa. 'You always did, you still do. That man doesn't have a clue what you need. Sometimes I wonder if even you do.'

And then Phillipa had Lucy's lips, biting with a ferocity which made her wince. It was madness, but already Lucy could feel herself wilting as Phillipa's tongue flicked at her own tongue-tip, teasing her lips further open as she forced herself closer, bringing them both further down into the soft sofa, her hand smoothing a path between Lucy's firmly clasped thighs.

'Remember the last time?' Phillipa breathed before resuming her assault. 'Remember the Lakes?'

As Phillipa kissed, Lucy opened herself more fully to her friend's attentions, relaxing her mouth fully to allow Phillipa the depth she sought, slipping her leg slightly away from the other so that the keenly massaging fingers might find warmer, higher access. And the memory of the Lakeside rendezvous did flash back now, as Lucy raised her own fingers into Phillipa's hair and pulled her closer: that night, only three months back, when Phillipa had ravished her fully for the first time. There had been drunken kisses throughout their ten-year friendship, but nothing as extreme as that night, when Phillipa had subjected her to the most painful, memorable orgasm she'd ever known. And yes, Lucy realised now, as she slipped fully back on the sofa to allow Phillipa to move her body atop hers, yes it had been wonderful, and Don hadn't even come close in the months since.

And now, on her home patch, Phillipa was, if anything, even rougher. It wasn't just the things she was saying; it was her whole manner, the sheer energy of the assault which astonished Lucy. Within minutes, Phillipa had removed Lucy's blouse, hitched the skirt up about her waist, and was kneeling on the carpet before Lucy, licking at her thighs, pulling up her stockings as far as they would go to better frame Lucy's exposed pussy. Lucy was powerless to resist, and was thankful for the constant stream of instructions, for without them she wouldn't have known what to do.

'Get your fingers in my hair and pull my fucking tongue right up you as far as you can,' Phillipa rasped before burying her face between Lucy's thighs. Lucy did as she was told, found a good grip in Phillipa's slightly sticky hairsprayed locks, and bucked her sex further up. A spontaneous orgasm was maddeningly close, and she could feel the hot tip of Phillipa's tongue stabbing at her pulsing clitoris. But her legs weren't parted enough to allow proper contact. Lucy shifted herself forward on the sofa so that her buttocks were off the edge of the thick leather cushion, then used one hand to raise and pull her left leg back as far as she could. Phillipa brought both hands to bear upon Lucy's sex, using her thumbs to flick at Lucy's puffed labia as her tongue now found freedom to roam over the distended, pinkened flesh, flicking at her unhooding clit before rasping the underside of her tongue down the glistening crack of Lucy's sex.

'This is just for starters, you little slut,' said Phillipa, and Lucy remembered the fierce fucking Phillipa had given her that last time, first with her tongue, then her fingers, and finally, with that rubber dick. It wasn't why she had come here this evening, but she knew now she couldn't, and wouldn't, stop it.

Phillipa was almost frantic with lust, her face pushing into Lucy as if her life depended on it. Lucy could feel the stirrings of her first come as her friend's tongue probed, slow, deep and strong, each stab of the tongue accompanied by a muffled grunt of intent. Lucy heard herself whimper.

'Please, Phillipa, please,' Lucy begged, and immediately, Phillipa raised herself between Lucy's parted thighs, leaned further forward and thrust her tongue into Lucy's mouth.

'Taste that darling,' she growled, lapping Lucy's lips and tongue with saltiness. 'Taste that and tell me that's not the taste of a woman who needs to be well and truly fucked. Go on. Tell me that's not what you want.'

Lucy's breathing quickened and became a succession of gasps as she tried to mouth a reply. She could taste the sweet bitterness of her own sex upon her lips, feel the coolness of the air upon her sex where Phillipa's mouth had just been.

'Oh yeah, I do, I do need it, I do,' Lucy managed to say before Phillipa's fingers stopped her begging further. And now, the restrained rhythm of Phillipa's tongue was replaced by a drumming beat upon Lucy's sex as two, maybe three fingers started to pound in and out, Phillipa's lips closed about Lucy's right nipple and suddenly, with dam-bursting power, the first orgasm came through Phillipa's fingers, pulsing across Lucy's midriff and knocking her breathless and she bucked and writhed against her friend's stabbing digits, her torso shifting further off the edge of the sofa as the climax neared, her pussy muscles spasming about her friend's fucking fingers. Lucy knew she was squealing, but her own noises, and Phillipa's exhortations, sounded distant and muted, as if it was all happening in another room.

'Oh yes, that's it, you push that pussy, Lucy, push it darling, then it's my turn, and you are going to fuck me just the same, aren't you? Aren't you!' Phillipa was shouting.

Lucy knew she was trying to say yes, trying to nod, trying somehow to confirm that she would indeed do as she was told, and perform the duty with relish. But the come was too strong to allow speech, and all she could do was cry out in ecstasy as the waves peaked, and her first orgasm in months crashed over her. She reached down, feeling for Phillipa's forearm, gripped it with a strength which made the girl shriek, and fucked herself harder on to the wet digits, the better to tease out the last throes of the climax.

Two

Don tried to keep his voice down. The girls would surely be able to hear him, but he was past worrying about sparing some tart's feelings.

'I specifically asked for Colette, didn't I?' he said slowly, weighting each word with the note of menace he kept for particularly awkward conversations.

The madame offered a perfectly reasonable explanation which involved prior bookings, due notice, and a junior Home Office minister. Don held the receiver away from him, quelling the urge to tell the old bag where to go. The agency had always been good to him, provided excellent girls at very short notice whenever they could. He knew it was just his temper getting the better of him again.

'Look, I know it wasn't arranged, but next time I'd be very grateful if you could at least send me another brunette.' He hung up.

Going to the bathroom, he paused at the door of the lounge, and checked what they were up to. The strawberry blonde, Pammy, was lying back on the sofa, dangling her sandals from her toes, allowing them to swing against her soles as she stared up at the ceiling. She was truly lovely. Maybe nineteen, angelic face, but a desperately dirty little thing when she got going. He still wasn't too happy about the other, who was shielding her eyes as she stood at the window, perhaps trying to figure out what the dark landscape held. She was in her mid-twenties, perhaps the same age as Don.

In all the time he'd been with the agency, he'd never ever entertained any girl who looked more than twenty. They should have known better than to send this one. She was certainly attractive enough, with beautifully plump breasts and a flawless arse. But she was also blonde, and not even natural. He hated that peroxide look.

He showered quickly, but didn't bother to shave the light stubble. He'd shaved at lunchtime. Pammy liked the feel of his stubble, or so she said. Not that he was concerned with her pleasure. She'd been here, and at the office, often enough by now to know what to expect, and he half hoped that she hadn't told the other one. It would be more fun.

Don had already looked out the paddle and crop before the girls had arrived. As soon as Lucy had left, he'd known he would have to call. The rage was subsiding now, but it wouldn't take long to resurface once he got started, and he knew it. Pammy would, as usual, take the brunt of it, but there would be more than enough for her friend. He suspended his breathing and listened carefully. The girls were silent, waiting for him.

With the cotton Japanese robe tied lightly about him, he was ready. Pammy had moved to the sofa where, only an hour ago, Lucy had been sitting. The older girl was smoking, her blouse carefully puckered, and Don was pleased to see a shock of red lace enclosing a glimpse of bronzed breast. He managed to conceal his interest as he walked slowly over to where she stood eyeing him warily.

'Put that out,' he said, his hands in the spacious pockets of the robe.

She looked at him without expression, slowly exhaling a fuzzy column of blue smoke. She glanced over at Pammy, who arched her eyebrows and nodded that it would be a good idea. The girl moved slowly, carefully across the thick carpet towards the ashtray on the mantelpiece. Her sling-backs were not the most practical footwear given the surroundings, but she carried off the move with as much grace as could be expected. Don moved behind her as she carefully extinguished the cigarette in the heavy glass bowl.

Don knew that the girl could see him approach her in the glass of the framed De Kooning sketch. He paused as he neared her, and glanced across to Pammy, who now had her finger on her bottom lip in true Lolita mode, and was smiling as much in challenge as curiosity. Pammy already knew pretty much what she was in for, but she must be wondering what would be in store for this newcomer. She would be waiting to see what Don would do.

He took another step forward. The girl was motionless, both palms now lightly grasping the high edge of the black stone fireplace. Don measured her up. She was about five-ten in the heels, and pretty solid of frame. She had the sort of body which women find difficult to keep in shape, so it was a fair bet she was fit. Her legs were long, her calves slender but visibly strong. She had broad hips beneath the lightly sequined dark-blue dress, and although her waist was remarkably pinched, the backless outfit diplayed an upper body which was certainly well toned. She had the look of an athlete. Don stepped the final pace and placed his hands lightly on her hips. He felt her breath stop, and he peered over her shoulder to find that she was indeed looking at him in the reflection.

'Let's get one thing very clear before we start,' said Don, almost in a whisper, but loud enough that he knew Pammy would hear, 'All I want is for you to do exactly what I tell you, when I tell you. If you do, I'll be happy, your boss will be happy, and you'll be happy. If you don't, no one will be happy. If you understand me, nod your head.'

The girl maintained his stare in the reflection, but did not move. Don moved his arms forward and raised his palms in front of her, slowly locating the dramatic, almost perpendicular plunge of her supported breasts. He felt her breathe in, and her chest rose, as if moving away from his grasp. He cupped her gently, easing his index fingers up and across to locate the stiffening buds through the cool cotton material. Her nipples were high on her breasts, and he suspected that she may have had implants; they were certainly heavy enough. She exhaled slowly, and when she breathed in again he caught the faintest waver in the flow of air.

'If you don't want to stay, you don't have to,' said Don, and now her nipples had strained enough for him to locate both with ease. She lowered her face, but maintained eye contact as Don gently gripped her nipples between thumbs and forefingers.

'If you want to stay, all you have to do is nod,' he said as he moved his head closer to hers, shifting his legs closer too so that their bodies were now touching. He detected a virtually imperceptible twitching of her arse as she breathed out again, and he tightened his grip on the now prominent nipples. She gasped. He squeezed harder, maintaining a steadily growing pressure. She had to be feeling that.

And then, with a pained gasp, she nodded rapidly, then slumped. Don grasped her body and pulled her close, turning her on her heels and spinning her to face him. She released a long, low groan. Don covered the fact that he was impressed by allowing her to slide down his body. She raised trembling palms to her chest as he stepped away.

'Have a seat, my dear,' he said then, and the girl raised herself slowly, still clearly getting over what must have been more painful than Don had realised.

Don indicated that she should sit beside Pammy, and she did so as he located the remote control and switched on the telly.

'Right ladies, I'm going to play you a little film. It's an appetiser I suppose. Pammy, you know the score by now my dear, so you can keep your friend right. Just make sure I don't have to interrupt anything when I get back. It's only twenty minutes. That should be manageable, I think.'

Don flicked the tape on, then stepped away. As if it were an afterthought, he paused at the door, came back in.

'Oh. I almost forgot. What's your name?' he said. The older girl stared at Don, and for a moment he thought he saw real hatred in the perfectly made-up dark-brown eyes.

'Joanne,' she said.

'Joanne,' Don said slowly, then again, as if tasting a wine. 'No. Em, Jemma. That's better. Pammy and Jemma. Yes. I like that. I'll be back in a tick. And remember,

23

ladies. Not a movement. You watch, and you listen, but you don't dare move, not even an inch. And don't forget. I'll be watching.'

Don turned away, and managed to conceal the smile until he reached the kitchen. Poor old Martin would be quite a celebrity at this rate.

He left the light off. The control pad for the cameras was behind a stainless steel panel above the extractor fan. Even in the three years since he'd bought this place, Lucy had never found it. Or not as far as he knew anyway. It excited him to think that Lucy may indeed know about the recordings he had of them. She wouldn't like it, that much he knew, but it was a thought anyway. She just didn't understand, never would. He needed this.

Quickly he checked the three tiny screens. All on, all clear. The material would be digitally stored. Tomorrow, before leaving for work, he would remove the filmdisc. It would be downloaded on to the master files in the office. He'd lost count of how many hours there were now.

Lately, he'd taken to editing the footage himself, co-ordinating the scenes to highlight favoured passages. There were so many favourites now. Pammy featured in many of the latest. She was quite expert at deep throat, and he'd even gone to the extent of setting up an additional camera inside the mantelpiece base, and that had yielded some superb footage of her bringing him off with mouth alone, hands tied behind her back. His cock pulsed at the fleeting image of her blonde curls merging with his trimmed pubes as her lips expanded over the base of him, straining ever wider in a futile effort to accommodate his rising balls, and that perfect shot of her recoiling, eyes still closed, as his member emerged from her throat and mouth, a fine strong spurt of brilliant white spunk streaming across her lips, nose and forehead in an almost artistic arc.

Double-checking the switches, the tiny screen flickered into life. The equipment seemed in order. One screen showed the girls next door sitting motionless, staring at the screen, where Martin was heavily endearing himself to the larger of the two Jamaican girls. Pammy was, as always,

24

smiling mischievously, but Jemma looked positively nauseous.

Looking at her directly now, at a remove, Don could see
that the older girl was indeed stunningly built, and had an
elegance about her which was unusual, even for the agency
girls. Perhaps she was a rich Daddy's girl who just did it
for the excitement – there were a few of them, and they
quite often turned out to be the best fucks in town. He
couldn't help but admire the way she sat, the poise, her legs
crossed just so, a finger slowly extended to check an earring
was hanging correctly. And then she glanced across at
Pammy, once, quickly, then again, lingering, wondering.
Pammy was absorbed in the tape, where poor old Martin
was now on his back and was having his balls rather
savagely massaged by the smaller Jamaican girl. Jemma
was clearly weighing up Pammy, perhaps imagining what
it would be like to end up in the sack with her, what
positions they would end up in, and how the man, Don
himself, would fit into it all.

Don slid the cover back across the console and crossed
to the unit by the sink. He took the small bottle of oil from
the back of the cupboard. It was, according to the label,
olive oil, but it was his special tonic, an invigorating lotion
mail ordered from India. He undid his robe and allowed it
to fall open as he unscrewed the top off the bottle and
poured a tiny amount of the viscous fluid into his open
palm.

Working the slightly greasy liquid into his scrotum, he
was careful not to let any on his glans. He was already
swelling thanks to the possibilities coursing through his
mind as regards the demure Miss Jemma. The familiar hot
sting in his ball-sac intensified, then slowly died as he
rinsed his hands.

He looked down at himself. The faint London streetlight
illuminated an orange torso, finely toned, and there below,
his penis was lengthening and thickening. The lotion was
always effective, and he knew that, when it came to his
'others', he sometimes relied on it. But it was worth it. He
closed and tied the robe. He would have to get back into

the room and seated before the erection was full. It would be embarrassing to walk in too excited. But, he smiled to himself as he left the kitchen, that was nothing compared to the potential embarrassment now facing Jemma. Lucy might have left, and there might be a lot of patching up to do. But that was all for tomorrow. This was now. This was tonight. And tonight, Don was going to party.

If Don had been preoccupying Lucy's thoughts when she arrived at Phillipa's, he was the last thing on her mind now. There was little she could concentrate on, given what Phillipa was doing to her, and the painful spanking she'd just endured would remain fresh upon her skin as well as in her thoughts for some hours to come.

Lucy had done exactly as she was told and, as a result, she now writhed upon the bed to order, caressing herself as Phillipa directed. It was impossible to guess what, if anything, Phillipa was actually doing as she calmly dictated Lucy's every move, and the blindfold, although comfortable enough, allowed nothing more than the merest hint of light at the lower edges. Lucy could feel the coolness of fresh sweat on her brow as Phillipa's voice seemed to get nearer.

'Keep those legs tight together dear, I don't want to have to tell you again,' Phillipa said with a schoolmarmish tone as she sat down, somewhere near the bottom of the bed, 'because you don't want another spanking, do you?'

Lucy arched her back and further tightened her thighs. The urge to spread herself again for Phillipa was unbelievably powerful, and she knew that her friend must know it. But she tensed her thighs together, aware of her throbbing clit being further entrapped, its pulsing seeming to echo throughout her whole body.

'You may answer, dear,' said Phillipa, and Lucy, her mind reeling, fought to remember the question. Get spanked again? Her arse was on fire as it was. No way.

'No, not again,' Lucy managed to say, and when Phillipa continued, Lucy was sure she detected a smile in the voice.

'Not again, what?' Phillipa asked, her voice high and strained.

Lucy resisted the sudden fury deep within her. It was one thing to be thrashed like an errant schoolgirl, but to be spoken to like one was almost too much. But there was no option, unless she wanted the whole charade to collapse.

'Not again, please, Miss,' Lucy said, teeth gritted.

Lucy's body shifted as Phillipa mounted the bed, and Lucy was aware, from the movement of air, from the growing scent of Phillipa, that her friend was astride her, on her knees, and shifting surely up the bed towards her.

Lucy continued to slowly tease her already hard nipples as she awaited the next instructions.

'Poor darling has a sore botty. Want Phillipa to make it better?' she stated rather than asked. Lucy nodded.

'Well, you'd better turn over for me dear, and let me see what's happened,' said Phillipa, and Lucy obliged. As she turned, her thighs brushed Phillipa's, and the coolness of the girl's moistened fingers was on her buttocks then, smoothing as she moaned in commiseration.

'Nasty. Nasty Phillipa made Lucy's botty all red, didn't she?' Phillipa taunted as Lucy sank her face into the cotton pillow and folded her arms beneath it.

'But Phillipa's going to make it much better. Much better. Just let me see it dear,' Phillipa instructed, and Lucy felt her friend's hands massage deeper, firmer into her burning flesh.

'Come on now, I can't help if you don't get your botty up for me,' Phillipa said, and Lucy dug her fingers down behind the end of the mattress, gripped the broad wooden support and levered her hips further up the bed so that she could comply. Phillipa's hands were slowly, purposefully palming Lucy's taut, stinging buttocks with a sureness of touch which Lucy had never experienced before. It was as if, and probably was because, Phillipa had experienced severe spanking herself, and knew exactly how to alleviate the pain. And whatever lotion she was using had an instantly calming effect, it's light scent conjuring citrus and coconut which ebbed and pulsed among the now heavy scents of the two women.

With her arse slightly raised now, Lucy's frustration grew. Her aching clitoris seemed to be further than ever from attention, and the spasming of her buttocks and pussy lips must have alerted Phillipa to the fact.

'Poor dear wants to spread out a little, doesn't she?' taunted Phillipa, and Lucy grunted into the pillow and tightened her grip on the bed frame. Phillipa was being careful not to allow her fingers even the most fleeting of touches against Lucy's inflamed sex, the occasional long stroke along Lucy's curved spine being the only departure from her glowing arse cheeks.

'Well, Phillipa's busy trying to make Lucy's botty better, so if Lucy wants to spread anything at all, she's going to have to do it herself,' Phillipa said, slowly and clearly, her voice loaded with expectation, her breathing slightly faster now.

Lucy drew her hands down below her and raised her trembling fingers to her own sex. It almost felt like another woman – she'd never been aroused to the point where her clitoris was so engorged. It seemed to have assumed the shape of a tiny penis, and Lucy gasped aloud when her thumb found it. She flicked the hardened bud down once, then again, and slipped her index finger into herself. She could come like this, right now, within seconds, but Phillipa clearly had other ideas.

'Now now, dear,' she teased, 'let's not be naughty. Phillipa didn't say anything about rubbing anything, or putting anything in anywhere, now did she?'

Lucy could only groan into the pillow again. What the hell was she supposed to do? It was torture, pure and simple.

'Just spread yourself for Phillipa while she tries to help,' she said then, and Lucy bucked herself up higher, parted her legs as far as Phillipa's knees would allow, then slid both palms as far down the sides of her sex as she could before slipping her index fingers under her labia and folding them back as far as she was able. She massaged up and down, and felt her clitoris bulge further from it's hooded covering as Phillipa's hands left her buttocks, and suddenly there was a splutter of liquid leaving a tube of some kind, and a simultaneous splatter of shocking cold

28

just at Lucy's coccyx. Her sharp intake of breath brought a giggle from Phillipa.

'That's nice and cool on Lucy's sore botty,' she laughed, and then Lucy was gasping into the pillow as Phillipa's fingers flicked up and down her exposed sex while the cold, thick cream slowly crept towards Lucy's arsehole.

One finger slipped inside Lucy's pussy, then another, but Phillipa then withdrew, turning her attention to Lucy's bud. Lucy wanted to throw herself on to her back and drag Phillipa's mouth over her again – the very thought of having her friend's tongue anywhere near her clit right now was almost enough to ignite another come. But Phillipa was now playing Lucy's bud like a harpist, rapidly drawing her fingertips across the bulging clit with one hand, roughly grasping handfuls of twitching buttock with the other.

Lucy held her breath as the thick cold cream suddenly seemed to pool in her slightly distended arse, and Phillipa must have been waiting for it to reach that point, for no sooner had the coolness registered itself on the sensitive hole than Phillipa was rimming eagerly, two fingertips pushing and circling against Lucy's twitching anus.

'This is going to be awfully sore if you don't relax, dear,' said Phillipa then, but how the fuck she was meant to relax when every fibre of her was set to snap with frustration was beyond her.

Phillipa forced her two slim digits into Lucy's tense arse as if to prove her point, and Lucy cried out at the sudden sharp sting as her ring was involuntarily stretched. Phillipa, with her fingers rigid and still, now focussed her other fingers directly on to Lucy's clitoris, at first gently squeezing the tender bud, then positively nipping it as Lucy slowed her bucking. Lucy didn't know if her eyes were open or not any more – the shimmering display of colours before her would have overridden any darkness, real or imposed. The pain was real enough, but the underlying reservoir of pleasure was, she knew, deep and worth waiting for. But it was touch and go: Phillipa must have sensed Lucy's frustration was peaking, because what she did next was enough to send Lucy berserk.

In a split second, Phillipa had withdrawn. The two fingers were pulled reluctantly from Lucy's arse, and her clit was released to replenish it's fullness. Lucy groaned long and hard into the pillow, and was aware of the mattress shifting, Phillipa's hair brushing the side of her face as she leaned over to whisper to her, hands briefly, gently, massaging her neck.

'That's enough for you dear,' Phillipa rasped, 'now it's my turn. You said you would, and now you'll have to, so turn over.'

And then Phillipa was up and off her, and Lucy's whole body seemed to shiver with a mixture of rage and bestial desire as she quickly turned on to her back and, not caring any more, parted her legs and roughly fingered her bruised clit. The bed shifted, the mattress heaved and bucked as Phillipa arranged her torso over Lucy, and then Lucy could smell her friend's sex nearing, the sweet saltiness tinged with – what was it? – some sort of strawberry and chocolate concoction, and Phillipa brusquely swept Lucy's hands away from her groin. Then Phillipa's hands were under Lucy's thighs, at the hems of her stockings, and she was hauling Lucy further down the bed, and Lucy shifted to speed the manoeuvre, and suddenly, despite the blindfold, despite the fact she'd never done anything as remotely disgusting in her life, Lucy found her tongue lapping at Phillipa's sex like a heat-mad bitch, and the two were locked together in a vice-like *soixante-neuf*.

Phillipa seemed not to be using her mouth on Lucy at all, and if she were issuing any instructions or orders, Lucy wasn't hearing them any more. She buried her head so firmly into Phillipa's thickly haired sex that she could barely breathe, but it didn't matter. She forced her nose into the dampest, deepest region of the smoothness before her, using her palms and fingers to spread the smooth arse cheeks, using her elbows to force Phillipa's thighs back for even greater access. And Phillipa certainly obliged, making space for Lucy to rub her blindfolded face roughly into her.

Lucy sucked at a puffed ridge of labia, then the other, then plunged her tongue as far in between as she could.

Her neck muscles felt ready to snap, but she pressed further, invading with her tongue as Phillipa had invaded with her own earlier. It was as if she'd been doing it all her life.

And Phillipa's arse too was smeared with the lotion, the tasty cream. Phillipa lowered herself further when Lucy's tongue tip poked at the tighter ring, and Lucy used her hands to better guide Phillipa's anus nearer.

Phillipa sat up, allowing her arse to hover above Lucy's darting tongue. Lucy's hands moved up to caress Phillipa's hips and back, and it was then she noticed the strange, shocking texture of cool rubber. That must have been what Phillipa was doing when she was instructing Lucy to masturbate – changing into her club underwear. It was some kind of basque, absurdly tight at the waist, but flaring out to highlight and project Phillipa's semi-exposed breasts. Lucy concentrated on tonguing Phillipa's anus as she felt her hand being roughly pushed against Phillipa's pussy. Lucy extended her index finger, and it was quickly enveloped in warm flesh. Lucy extended another, then another, then her four fingers were sheathed inside Phillipa's lubricated pussy, and Lucy was suddenly aware of what she could do with her thumb.

Phillipa was voicing her pleasure now, and although her movements were slight and regular, Lucy realised that her friend was nearing a climax. Lucy kept her hand still as Phillipa tensed and rose, relaxed and fell on Lucy's fingers, with only the slightest increase in pace. Lucy pressed the flat of her thumb against Phillipa's wet, slackening arse, and the deeper groan confirmed what was now inevitable. Lucy raised her mouth to her wet thumb, got her nail between her teeth and sheared off the end. It might cause damage. And then she plunged her slippy thumb into Phillipa's arse with a vigour which clearly caught her friend by surprise. Phillipa released a shrill cry of pained delight, and raised herself away from Lucy's face. With more room to manoeuvre, Lucy raised her other hand to assist the frantic finger-fuck. Phillipa dropped forward, plunging her face into Lucy's sex.

31

Now it could happen. It was peaking for both of them, and Lucy knew it. Lucy flicked her blindfold back, freeing her hand momentarily before plunging it once more into her friend's arsehole. There was no way Phillipa would see her doing it and was surely past caring even if she did.

The sight astonished Lucy. Don had forced her to watch porno with this sort of thing in it, but she'd never, not even in her wildest fantasies, ever seriously imagined that she would, one night, end up with one hand buried to the wrist in her best friend's pussy, her other hand frantically reaming a deep, darkly distended arsehole.

Lucy's come was sparked by the sight, and her own writhings seemed to complement and bolster Phillipa's. As the two fucked and ground ever harder on to each other, their cries intermittently muffled by one another's flesh, Lucy couldn't have told anyone what she thought about Don any more. In fact, with her body full of another woman, and another woman full of hers, she would probably have had trouble remembering who the fuck he was.

Lucy was now as far from his thoughts as she could be – with Jemma stripping in front of him, and Pammy straddling him, easing herself up and down on his cock as he lay back on the sofa, it was pretty much as perfect a way of winding down as he could imagine.

Pammy knew better than to draw his face towards her or in any way obstruct his view as he scanned the long-legged blonde stepping out of her dress. Her legs were heavy at the thighs, thick ripples of muscle within the cream stockings, and she favoured the high wearing of the legwear, the delicate lacework of the hems pulled up almost to her crotch and the crease of her buttocks. Perhaps the girl had had experience as a lap dancer, or a stripper, because she certainly knew how to move herself, and Don had to stop Pammy more than once when orgasm sparked at the sight of the blonde's arse cheeks tensing and relaxing as she stirred her hips circularly, fucking an imaginary dick.

And he could see, even with her panties still on, that she was shaved. There was no doubt about it – her labia were pronounced against the sheer silk of the underwear, the merest strip of darkness along the material proving her own excitement as she performed for the couple on the sofa.

Pammy grabbed Don's cock as he raised her away from him, and continued stroking him at the pace she had set when he was within. She moved herself off him, biting on his neck without obstructing his view of Jemma, whose panties were now gently toed away as she stepped closer and drew her scarlet-painted fingers along her inner thighs, watching herself as the already distended pussy lips parted, and the glistening pink of her inner flesh was made visible.

'Look at that,' said Don, and Pammy turned to watch, still firmly, slowly working her fingers along Don's cock.

'That's nice,' Pammy said, loud enough for Jemma to hear, and the blonde responded, parting her legs still further, drawing her fingers close and hard up her own sex, her reddened lips pouting in an obscene kiss towards the both of them.

'Turn around,' Don ordered, and Jemma did so, smooth, professional, even in her heels, two steps bringing her magnificent rear into full view as she bent down, grasping her arched ankles, and relaxing her arse cheeks so that the darkness of her arse was on full view, and the parted, shaven ridges of flesh below were framed by the light from the recess beyond.

'You want to lick that pussy, don't you, darling?' said Don, and Pammy grunted hard, gripping Don's cock painfully as she did so.

'Get over there and lick her out,' he ordered then, and Pammy removed herself from the sofa, pausing only briefly to draw the full length of Don's cock into her mouth with one impertinent act of defiance which at once angered and shocked him. Her expression was rabid, removed from normality as she crawled over to Jemma, who by now had smoothed her palms up the back of her legs and was massaging her own buttocks.

Don shifted further back on the sofa and resisted the urge to rub himself. It was just right: they were facing the far wall, where one of the cameras would capture them frontally. The other, inside the left pillar of the fire-surround, would provide the side-shots.

Pammy, her own black hold-up stockings still neatly in place despite her enthusiastic fucking of Don, paused at Jemma's rear. Bowing her head almost to the floor, she arched her face about the older girl's right foot, gnawing at the heeled ankle. Jemma, now fully upright, brought her palms to her arse and massaged her cheeks harder, parting them, raising her opened sex for attention.

But Pammy lingered, slowly running her open palms up the long legs sheathed in creamy nylon, gripping lightly at the lacy hems as if ready to rip them down. But she didn't. She raised her face up the right leg, working her head as she kissed the calf, the sensitive spot behind the knee, then further up to the woman's thigh, where she started to lose control, biting lightly into flesh and drawing small squeals of pain from Jemma.

'Get licking,' Don commanded, and he could not resist bringing his palm to the head of his straining dick.

Pammy needed no second order, for she buried her face between the raised buttocks with a sudden violence which almost toppled Jemma, and she twisted and worked her face against the tight globes of tanned skin, her hands clawing the arse cheeks apart as she sought some contact with the hard-to-reach pussy.

'Wider,' Don said, but the girls were getting lost, absorbed. He got off the sofa and knelt behind them.

'Get your legs wider, Jemma,' he commanded, and the girl did so, her feet straining to maintain balance on the heels, her knees slightly buckled now to facilitate Pammy's attention. And the smaller girl had now found a more satisfactory contact, her widened mouth closely working deep into the standing girl's sex.

Jemma lowered her palms to Pammy's head and started to work her groin against the girl's face, gasping, eyes closed, her torso swaying as balance ebbed, the rhythm of her thrusts increasing as the two settled into a mutually suitable pace. Don couldn't see Jemma's sex, couldn't see Pammy's mouth, so he slapped Pammy's behind to interrupt, and soon had them back at the sofa, the older girl comfortably reclining, holding her own legs apart and high as Pammy continued the exploration, and now the view was better, and Don could pay some attention to Pammy as she serviced her colleague.

He slapped the paddle against an open palm. Pammy didn't look up – she knew what it was. But he noticed Jemma glance briefly towards him as he knelt on the carpet behind Pammy and, although there was fear in her eyes, he knew she was into it.

'Here, use this,' Don said as he placed the slender white dildo on the sofa beside Jemma. As Pammy removed her face from Jemma's sex, noisily gasping for breath, the older girl grabbed the toy and raised it in front of her, as if examining it before allowing things to go further. She scanned the modestly sized rubber implement, her expression unimpressed as Pammy suddenly reached across and started to mouth the end of it, sucking it towards her. Jemma looked genuinely disgusted, but released her grip on the tool and lay back, eyes closed, waiting.

Don had manoeuvred Pammy's raised arse to an angle he knew would allow the far wall camera to perfectly capture the openness of her aroused sex. She still hadn't been touched, but already her pussy was engorged, a rosy glow on her buttocks.

The paddle was like a miniature canoeing oar, the expensively tanned leather surprisingly light, the hardwood frame strong. The surface of the instrument was slightly curved, so that, if used skilfully, contact with skin, particularly buttocks, produced a tremendous crack which sounded much more painful than it actually was. Pammy wouldn't even notice it – it was an appetiser for her, and she would already be longing for the rod. But Jemma, by the wariness he had seen in her eyes, was not familiar with corporal punishment, and he relished nothing more than the prospect of breaking in the uninitiated.

The first blow echoed about the room like a gunshot, and Jemma's eyes snapped open in alarm. Pammy jerked her cheeks up insolently and giggled, as if she had just been tickled. She was busy too, working the tapered end of the dildo up and down Jemma's opening lips with flicks towards her barely visible clitoris, and the older girl had brought her own fingers down to unhood her bud. Pammy brought the tool down, then stuck it into the older girl's pussy with one slow but strong movement, twisting it as it disappeared. Jemma sat forward slightly, the angle of the entry somehow paining her, and Don landed the second blow on Jemma's right cheek just as she withdrew the dildo.

Pammy glanced back at Don, and he was mildly annoyed to see her now smiling broadly, although he'd put quite a bit of effort into that one. Her expression was challenging him to do better, but he didn't want to use the rod on her just yet. Jemma had to witness a paddling before the harder stuff.

Don shuffled a little further back to get a greater swing, and the third crack, on her left again, was a peach – Pammy sank the dildo back into her colleague, harder now, just as the blow registered, and Don clicked what she wanted to do. The slender white toy, now gleaming with wetness, was drawn out again, the tip poised at the deepening crimsonness of Jemma's flesh.

He gave Pammy another to her left cheek, and this time she pumped the tool deep into Jemma, drawing a cry from the girl. Don cracked the paddle down again, the tool was back in again, and then the rhythm was established, and he swung his arm back and forth, bringing the weapon down on the reddened globes of Pammy's arse with a ferocity which she matched with strokes of the dildo, the older girl now starting to pull and tweak at her still-hidden clitoris as her climax neared.

But he wouldn't allow it.

'Stick that thing up her arse darling,' he said, his own voice quavering with the excitement of it. Pammy pulled the tool from the gleaming pussy lips and eagerly twisted it down towards the girl's tighter ring.

Jemma sat up, her knees drawing down instinctively.

'No, I don't do that,' she said, angrily defensive.

Don caught her stare, and the determination he saw there was steely, sure. It might all fall apart now. He drew the two-foot cane slowly through his cupped palm, feeling the cool wood.

Pammy, with the white tool tightly in her grip, was herself kneeling upright, unsure what to do.

'I'm sure Pammy can persuade you dear,' he said then, but Jemma's jaw was set, her eyes darkening with fear and rage as he brought the rod across Pammy's arse as a mild reminder that he was still in charge.

'I don't think so,' Jemma stated with some certainty, her calves now drawing beneath her as she closed off the access, trying to bring a curtain down on the whole scenario.

Don feigned a sudden wave of sympathy.

'All right dear, but you must at least let Pammy have just a little lick,' he said, smiling, 'she simply can't get any satisfaction otherwise, and I'd be most grateful. You never know, you might even enjoy it yourself.'

Don felt what he imagined to be a suppressed giggle rippling through Pammy's back as she eagerly palmed at Jemma's closed thighs, easing her hands to part the limbs once more.

'OK, but not that,' the older girl reiterated, nodding at the discarded sex toy on the sofa.

'It's all right. I don't need that,' Pammy said as Jemma raised and spread her legs once more, her dampened pussy tightening.

Pammy used her fingers to draw down some liquid from Jemma's pussy, and then she was gently poking with her index finger, not penetrating the girl at all, but merely softening the tension, licking at the concealed clitoris as she maintained a gentle probing. Jemma was flushed now, a mixture of fear and arousal, and Don resumed caning Pammy with mild, irregular strokes, his attention being drawn to the expression of mounting lust on Jemma's face as Pammy drew her tongue down the delicately ridged labia and then began stabbing at the girl's arsehole.

Jemma, unbidden, hauled her legs up higher, shifting herself forward so that her arse rose higher, and Pammy was delving deeper. Don could tell from the movement of Pammy's shoulder that she was finger-fucking the girl, but what orifice, he couldn't tell. He started in earnest on Pammy's behind, bringing the cane down harder across her cheeks. With every stroke she tightened and then relaxed, the streaks now rising on her flesh, red bands contrasting beautifully with the darkness of her stocking-tops.

'Get on all fours,' ordered Don, and Jemma opened eyes which were drunk with lust.

With Jemma raised on the sofa, crouching, her arms along the ridge of the back, her arse easy for Pammy to access now, Don shifted to the side to make sure the cameras would get this. Her arse was magnificent – flawless, tight and virgin. Pammy had rimmed a slight depression, but it was clear the girl was as tight as a drum. Pammy glanced up at Don, her hand hovering over the dildo. Don shook his head and raised a finger.

Pammy resumed drawing long licks up Jemma's buttocks, coating her crack and arse with a mixture of their juices, and as she probed again at the darkened tight hole, she introduced her finger, slowly, along with determined stabs of her tongue, so that when she stopped the tonguing, her finger was inside, and now she could concentrate on slackening the orifice.

Don ditched the rod. Although she had not protested one iota, he could tell that she would be unlikely to work tomorrow – her buttocks would be red for some time to come. He briefly stroked himself – pre-come had already trickled as far as his scrotum, and the lotion had been completely absorbed. He was painfully stiff. He positioned himself behind Pammy and slowly fed his cock into her pussy. She immediately started to buck back against him. Her arse was pulsing, full and damp, and he had no difficulty slipping his thumb in to the hilt, and he kept it inside, grasping her cheeks with his free fingers and using the grip to better direct the rhythm as she quickened, her own finger now deeper inside Jemma.

And the older girl was enjoying it now. Her hands were gripping the corners of the two-seater sofa as if her life depended on it and, from the sounds she was making, he guessed that she was biting the ridge. Pammy had two fingers inside the girl's bum and was now slowly pumping them back and forth, Jemma's ring gripped tight about them. Pammy, now heading for her first come, bit into the older girl's left buttock with groans of delighted relish as she retrieved the dildo and brought the slender smooth head towards the girl's rear entrance.

Pammy glanced back again at Don, and he nodded. Pammy delved her tongue in again, her fingers still pumping, and Don watched, enthralled, as the saliva was spread and smoothed, deepening and distending the ring as the white cool head of the tool was gently poked into the darkness.

Jemma released a squeal of shock, and brought a hand down behind her, frantically palming to locate the toy, and when she grabbed it, Don feared the game was over. But rather than ditch it, as he fully expected, Jemma whitened her knuckles about the thick base of the toy, released a long throaty groan, and sank the dildo inside her own arse. Her buttocks clenched with the shock, instinctively gripping the intruder, and it was Pammy who helped her ease the tension, smoothing her tanned, flawless cheeks further apart, closing her own fingers over Jemma's, encouraging her to twist the dildo as it was slowly, painfully drawn out again before being returned, this time an inch further.

Don stopped fucking Pammy. Her pussy was starting to spasm about him, and she would surely draw his load if he wasn't careful. He allowed his cock to slide up and down the cleft of Pammy's buttocks as Jemma started to fuck herself properly with the tool, crying into the sofa as she found a rhythm, her anus now slackened to a comfortable degree as she frantically worked the whiteness in and out, Pammy flicking at her clitoris. If he was going to do it, it would have to be now, before she came.

Fifty seconds later, Don was grimacing, anxious to hold back his come as long as possible. The position was awkward too – half crouched over Jemma, whose raised arse was poised over Pammy's face, his cock was firmly lodged in Jemma's bumhole. She had resisted at first, protesting at Don's thickness, but Pammy had helped further lube the older girl's hole as he eased himself in, and now that he was in, she had tightened about him, and he would have difficulty pulling out, even if he wanted to.

Don leaned further over Jemma's back and forced her torso down so that he might get some fingertip support on the sofa, and as soon as he found it he started to stroke deeper into her, the tight grip of her anus about his shaft like a firm hand.

'Yes . . . oh yes, please, yeah . . . fuck my arse you dirty bastard,' she cried, and he started to come.

He had instructed them carefully beforehand, so when he indicated that his come was imminent, Jemma rolled over on to the sofa, groaning, and leaned up, quickly grabbing Don's jerking cock. As Jemma's face neared, Don knew the timing was just right. The older girl's lipstick was a mess, her mascara running where tears had breached it, and with her mouth open, tongue half-out, a slight frown on her forehead, she looked every bit as filthy as Don wanted her to be. Pammy's face was there too, her tongue already out, her eyes shut, but still that half-smile playing about her face. The faces met below his cock, Jemma's fingers tight about his shaft and vigorously massaging his length as Pammy's finger poked at his bum.

His come shot across them both in a snaking pearl-string, much of which found Jemma's mouth directly as Pammy watched, open mouthed and loving it. Jemma took Don's spasming penis into her mouth as his flow ebbed, sucking the final spurts from him as Pammy tongued his tight scrotum.

He exhaled long and loud, groaning as the climax faded, leaving him breathless and gripped with an overwhelming fatigue. He slumped on to the sofa between the girls. They fawned over him, moaning theatrically, noisily licking his come from one another's faces.

Don closed his eyes and thought of Lucy, and the wave of disgust rolled over him, just as it did every time. But almost immediately, he thought of his cameras, and hoped that this one had been captured well. Then he got up, chest still heaving, retrieved the paddle, and ordered Jemma to her knees.

Three

Lucy was at her desk before the sun rose. Her arse was aching dreadfully, and only a liberal application of cooling talc had helped to soothe the burning tingle about her anus. It was difficult to concentrate on what she had to do – the flashbacks from the evening before with Phillipa were frequent and vivid, and if they lingered for even a second too long she was aware of a spasming deep in her groin.

It had been an altogether monumental session. Lucy knew she would never forget it, and that her relationship with Phillipa would never be the same again. There had been the spanking, the fisting, then that bloody dildo. The thought of it now made Lucy cringe inside, both physically and mentally, but at the time it had seemed perfectly natural, even sensible. Phillipa certainly knew what buttons to press to get what she wanted, but she didn't half take her time about it. Lucy blinked away the sleep and tried to focus on the agenda she'd quickly drafted on-screen.

What sleep she'd managed to get had been short and disturbed. The visit to Phillipa, while educational and enjoyable, had not gone according to plan. The intention had simply been to chat, to seek some objective advice. But Phillipa wasn't objective – that much was now clear. That her friend harboured such intense passion for her was something of a shock for Lucy, but that would have to be dealt with later. For now, she needed advice more than ever before, and there was only one person left who could help.

Thierry Levant had been Lucy's first lover. Following her final year at school – before she would be permitted to attend university – she'd been placed in a menial secretarial position at his headquarters, then in Geneva. The job had been a necessary evil as far as Lucy was concerned – Daddy had recommended Levant's firm personally, insisted that she reside in Switzerland for at least one year before making any decisions regarding further studies and career. It had seemed absurd and mean of him at the time – Lucy had plenty of friends lined up for a variety of interesting Oxbridge colleges, and would have been delighted to accompany many of them for the laugh if nothing else. But Daddy had insisted – you'll get out and taste the real world before you make any choices.

So Lucy had arrived at Levant Incorporated with a basic grasp of German, good French, a miserly allowance set up by Daddy, and a year to kill. Her job was meant to involve liaising with middle-management in England, conveying their messages to interpreters in the many departments scattered throughout the ten-storey building. The company had interests all over the world, but a heavy concentration of representatives in London.

The work itself was all as dry as dry could be – reams of statistics would come churning through the fax machine. Lucy would wait until the printouts had finished, then register the delivery, read the covering letter, and pass it to the relevant interpreter. It was mind-bendingly boring, and within three painful weeks she had had enough.

She called home and pleaded with Daddy. He was disappointed, felt that she could have stuck with it a bit longer, but Lucy had insisted – either she be given some more challenging work, or she would be home that weekend. Daddy had harumphed something about having a word, then hung up. Lucy had suffered another two days of tedium, wondering whether she would be left to die of boredom, when, on that Thursday afternoon she would never ever forget, a spotty young man, beaming with shyness, had asked Lucy her name, and when she confirmed it, asked her to follow him.

The office on the top floor – if it really was an office – was vast, but contained virtually no furniture. There was a two-seater sofa in one corner with a glass-topped circular coffee table in front of it. The only thing in front of the windowed wall running the length of the room was a huge teak desk with nothing on it except a mobile phone and a tall, thin oblong crystal vase which had been filled to an inch from the brim with clear water. The midday light, brilliant and stark, reflected off the desk surface, glaring so strongly that Lucy had to squint, and made out only a shifting patch of darkness when a door opened in the wall to her left and Levant entered.

Lucy instinctively clasped her hands in front of her and stood erect. The man walked across the room towards her, but he might as well have been a ghost, for his steps made no sound. He stopped several feet in front of her. He was very tall, broad shouldered and slim, but the glaring sunlight provided her with little more than a blue-edged silhouette. She'd seen enough photographs of the man to know what he looked like, but they seemed now irrelevant. Even the pictures of him with Daddy five, ten, even fifteen years ago now flashed into her mind with a new and frightening aspect to them.

'Lucy,' he said, his voice so low it was as if he was simply voicing a thought, 'I hear you are not happy.'

Lucy lowered her head. She felt suddenly ashamed of her complaint, of her use of Daddy. She should have taken her concerns to him directly, not compromised the old friendship in such a childish way.

'I hadn't intended my father to raise the issue with you, Mr Levant,' Lucy began to reply, but he raised a palm as he passed her.

She turned to follow his careful, silent progress as he crossed to the opposite corner of the room. Now, with the sunlight behind her, she could see him. He was wearing a dark, loose tracksuit, and from the dampness of his hair it seemed that he had just showered, or had perhaps been exercising. He leaned down, bending from the waist, to adjust some control, perhaps the heating. It was very warm in the room, just as it was in the rest of the building, but in here the heat was palpably dry, almost static.

When he rose and turned towards her again, it was the first time she had ever seen his eyes in real life. Even at a distance, they were riveting, primarily grey, but flecked with sparkling points of blue-green about the blackest of pupils. He paced back towards Lucy, and she was aware not only that she could not remove her eyes from his, but that he was searching her face closely. He paused briefly before her, that same distance again, and he stared down at her feet, then brought his eyes up her body in a slow, meandering stare which was analytical, critical, not in the least lascivious.

Lucy felt herself wilt under the gaze. It was as if he were looking for something specific. She was wearing a light pastel skirt, flat canvas pumps, a flared white blouse. No make-up today, and no jewellery. She hadn't been bothering – the air-conditioning in the place had affected her skin slightly, so she'd shunned cosmetics for the past three weeks. She felt herself wondering how plain she must look. And then he was away again.

He crossed to the desk and lifted the small cellular phone. He stood, back to her, surveying the cityscape as he spoke, but so low that she couldn't make out a word. It was a one-way, ten-second conversation, perhaps with his secretary who commandeered the huge ante-room which served as a reception area. He replaced the phone carefully on the desktop, then sat down and beckoned her with a double-flick of his raised fingers. Lucy, mildly angered by this gesture, did as she was bid. It was like being called to see the headmistress. She took the nine paces slowly, her legs stiff and awkward with nerves, and paused before the desk. The sun had shifted further again, and his features were once again diffused by the strength of the light streaming through the thick glass wall behind him. She reclasped her hands and stared at him.

'Lucy, I should explain something to you. I didn't greet you when you arrived here because your father wanted you to go directly to work, and wanted you to work as others

45

do, without favour. I was very happy to honour your father's request because he is a friend. I can count on one hand the people I consider friends, so I do what I can for them.'

He paused and shifted his seat closer to the desk. With his elbows he created a pyramid atop which his long, thin fingers gently tapped each other's tips.

Lucy stared down again. She was causing trouble. Daddy was probably furious and embarrassed and would give her the silent treatment when she went back for Christmas.

'You look worried,' he said.

Lucy grimaced, sought words to frame her confusion and regret. She'd rarely felt so lost.

'I just want to do something else,' she pleaded, 'I mean, it took one morning to work out what was required, and I've been doing it ever since. I think I'm capable of more.'

He sat back in the seat, the fingers entwined and held to his chin. She could hear a smile in his voice.

'We are all capable of many things,' he said then, 'and that is perhaps what worries your father more than anything else.'

Lucy frowned at the man as he stood and faced the window once again.

'You are my responsibility as long as you are here,' he said with a severity which at once alarmed and unsettled Lucy, 'and I take my responsibilities very seriously. I note, for example, that you have done little apart from work since your arrival.'

He'd clasped his hands behind his back and was standing motionless.

'I'm here to work,' Lucy stated, trying to firm up her voice. She didn't like his tone, the way this was going. Was she being chastised for doing what she'd been sent here to do?

'I've been watching you very closely. Very closely indeed. You do some shopping, you return to your apartment, you watch some television with your flatmate, you retire early.'

Lucy's mind raced.

'Pardon me, but what I do in my own time is my own business,' Lucy heard herself stammer slightly, but there was no doubting the anger in her voice. He turned and moved to the corner of the desk.

'No dates yet?' he asked, but the tone suggested that he already knew the answer.

Lucy bristled. She crossed her arms, set her jaw, and took a deep breath before answering.

'Mr Levant, I'm not one to jump to conclusions, but it seems you've been spying on me. Don't you think that's taking your responsibilities a little too far?' she demanded. Her tongue-tip was touching her upper lip, the way it always did when she was about to lose her temper.

'Spying?' said Thierry. And then he looked down at his feet and he let out a long, thoughtful groan, as if weighing the word, searching for a dictionary definition against which to compare his own interpretation. 'It's not the word I would use perhaps, but I suppose, technically, yes, I suppose I have been.'

He perched himself on the end of the desk, smiling at Lucy, awaiting a response. She felt her jaw slacken and drop.

'You *have* been spying on me?' she said, her voice rising with incredulity.

And then he laughed. He threw back his head and he emitted a high and surprisingly loud laugh which seemed to echo about the long room.

'Have none of them actually asked you out at all?' he asked. Lucy felt her cheeks blaze. There had been advances made, sure, most of them coming from slick-suited middle-management types who wore their sleeves high to show off chunky gold watches. She had experienced no trouble whatsoever in rejecting every offer thus far.

'I suppose they are frightened to pursue you too keenly. They know who you are, and they know I am looking after you,' he said, the mirth still there.

'I can look after myself, thanks all the same,' Lucy managed to say through tightly clenched teeth.

'Of course you can, my dear, but I fear that you are not yet familiar with the evil intent of many men, and believe me, there are certainly many of them. You would be a prize indeed. There must be few men who would not give much, and perhaps everything, for the chance to paint their fantasies upon you.'

Lucy wanted to leave. It was too much. She lowered her eyes and shook her head.

'I'm sorry Mr Levant, but I think I should just –'

She turned from the desk and started to walk away, but there was a momentary confusion – where was the door? The sunlight glaring on the plain canvas-covered wall obliterated any tell-tale frame, no visible handle. She stopped, waited.

'You should just what?' he asked.

'I should just go home,' Lucy said.

'Enough of this game,' he said then, and Lucy heard him move. Was he coming to get her? Was he going to do something to her? She turned, alarmed, to find that he was seated again.

'Come over here,' he ordered, his voice humourless, a new note of impatience there.

Lucy obeyed. Her body was shaking, but from excitement or raw anger she couldn't tell.

'Place you palms on the desk,' he said. He was rummaging in a drawer somewhere beneath the desktop.

Lucy felt her eyes widen, her breath quicken as she advanced to the desk. She slapped both hands on the thick teak so hard that he visibly jerked back in the seat.

'How dare you order me to –' she began.

He stood up, suddenly tall and looming, and slapped his own palm down on the desk as he barked 'Get your hands on that desk and shut up!'

She froze, the breath blasted from her by the ferocity of his response. It was unbelievable. Options raced through her mind. She would call Daddy, she would call the police, there had to be some kind of union in the place. But she was fully aware that so long as she kept her palms against the smooth wood, the options all lay with him. Her fingers drew back in the momentary hesitation. He was motionless, staring, daring her to remove them fully. She fought to stare him out, but the power of the grey eyes seemed to bolster as hers drained of resistance, and she flattened her palms with an audible groan of frustrated defeat.

'You have always been a stubborn child,' he said, and she could only stare in amazement as he leaned back beneath the desk and rose again with what appeared to be a table-tennis bat in his grip.

'I have responsibility for your wellbeing while you are here, and that includes your punishment. You should be grateful for the chance to work here, to gain experience. You should be grateful for the chances that have been presented to you by caring parents and their friends. Instead, you whinge, and even have the – What is that word? – yes, the precocity to bring your meagre complaints to me. You have no idea who you are dealing with, young lady.'

Lucy forced herself to exhale, then inhale. It had to be some form of nightmare and she would soon awake. She closed her eyes and felt the cool wood beneath her hot hands, the faint warmth of the sunlight on her bare forearms, and she heard him continue his lecture as he rounded the desk and moved behind her. She could stand up, turn and bolt, but she knew now that she didn't want to. For the first time since she'd entered the room, she acknowledged the warmth between her thighs, the familiar tingle of arousal. Could he tell? It didn't matter.

'Don't worry, my dear,' Levant said, then with a barely concealed glee which made Lucy's jaw twitch with fury, 'I took the precaution of checking with your father what should be the nature of any punishment, and he assured me that you are well acquainted with what he calls the slipper.'

Lucy jumped as Levant slapped the bat against his own palm. It sounded alarmingly hard, but there was a rubbery resonance to the impact which was indeed familiar.

'Curious people, the English,' he continued as he pressed a hand into the small of Lucy's back to guide her further forward over the desk. She acceded slowly, but that had as much to do with the nervous rigidity in her frame than any resistance.

'I've never seen the attraction of using something as unattractive as domestic footwear for chastisement, but I suppose it's a matter of taste,' he said as he slapped his hand with the bat once again.

Lucy dropped her forehead on to the desktop and slid her torso further over the flat, smooth surface under his guiding hand. He wasn't pushing her, but she knew now that resistance was pointless – she'd had her chance, and blown it. With arms outstretched, her palms slipped over the far edge of the desk. She gripped the thick table-top, even her fingers stiff with fear. And now, so far was she prone that the crease of her thighs was pressed hard against the desk rim, and it would take only the slightest movement for her to bring her pubis against the hardwood, but not so slight that he wouldn't notice.

Something lightly traced a line across the small of her back, then down around her right buttock. It could have been a finger, but was more likely the edge of the implement he was about to use to punish her. She took a deep breath and waited, but the slow movement continued. She was aware of him moving closer, his breathing low and barely audible.

'This will hurt you, Lucy,' he said with a decidely false note of commiseration, 'and I apologise in advance for any pain you may experience, but you have to understand that pain is part of experience, and experience is what you were sent here for.'

'I wish you would get on with it,' she said then, and she heard a breathless chuckle of surprise from him in the instant before the paddle came cracking down on her right buttock. Lucy inhaled sharply and groaned as she exhaled, a sound of anger and contained pain.

'Tell me Lucy, are you still a virgin?' he asked, so casually that he might as well have been asking someone the time.

Lucy gripped the table tighter and jerked back her hips, taking the opportunity to part her legs slightly so that her mound would be near the rim of the table.

'You're the big man of the world, Mr Levant, why don't you tell me?' Lucy replied, enjoying her defiance now. If he wanted a game, she would give him one.

Again, he laughed, but as he did so he smoothed the place he had just struck, and Lucy could feel the long fingers briefly, tentatively testing the tautness of her flesh.

'I think you came to see me today because you are frustrated, and frustration can be a terrible thing,' he said, and the paddle came down again, this time on her left cheek, and with considerably more force than the first stroke. Lucy gasped, but cursed her weakness. She'd been spanked a lot harder than this before, by her mother as well as her father, but never in such intense, titillating circumstances. It wasn't as if she'd actually done anything wrong, but she knew full well that this man was deriving satisfaction from her predicament.

'Well then,' he said, and she felt him move further back, perhaps to get a better trajectory for the strokes to come.

Fingertips briefly pressed her inner thigh, requiring that she part herself further. She did so, and the extra space allowed her to find the table-rim with her throbbing clitoris. It pulsed gratefully at the contact, and Lucy knew that she would have to make best use of the paddle strokes to allow her to find stimulation.

She hadn't long to wait. The next stroke was a beauty across her right, lower than the first, and decidedly painful as it caught the crease of her thigh and buttock. She released a yelp which annoyed him, for his hand came up to her head, his fingers snaked through her unpinned hair, and there was a finger, a thumb on either side of her neck, just behind her ears. Another blow to the left, but with an uncanny symmetry. Lucy jerked her hips forward as the blow landed, painfully bumping her clitoris against the cool wood.

'I think twenty will be enough for you,' said Thierry as the fifth cracked across her right thigh, and this time she found the rim in perfect time, her bud sending the familiar signals of an impending come should the rhythm be maintained.

51

And then it happened. It came so quickly that she was vaguely aware only of his voice counting towards twenty, and he was somewhere in the low teens when she started to buck against the table of her own accord, the pain searing across her thighs and arse as the thrashing intensified, each stroke harder than the one before. She didn't know how obvious her pleasure was, or whether it would have mattered at all, but by the time her come had peaked and ebbed he was on the other side of the desk, the slack training pants already lowered to free his swaying, rigid cock. She knew exactly what to do.

He slumped into the swivel chair and leaned back as far as he could, his cock and balls exposed at the edge of the chair. Lucy stood up, the pain still pulsing in waves which threatened to overwhelm her. She kept her hands on the desk for support as she staggered around to the other side. Levant removed the tracksuit as she neared, and by the time she dropped to the floor in front of him, he was naked.

He cupped her face in his hands and smoothed her lank hair away from her forehead.

'Have you done this before?' he asked with what sounded like genuine concern.

Lucy didn't feel as if she could lie to this man. Something about him seemed to strip her of pretence, of the ability to deceive. She stared into his eyes, close and sparkling with excitement.

'No,' she said, but before he could comment she had the long, thin cock in her hand and lowered her mouth on to it.

Levant released a long, pained groan as Lucy brought her other hand to bear upon his length, and she stuffed the thing as far into her mouth as she could. She gagged, pulling it out as the urge to retch gripped her, but her hands were already working him up and down with a rhythm which seemed to come naturally, and his hands in her hair gently encouraged her to try again. She opened her mouth as she weighed up the size and shape of the thing, imagining it inside her, filling her pussy. Perhaps he would do it, if she did this well enough.

She carefully lowered her mouth over the hard head of Levant's cock and held his shaft still and tight as she concentrated on sucking it as hard as she was able. Her cheeks puckered with the effort, and she soon had to pull away to catch a breath. The reek of him was intoxicating, a smell not unlike her own sex, but distinctive, animal. She sat back on her heels and looked at her own hand stroking the long cock. It was obscene, the most disgusting thing she had ever seen in her entire life. She'd never ever seen one so close, and so starkly lit, in daylight like this. She wanted it inside her, and she wanted it now. Her pussy was cramping with need, but when she started to raise her skirt, Levant sat up and his hands on her shoulders were firm.

'No, my dear. No no no,' he said, and the smile was there, a smile of drunken lust, 'everything at the proper time, and in the proper place.'

Lucy snarled with frustration as she resumed wanking him, but her other hand was soon massaging herself through the cotton of her skirt. He couldn't have stopped her doing that. Wild horses wouldn't have.

He was further back in the seat, gently jerking his hips up and down as Lucy once again brought him into her mouth and settled into a rhythm which he obviously approved of.

When he started to come, Lucy sensed it. She quickened the pace of her strokes, and the groan confirmed that her instinct was right. She pulled her mouth away from him as the milky come appeared, a thick, almost syrupy globule of liquid which seemed to totter atop his helmet before trippling down over her knuckles like candle wax.

The whole thing appalled and enthralled her so much that her own approaching climax was lost, and she slumped back on her calves, pulling her hand away from him.

He was lost, his head arched back, his breathing now slowing as his cock wavered, spasmed some more fluid forth, then wilted dramatically to lie atop his hairy thigh.

Lucy looked down at her hand. It was shaking, and the fluid was thick, not dripping. She didn't know what to do with it. She stared at it. Revolting. She turned her hand on to the dark green carpet and drew it along the thick fabric. The sperm smeared across the pile in glue-like ribbons.

When she looked up, Levant was looking at her like no man had ever done before, and she knew that he was in love with her.

For the remainder of that year she was his lover. He taught her everything he knew, told her stories of his travels and dealings with some of the most powerful and feared men in the world. She adored him, and thought her life must surely end with the completion of the twelve-month assignment.

But the relationship never really had ended. Neither of them had been able to make the final cut, and so Lucy had returned home, had gone to university, then immersed herself in business, but always made a rendezvous somehow, somewhere, usually in the autumn.

Their first reunion, in Marseilles, was still brilliantly clear in her mind. As his yacht had slipped slowly from the harbour, she'd released herself from his embrace and delved into her pocket.

She had feared he might laugh at the ring. It wasn't expensive – a simple gold band – but she'd had their initials entwined on the inner surface.

He was clearly moved by the gift, tears rimming his lids as she slipped it over the little finger of his left hand. It fitted perfectly.

'I will never remove it,' he'd said. 'Never.' And he'd then taken her to his quarters and made love to her as they sailed into the night.

Four

Minami had seen the faces in her sleep, yet again, and they grew in detail with every vision.

She didn't know when they would arrive, but she would have to be prepared. Even her limited experience of foreigners had taught her that they were so different, in so many ways, that nothing could be assumed.

The faces disturbed even her meditation, and she closed the shrine earlier than usual, unable to concentrate. What puzzled her was how the approach would come. Minami's house was only known to a favoured group of mostly very senior management from the city's larger companies and, of course, the local yakuza, who made sure she was safe in return for modest annual payments. The thought of foreigners arriving was worrying. Would they just turn up at the door? Surely not. If they did, they would be politely refused admittance.

Naomi had listened, nodding occasionally, when Minami outlined what she wanted her senior girl to do. Naomi would probably relish the assignment – she was particularly fond of foreigners, especially the American troops stationed at the local naval base, and had never made any great secret of the fact that she liked the dark-skinned men. They did not appeal to Minami, but she realised that she was not dealing with her own preferences.

So when Minami arrived at work that morning, annoyed that her routine was being so disrupted by thoughts of these strange faces, Naomi was waiting.

Minami could tell that the girl had been up all night, even though she was supposed to be on the day shift. The pair sat opposite one another across the low table and it was some minutes before Minami asked how the search had gone.

'I have two,' the girl replied quietly.

'Suitable?' Minami asked. Naomi hummed a note of indecision and tilted her head to the side, but Minami could tell that the girl was confident in her choice.

The pair sat a further ten minutes in silence before Minami rose and waited for Naomi to lead.

Naomi was tall for a Japanese woman – in her mid-thirties, she was rather heavily built, and it was a physical atttribute which she had taken full advantage of in her career choice. The clients loved her broad shoulders, her strong, stocky legs. She was frequently requested for special assignments, jobs which required her perhaps to vacation with a client, or visit them in their hotel rooms. She was by far the most experienced girl in the house, and her fees were measured in amounts which the other girls could only dream about.

The two men outside the room were suitably deferential when they saw Minami approach – they would certainly have heard of the Mama and her girls, but they would never have expected to get into the house, let alone ever set eyes on her. They averted their gazes from her, and stayed in rigid bowing positions as she followed Naomi into the only Western-style room in the house.

The floor was linoleum, black and white check, and the walls were windowless, painted stark white, a long narrow mirror running the length of the left wall. The room had a clinical smell about it – for good reason – but none of the equipment was currently being used, all of it carefully stored behind the sliding panel doors which comprised the right-hand wall.

The foreigners were sitting in opposite corners at the far end of the room, him lying, while she had her knees pulled up to her face. The girl was a mess – her eyes were red and swollen from hours of sobbing. Minami noticed that the man had tried to make a pillow of his bound hands, but it must be difficult with the handcuffs so tight about his thick wrists.

As the women entered, the coloured man started to get up, and it was Naomi who beckoned the guards. They moved slightly ahead of Minami, hands clasped in front of them as they stared at the man. He got to his feet unsteadily. He was huge, perhaps six foot seven, and massively shouldered. Coffee-coloured rather than black, he had a friendly, partially toothless smile, and Minami noted that the gap was fresh, the gum bright pink, a smear of dried blood noticeable on his lower lip. Upright, the man did not move forward. He released a stream of questions, smiling for the most part, but the nervous grins were interspersed with frowns and sudden pitch changes which betrayed his fear. Naomi translated the gist of the man's gripes and queries, but Minami didn't want to hear them. He raised his hands, pulling at the handcuffs, and Minami instructed the men to placate the dark stranger.

The men advanced swiftly, and with several sharp kicks to his shins, and a couple of punches to emphasise their point, the huge man found the floor again, groaning loudly.

So theatrical, these foreigners, thought Minami. Always shouting, gesticulating. They had the pain threshold of kittens.

The girl stood, as directed by Naomi. She looked terrified. She had not been harmed, said Naomi, but had had a lot to drink the previous night. She was also having hysterical outbursts, fearing she had been kidnapped.

Minami smiled. Kidnapped!

The girl was small for a foreigner, perhaps only a little taller than Minami herself. Despite her bloated eyes and wet, red nose, Minami could see that the girl was pretty.

Minami considered Naomi's description of how the pair had been found: Naomi and Tomoko had toured the bars for some time, trying to fend off the persistent salarymen, and had eventually ended up in the Shot-Bar, a popular late-night club which was frequented by a mixture of Japanese and foreigners. The couple had been drinking at the bar when Naomi introduced herself and told them of the party. There would be something to smoke. The man had been especially keen, the girl less so, but he had persuaded her that an hour or so would do no harm. Once outside, the guards had taken them easily, the man too befuddled with alcohol to offer much more than token resistance as they slipped on the hood and cuffed him. He had probably imagined the dark-suited gang members to be drugs squad operatives, and didn't want to make things any more difficult for himself. No, they could not know where they were. Yes, their employers had been notified that they were ill, unable to work for several days at least. No one would come knocking at Minami's door. The foreigners would not be missed, except by their flatmates, and even if they did approach the police, Minami would have a quiet word and the search would be sure to come nowhere near her or her house.

Minami wondered if the couple would be suitable. She didn't know for sure, and had to trust in the judgement of her top girl. They seemed young and fit enough. They would do. She instructed Naomi to make sure that the foreigners were fed and given sleeping mats. They could be allowed to rest briefly, and then the girls would start the preparation.

The man resumed his vocal protests as the men slid the door shut behind them. Minami wondered when they would arrive. She closed her eyes, and the face of Loo-see was there, clearer than ever. It must be soon. Very soon. Naomi did not know, and had not asked, why the foreigners were needed – she would not dare. But she must be curious. Minami-san quelled the vague urge to unburden her premonitions to the head girl – little could be achieved by it – but she knew in herself that the foreigners would appear, and that when they did, they would want something familiar to play with. If anybody could judge what the foreigners liked, it was surely Naomi. Minami knew her girls well, and she saw the light in Naomi's eyes refract in that way which told her that the choice was right. Now it was simply a matter of waiting.

* * *

58

Don nodded sporadically, holding the gaze of the boring old bastard opposite. The meeting had dragged on way past the three o'clock deadline he'd suggested. The deal was done – what else could there be to talk about?

But he knew that Lucy was preoccupying him. The curt message waiting for him in the office when he got in that morning – staying 'a couple of days' with 'a friend'. She knew full well he would not regard that as an adequate communication. He'd often had to remind Lucy of her position – the status of her father, as an ex-government minister, made her as attractive a target for potential kidnappers as they could wish for, but she'd never taken the warnings seriously. Even if she didn't give a shit about him, she could have slightly more regard for herself.

The mayor wittered on as Don wondered where she might have gone. The old fool was on about some hospitality package the city council had arranged for him and Martin. With the deal now done, requiring only Home Office permission to allow the opening of two major hypermarkets in the region, the city was pushing the boat out for Don in an effort to show how thrusting and dynamic the crumbling industrial centre really was. There was talk of a special surprise, and much laughter which Don struggled to contribute to. He couldn't care less. He wanted to go home.

A 'friend' – she'd never been so vague before. There would always be a name, or a place. She'd done it on purpose to wind him up. He'd called her office, but all Lucy's PA could tell him was that she'd briefed senior staff in a short meeting, said she was taking a short trip, and would be back in a few days. That was it. She wasn't to be contacted unless in a dire emergency, and even then, any messages were to be forwarded to her e-mail intray and she'd deal with them from there.

So Don had left an e-message. A specific, unequivocal message. 'Call me the instant you get this,' he'd written, and it had been received by her office terminal with a maddeningly cheery electronic ping.

The mayor was smiling still, but Don, with a start, realised that the wrinkly grin was strained, and the old man's white eyebrows were raised, trying to raise further still. He must have asked a question. Don summoned a laugh, shook his head and apologised.

'I was miles away, I'm so delighted with the way things have gone. Sorry, what was that?' Don felt his cheeks redden.

'The minister. The presentation on Friday. Are you happy with arrangements?' asked the little man.

Don took in a deep breath and recovered himself quickly.

'It's probably safe to say that the right honourable member is as good an ally as one could wish for. He's been most accommodating in the past, very sympathetic to our cause in the northern regions. What my father-in-law might call a very safe pair of hands.' Don said, smiling.

The mayor smiled, as did Martin and the other councillors. Lucy's father. It was incredible how the mere mention of him was enough to stop conversations dead. It was as if the prestige of having been private secretary to royalty carried with it some shamanistic power which mortals could not understand, let alone discuss. The fact that Major Bowden had developed an increasing dislike for Don since his marriage to Lucy was neither here nor there, and Don was very careful never to imply that the Major had direct interests in Don's burgeoning retail empire, although he did possess a significant eight per cent of shares. But facts were facts – the Major was his father-in-law, and people could read into that what they would.

'I'm sure everything will go swimmingly,' said the mayor as he rose, 'and I hope you will enjoy your stay here. Please be sure to inform my assistant of any needs you may have. Anything at all.'

And with that, the council entourage was up and away. As soon as the door of the small conference suite had closed, Don wrenched at his tie. The air-conditioning in the hotel must be wonky. Martin slid a glass of iced water across the thick glass table. Don stared into the tracks of condensation left on the surface. Where the fuck had she gone?

He sipped at the metallic water and watched Martin as he rose and went to the window. The view of the city was obscured by a murky brown mist. The cranes at the riverside were barely visible. Don stared at his closest aide. The memory of the videotape brought a rush of nausea which transformed itself into a clawlike grip of guilt. Martin had never been anything less than totally loyal. Six years they'd worked together – longer than he and Lucy had been married. He trusted Martin more than he did her.

'Kelly's people were in touch again today,' said Martin quietly, as if to himself.

Don sighed. The pay-offs, the backhanders. The nefariousness of it all sometimes threatened to wash over him, but business was business. Devil take the hindmost; where there's muck there's brass. Dad's stock phrases seemed to hover in the air before him, ready for all occasions, a perfect excuse every time.

'Get it sorted out?' asked Don.

Martin didn't take his hands from his pockets. He seemed to be staring upwards, into the brighter sky above where the river would normally be visible.

'I told them, no cash under any cicumstances. I offered them Magno. The boys at accounts are sending on the figures. They'll get back to us tomorrow, lunchtime latest,' Martin replied, tired and disinterested.

Magno was a small publishing firm which had been part of Don's portfolio for some years. It was floundering, but might realise half a million or so if broken up and sold wisely. It was more than enough compensation for the backroom consortium which had steamrollered the planning permits through the council's approval procedure, but by the time it was divided up between the various players, this one would get a hundred grand, that one fifty. Perhaps the mayor would find himself in possession of a Spanish villa bequeathed by a grateful citizen, and perhaps the director of planning would discover an offshore account he never knew he had. Perhaps. But it would all be so far removed from Don that he would never ever know the details, could never be directly connected to any of it. And that was thanks to Martin.

'Fine,' said Don with a finality which snapped Martin away from his survey of the dimming sky, 'let's get out of here. Do you know the town at all?'

Martin moved back to the table and slumped back in the steel-framed chair. It wobbled slightly after he sat down, like a gigantic baby-seat.

'I know you weren't really listening,' replied Martin, 'but the old boy has lined up some sort of entertainment for us at the new Riverboat. Fancy a shot at the tables? Long time since we've done a bit of blackjack.' Martin was trying to enthuse, but he was clearly tired himself.

'I suppose we should show face if it's arranged. I'm talking about later.' Don retorted, and the impatience was clear in his voice. Martin leaned on the table, chubby hands clasping into the basket he always arranged when he was about to ask something serious.

'There's something you're not telling me,' the aide said, and Don resumed his examination of the droplets of water on the table. He couldn't tell Martin. Close as he was, this was too personal. It was beyond the line he'd always drawn with anyone he worked with.

'Look,' said Martin, slowly karate-chopping at an imaginary line on the glass, 'if it's this deal, I don't see what you're worrying about. We've done this a dozen times before. The presentation on Friday is a formality. The minister will loathe having to remove his nose from the Home Secretary's arse for more than a couple of hours, so he'll turn up, give us the rubber stamp, and that's it. What's to worry about?' Martin seemed almost angry, as if the doubt on Don's face was a form of personal rebuke.

Don lit a cigarette. He only allowed himself to smoke in the evenings, and even then, it was usually with a drink. He exhaled a long, billowing plume above the glass table-top. Martin sat back, arms folded – he hated smoke.

'Remember the chap we used during the Suffolk deal?' said Don.

Martin leaned forward, frowning.

'The Irish lad, forget his name,' said Don as he stood up.

'What about him?' asked Martin, genuinely curious.

'He was good, wasn't he?' Don asked with an affirmative tone which made Martin groan aloud.

'The guy was an arsehole. Don, do you know how much trouble he was? It took weeks to –'

Don pointed his cigarette at Martin, 'But he was good. He did what we asked. He found out who had bugged the office, and if he hadn't, those stores would never have been opened.'

Martin raised both palms to accede the point and waited for Don to continue.

'I want you to get him back. Lucy's up to something. I don't know what, where, why or anything else, but something's wrong. Get him. Tell him to find her, find out what she's doing.'

Don turned to face Martin again, and his aide's face was crumpled with concern.

'What's happened?' Martin asked quietly.

'Nothing's happened. Not yet anyway. But I need to know where she is,' Don said as he paced back to the table.

Martin had been in business long enough to train his facial muscles, his expressions and manner of moving to such a diplomatic pitch that little if anything of Martin Tyler the man ever showed through. But Don could see now that the man was shocked. Of course, he would be. Don was asking him to arrange to have Lucy, his own wife, spied upon by a man they had previously used to trace moles and organise industrial espionage. Don held Martin's stare until the older man finally cracked and lowered his gaze to the gleaming table. Don was sure he saw a slight shaking of the head, but even if he hadn't, the expression of disgust on Martin's face said it all.

'Just arrange it, please,' said Don. 'And now, my good friend, it really is time to get the fuck out of here.'

Naomi couldn't wait to get back into the room. She had slept fitfully for five hours in the staff quarters, her thoughts circling, like a mosquito, about the physique of the man they'd brought to Minami. She was delighted that the Mama had agreed to keep him, although why on earth she wanted the pair was still a mystery.

Quickly, but carefully, she dressed with the dark man in mind. Minami had approved her wearing western dress – normally forbidden – for the duration of the couple's captivity, and so she intended to take full advantage of the chance.

She removed her best black rubber dress from its dustguard – she'd perhaps put on a little weight since she'd last worn it, and hoped she could get into it all right. Her new, brilliantly gleaming patent leather boots were still in the box – she hadn't had the chance to wear them at all. Her belts and cuffs and other bits and pieces were all safely boxed in her corner of the girls' changing room, but she had a nagging feeling that there was something special she had forgotten.

She secured the thin rubber stockings with the clips extending down from the corset, then got the dress on before donning the boots.

Scanning herself in the mirror, she conceded that she had perhaps gained two or three pounds since she was measured for the outfit, but the dress was so tight, so flattering, that her bust was, if anything, enhanced, her belly and hips ever more western for the extra weight. And with the boots on, her lengthened legs transformed her entire shape, giving her the sort of figure she knew the foreign men went crazy for – it was like her idol, Marilyn Monroe, whom she had always wanted to be. She'd had a little belly, and generous, broad buttocks. Naomi half-turned and raised herself on to tip-toe, and was pleased with what she saw.

It would not be today that she would get to fuck the man. Perhaps tomorrow, perhaps not until next week. Minami would dictate the time and the place as well as the manner, but it would happen, and Naomi felt herself shiver inside at the prospect – he was huge. She could tell just by looking at him that he had the sort of cock which made her knees liquify with outright lust, and sooner or later it would be hers to do with as she wished. That would be her reward for this frustration, and she fully intended to make the most of it.

Applying her make-up, she tried to concentrate on what she was doing, hoping it might make the time pass faster, but the watch on the dresser before her was stubbornly slow – still half an hour to go. The girls would have bathed and cleaned the pair of them, equipped the room. The captives had been given rice and soup, but just enough to keep their mind off their stomachs. They would still not have been allowed any form of contact, and Naomi knew that by now, the girl in particular would be desperate for warmth, security of some kind, in the huge man's arms. It still wasn't clear if the couple had just met in the club that night, or if they were a more permanent fixture. It didn't matter. All that mattered was that Minami had some use for them, and that involved Naomi having to prepare them.

Twenty-five minutes to go! She touched her fingertips to her hair. The gel had hardened into a flawless shell of shining black, secured at the peak of her crown with a broad leather thong, the perfect pleat trailing down to just above the nape of her neck. The collar, plain-studded, was comfortably tight.

She crossed the room once more, careful to stick to the boarded section of the floor where her heels could not damage the delicate tatami mat below. It was maddening. She seldom got so excited, unless she was out on the town, in her own time. It was simply so disconcerting to have a foreigner in the house – it was almost as though she'd been allowed to have her cake and eat it. She sat down carefully on the three-legged stool and squeezed her thighs together, hard, but the action only intensified the warmth.

She stared at herself in the small mirror. Her eyes were glazed with expectation and desire, her lips, even below the glossy scarlet, pulsing with impatience. It was no use.

Standing up, she carefully drew up the hem of the rubber dress. It stretched reluctantly, but it would give enough. With the rubber tightening her waist further, she sat back down and looked down at her sex, the trimmed pubic hair short, fantastically wiry and shiny, the clean cool rubber sheathing her full thighs, the straps of the corset already leaving tell-tale marks on her flesh.

It had to be quick, and it had to be clean.

With the thumb of her right hand pressed down hard on her clitoris, she closed her eyes and remembered them, pretty much in sequence: the very first black man she'd ever been with, a slovenly drunk who had paid her half of what she asked for – his smell was still in her memory, a repulsive sweet-sourness which had made her sick, but also, alongside the smell, the sight and feel of his cock as she sucked it to delivery; the handsome youth who had worked at the language school had become a boyfriend for almost a year, and she could still recall the contours of his manhood, the thick vein like a cable down his length, his tendency to piss immediately after coming, despite his erection still being full; the middle-aged executive who'd been introduced by a friend, and how friendly and sweet he was until he got her into the love hotel, chained her to the wall and beat her with his trouser belt until she was screaming for mercy, only to fuck her viciously instead, first with his cock and then his fist.

She had suspended her breathing. She could do it at will – it intensified orgasm, but only if her timing was perfect. Her lungs were ready to burst, her thumb was quivering with the pressure now being exerted on her stationary bud, and so she summoned the memory which did it every time.

The soldier from the base she'd spent a full weekend with last year – his face was still clear, close and glistening darkly with sweat as she sank herself on to him again and again, savouring the thickness of him inside her as her pussy walls caressed him, his mouth sucking hard on her nipple. She grasped his hair between her fingers and whined with the onset of the slow, grinding climax, feeling his dick jerk further, spurting into her, and that moment, when she relaxed fully and sank on to his full length, was one she would never forget, her senses slipping on to the brim of unconsciousness as her body went limp.

Naomi shuddered, eyes shut, as the memory-induced orgasm tore through her, and she had to grip the edge of the stool to avoid toppling backwards. She took several deep breaths, stood up, rearranged her dress, then checked the clock. Ten minutes had passed.

With her lust now partially sated, Naomi would be more in control when she did face the captive, more restrained, just as Minami-san always advised.

But when she did get him? Naomi closed her eyes and felt a chill after-shock of the come pulse through her groin. Be patient, she told herself, be patient and you will have him.

Lucy could tell that Thierry had not quite concluded his business, but he had obviously gone to some lengths to ensure that nothing would disturb their unscheduled meeting.

Lunch, in the fashionably spartan restaurant overlooking the bay, was disrupted only once – Thierry had excused himself from the table, accompanied his assistant to the door, and even his slight hand gestures made it obvious that he did not expect to be interrupted again.

He had thinned about the face, and his neck was almost certainly a shirt-size smaller than when they'd first met, but Lucy could feel the familiar palpitations when his eyes met hers. Thierry Levant was not, never had been, a conventionally handsome man. His eyebrows were thick and almost met, and his nose, Roman and prominently boned, was askew as the result of a teenage ski-ing accident. At six foot one, broad at the shoulders and hips, he looked as though he should be a heavyweight, but he was not. His was the body of an ageing swimmer. As if to compound the aquatic impression, his hands were long and feminine and always moving, like fins, and his eyes were as dark and deep as those of any dolphin or seal. He was, if not handsome, an extraordinary looking character, and that, for Lucy, had always been a vital element in the attraction.

In spite of the slow elegance with which he moved, and the high, almost girlish laugh he occasionally released, Thierry was very much a man's man – he was, she knew, feared and admired in equal measure by his peers and competitors. She knew that his parents had abandoned him when he was three, and he'd been brought up in Marseilles by a seriously violent aunt and uncle.

At sixteen, he'd left for Paris. The uncle was found mugged and dead some three months later. Thierry had been interviewed, but managed to provide solid alibis, all of whom seemed to be connected to one of Marseilles' more prominent underworld gangs. When, at only twenty years of age, the shipping company he'd been working for went bust, Thierry and his friends bought it for ten francs. Within five years it was the largest company on the port, Thierry was the Operations Director, and his bosses were some of the most feared men in Europe. Another five years on, Thierry was the Managing Director of the company, the bosses were retired or dead, and politicians were calling to make appointments to see him. That much Lucy knew – Daddy had told her. How he had done it was another matter, and she knew she would never ever ask, and he would never ever tell. But now, to look at him dabbing at his lips after finishing the small portion of parboiled vegetables, one could easily put this man down as a gentle ex-civil servant, a congenial central European village vet or doctor. But when she met his eyes, those black, grey-lined eyes, she shivered inside.

'You make a habit of surprising me Lucy,' he said, 'the last time it was Warsaw, you turned up right in the middle of that summit. Remember?'

He was smiling at the memory, and Lucy did too.

'Yes. Haven't I apologised for that enough? I didn't realise it was so important,' she said apologetically, but he was already laughing aloud.

'Thank God you did. It was incredibly boring. It was as if my prayers had been answered, only I hadn't remembered praying in the first place.'

Lucy sipped at the white wine. It had become warm. The view was stark; blackest black rock for a shore, unbearably bright blue sky, and shards of land jutting at improbable angles for indeterminate distances into the slightly choppy sea. It was a strange and unsettling landscape. Thierry's voice lowered, became loaded and cautious.

'I have two more days here, then I'm off to sunny South Africa. What are your plans?' he asked, and when Lucy looked at him he was still and staring, calm, expectant.

68

'Are you asking me to come with you?' she said, but she didn't smile, and neither did he.

'No. No, I'm not. I don't think my wife would appreciate it,' he replied, but he didn't let his eyes waver from hers for even a fraction. Lucy smiled.

'Lucy, I can be honest with you, because with you I am myself, and always have been. You know that I love you. I always did, more than any other woman I ever met. More than my own wife. But you were not available to me. You had other plans, always other plans. Now, you have done well. You have your business, your status, your successful husband. You have everything you ever wanted. You will have to forgive me being frank, but I cannot imagine why you came here, why so quickly, so – What is the right word? – so . . . unhappily.'

Unhappily? She should have known better than to even try and conceal her concerns at all. But the meeting was so perfect, so relaxed, she couldn't bear to broach the subject of Don and her crumbling marriage. She felt now that there was really no need. It had been a silly idea in the first place.

'I just needed a break. You know how it is,' she said chirpily.

'Yes, I do,' he said, and she watched his suspicions dissolve under her warming, intensifying smile.

It was when he got her to the room that she realised he was more than suspicious – he was angry.

She'd worn the type of simple outfit she knew he favoured: black pin-stripe suit jacket with knee-length skirt; thin tan stockings, held high on the thighs by white garter belts; thin white cotton panties which he had a special soft spot for; almost flat-heeled black brogue-style shoes, which reminded her of the footwear she was forced to wear at boarding school.

So when he'd ordered her to sit on the hard-backed chair in the lounge rather than proceed directly to the bedroom, she waited patiently, legs together, ankles touching. He would be getting something ready, fetching something, and she would wait like this until he returned. She felt the fear grip her spine and guts when she remembered the marks which would surely still be obvious on her buttocks – Phillipa had left her mark in more ways than one, and Thierry would demand an explanation. He would surely be enraged that she had allowed anyone else to punish her in the way that he felt was exclusive to him. Then again, he might like the notion.

When he did return, he was carrying a riding crop which she had seen before. He flung it on the sofa and crossed to her. She dared not look at him, the déjà vu sweeping over her, that first day in his office resurfacing in her mind, clear in image and atmosphere.

'Stand up,' he said quietly, and she did so.

He raised both palms in front of her chest, slowly palming his large hands over her breasts, then hooking his fingers about the lapels of the lightly pin-striped jacket. Lucy closed her eyes and raised her face to his, and his mouth was on her then, his lips forcing hers apart, his tongue exploring her. She started to raise her arms to draw him nearer, but he sensed the movement and grunted that she should not do so. He continued to kiss her as he suddenly ripped the jacket open, the buttons scattering as the fabric parted to expose her, and then he was on her breasts, tongue lashing at her nipples, nibbling, sucking so hard that Lucy felt ready to pass out.

He fumbled with the catch on her skirt as he resumed kissing her neck, but his patience was thin, and the skirt was soon wrenched from her. The zipper burst so that she stepped back and allowed the material to drop around her ankles. He lifted her clear of the clothes, and then he had her on the sofa.

Lucy struggled to unbuckle him, his hardness already evident, straining against the fabric of his trousers. She was on her back along the sofa, and then he had her leg raised over the arm-rest and his hand was gripping her sex – not stroking or rubbing, just gripping – and she further parted herself to allow his hand access as he grasped the panties carefully, pulling the material away from her so that his fingers could loop beneath. Then, with such force that her

70

hips were raised from the sofa, he tore the flimsy material from her.

Lucy was aware of him moving the crop from beneath her as he mounted her, kissing her passionately once again as she managed to free his dick. She attempted to wank him, longing to feel the familiar shape of him, but he moved her hands away again, and she brought them, clasped, behind her head as his sex moved towards hers and she knew that he would find her quickly, as he always did on these initial outbursts of lust.

Suddenly, he was off her, and when she opened her eyes he was removing his trousers, the shoes and socks already discarded, his cock reddened and straining as he turned to her. She held his gaze as he removed the shirt. The crop was on the carpet at his feet, and she saw him glance at it, but he didn't reach for it. Instead, he brought Lucy's legs together, then slipped his arm under her joined knees and raised them – she gripped the arm-rest and strained to help raise herself as he mounted the sofa. He continued to push her joined legs until her knees were almost at her face. She still had the shoes on. She closed her eyes, and half-forgotten snippets of encounters with older girls at the boarding school flicked across her mind.

And then, with both palms kneading her buttocks, his face was on her sex, his tongue lashing along the crevice of her arse and pussy, flicking rabidly at her pulsing lips, a finger smearing saliva across her anus. The motion of his head on her was steady, face pushing into her with a desperation he hadn't demonstrated before.

The sudden tension at her buttocks made her wince – he had gripped her stockings, and was hauling them higher up her legs, tearing at the sheer material with his fingernails, pulling the white garter belts between his teeth, and all the while his tongue was fanning out her inner flesh, his lips pressing hard on her clitoris as she started to lose breath, the climax approaching.

If he sensed her imminent come, he didn't acknowledge it, for as Lucy shuddered, goose-bumps erupting in a wave which started at her belly, he raised himself and, with a

71

brutal stab, sank his cock into her pussy. Lucy cried aloud and attempted to part her legs, but he had her held firmly at the thighs, and obviously wanted her tight, constricted like this as he pumped in and out of her. She felt his hardness quicken and deepen, his balls slapping maddeningly against her arse as he peaked. He brought his cock from her to milk himself on to her arse and thighs, and she felt the warm dampness being spread upon her flesh as he massaged his liquid into her with the tip of his cock.

He backed off, got to his feet. Lucy allowed her legs to fold back down on to the sofa. She wanted to get up, to take him in her mouth, to feel him close again, but she was too drained to move. He paced across to the table below the large, framed mirror, and she watched as he poured and drank a little iced water before returning.

Thierry's cock was still rigid, and he didn't even look at her as he reached down for the crop.

'Right my darling, let's see what you're made of,' he said then, humourless, frowning.

Lucy didn't have to be told twice, but the strength of the first come had sapped her energy, and it was with some difficulty that she got to her knees, flopped her arms over the back of the sofa, and raised her come-spattered buttocks for the punishment she yearned.

The club was uncomfortably hot, and Don had long since removed his tie and unbuttoned his shirt. The young man assigned to them by the council had certainly been helpful enough in locating discreet entertainment, and the turgid but necessary process of sharing a few drinks with the young ladies was nearing its end. The complimentary suites were already reserved at the hotel, and cars had been arranged for midnight.

Don tried to ignore the attentions of the girl to his left. She was attractive enough, but seemed unable to keep quiet for more than thirty seconds at a stretch. He would find a suitable way of shutting her up as soon as they got to the suite. The brunette to his right was annoyingly standoffish and seemed nervous of him. Not that he'd done anything to unsettle her. The stage-show, a sequence of increasingly raunchy pole-dancers, had been entertaining, but Don had watched it with as much interest as he might devote to a second-rate movie, chatting to Martin rather than spend time building relationships with these females who would, in a few hours' time, be of no further use to him.

But Martin had taken a real shine to the little blonde, the youngest of the trio. She was a looker right enough – petite, finely featured and genuinely friendly, unlike the others, who seemed to put on their manners and conversational style along with their make-up, thickly, obviously. He'd been away for about fifteen minutes with her, and Don was starting to wonder if perhaps they'd sneaked off back to the hotel to bag the best bed. The brunette seemed to read his thoughts.

'I wonder what's happened to your friend?' she asked, clearly hoping to irk Don into some form of conversation.

'He was sent to boarding school at a tender age and developed various neuroses,' Don replied without looking at the twenty-something. She sipped at her empty glass and returned it to the table with just a little too much force for Don's liking.

'You look tired, dear,' he said, and when he looked at the brunette her eyes were wide and hurt.

'Why don't you go home and catch up on your beauty sleep?' he smiled. The girl's jaw dropped slightly, but the gesture was not theatrical – she was genuinely hurt. Don laughed.

'Look, you needn't even try angling for a sympathy vote, because it's something I'm pretty short of at the moment. Fact is, I don't fancy you, and worse than that, I don't think I could fuck you if my life depended on it, so why don't you just stop wasting your own time as well as mine. I suggest that you leave. Now.'

The girl stared at her raven-haired friend, perhaps hoping for some show of support, but it wasn't forthcoming. The other girl was giggly and past caring. It was all a joke to her. The brunette shuffled along the alcove, stood, straightened her peacock-blue cocktail dress and strutted for the exit. Don pulled the other girl close, reached below the table, grabbed her right hand and brought it to his crotch.

'I hope I made the right choice,' he said. The girl glanced up and smiled broadly, revealing an admirably straight and gleaming set of teeth along which she was running her pink tongue-tip.

She palmed her hand across to where Don's cock lay flaccid against his inner thigh. He felt her fingers tighten about him, and was surprised at the strength of the jerking of blood which greeted the pressure. She too noticed the effect, and drew her hand further along his thigh to where the ridge of his glans was now growing prominent against the thin suit material.

'I'm sure you'll find that you did,' she said then, and Don leaned back further, the better to allow her room for exploration as Martin rejoined the company, his little blonde friend nowhere to be seen.

'What happened to the girl?' asked Don, and Martin's face registered a certain distaste at the question.

'Her name's Helen, and she's chatting to a friend,' Martin replied, avoiding Don's eyes.

The brunette, Charlene, continued her massage of Don, and although it was all happening well beneath the broad table, it was obvious from the slow flexing of the girl's arm that she was stroking Don with a steady rhythm. Martin topped up his glass from the large, heavy pitcher containing the lurid blue cocktail. He proferred the pitcher to Don, who slid his glass forward.

'She's getting paid to be with us, not chatting to pals,' said Don, and Martin gasped in annoyance.

'Leave it out, will you,' he said bitterly, 'she's trying to get some stuff.'

'Stuff?' Don repeated, but he knew full well what Martin meant. A bag of coke no doubt. Martin was quite partial to a little sniff now and then – he claimed it helped him. Don had always resisted the urge to partake despite the widespread availability and usage among colleagues. He

74

considered it a sign of weakness to rely on powder for effective performance, be it in business or elsewhere.

'For herself, I hope?' Don persisted, but Martin didn't rise to it. Instead, he leaned across to Don and whispered.

'Our man in Iceland,' he smiled at Don, as if ready to impart some meaty gossip. Don leaned closer, but not so far that the girl's steady, insistent massage would be interrupted.

'He's gone missing,' Martin said, his eyes searching Don's for a response.

'What? Missing . . . How?' Don staggered the words out through clenched teeth.

'His mobile isn't responding. The GPS system has it located at his chalet just outside the city, but he isn't there. Something's happened.'

Martin sat back and sipped at his cocktail.

'So what now?' Don asked. The girl's hand had suddenly become an annoyance, and he brushed it from his lap angrily.

'I don't know, Don,' Martin replied chirpily as he dropped a thick, coloured ice ball into his glass. 'You're the boss. You tell me.'

Don had to struggle to ignore the impertinence in Martin's voice. The bastard was enjoying this, no doubt because he had obviously objected to Don's trailing Lucy at all. But Don had always tried to stick to the agreement that work was work and play was play, and the two should never, as far as possible, overlap into their friendship. He also knew that this business with Lucy was the thing which could smash the friendship once and for all – Martin, in his own way, loved Lucy intensely, and Don knew it full well. Perhaps he had been wrong to order observation of her, or maybe he should have ordered it privately, keeping it away from Martin. But Martin was the contact, and Don wouldn't have known where to begin trying to get in touch with the Irish lad. Jesus, he still didn't even know the character's name or who he worked for.

Helen's timely return diffused the inevitable argument, and Don resigned himself to waiting for the morning to find out more.

The petite blonde smiled charmingly at Martin, who rose from his seat as she moved in beside him. Every inch the gentleman, poor old Martin couldn't help himself. He never ever could get it into his head that these girls who smiled and flirted and moved just-so were only ever doing it because they were being paid substantial amounts to do so. If they were out for a night they wouldn't look at Martin twice, and the poor wretch didn't know it, otherwise he'd surely never extend energy and time on them.

Don watched, transfixed, as Helen whispered into Martin's ear, and his friend giggled and nodded and lifted his glass, draining it at one draft.

'I think we'll head off now if that's all right with you guys,' Martin said, and Don nodded and the girl's hand was back on his thigh, and he wondered what on earth he was going to have to do to Charlene to make it any different from any other night.

Five

The two days had disappeared, a seamless stream of lunches, dinners, but most of all, lovemaking. He had taken her to the uplands, where the jagged, fierce mountains seemed almost alive, their contours stabbing into the brilliant blue sky. The surreal, steaming lakes, the pungent sulphuric breezes. It was like summer in Hell.

She couldn't get enough of him, and the feeling was plainly mutual, but there was a desperation about him which at once shocked and worried her – he seemed to be grasping her tighter, thrusting harder, pledging his adoration of her so much more intensely than ever before.

He took her through Reykjavik, showered her with gifts. She hung on to his arm and savoured the radiant happiness, all the more precious for being finite. And then came the night, when he disappeared for an hour or so, catching up on business from a reserved office and she prepared for him, pampering her body with care, and he came back, ready for her again.

But the first sign of the end of the idyll came on the morning of their third day. She still hadn't contacted Don or the office, and had no intention of doing so. It was late morning, and they had slept late. She was at breakfast, watching the bay from the table at the window as she waited for him to finish the call he had taken in the bedroom.

When he did emerge, still robed, hair tousled, Thierry looked sterner than Lucy had ever seen her. She added a little more cream to her coffee and watched him as he paced over to the window, then slid the balcony door completely shut. The midday sun was already watered and weak and making its early descent. It would be dark by late afternoon.

'Penny for your thoughts?' Lucy asked, but the look the comment drew was anything but amused. He stared at Lucy carefully, hard, for a second or two, then crossed to the table and sat opposite her. He framed his fingers into the familiar basket, worry creasing his forehead.

'Lucy, you would know if you were being followed, wouldn't you?' he asked, but there was no trace of mischief about his expression.

'Well, I don't go to any great efforts to disguise myself, if that's what you mean.'

'That's not what I mean, and you know it. I'm telling you that you've been followed. There's someone here asking questions about you. And asking questions about me.'

Hence his concern. Thierry had never made a secret of the fact that he hated Lucy's tendency to travel alone, and at short notice – he called her attitude 'cavalier'. Thierry, by contrast, had his itinerary worked out to the nearest hour at least two months in advance, and even if he changed it, it would be according to a supplementary plan which only he knew details of. Of course, Thierry probably had plenty more enemies than Lucy, but she always regarded his worry as unwelcomely paternal.

'Journalist?' Lucy asked. Thierry nodded, eyebrows arched in acknowledgement of the suggestion: he had managed to keep his recent marriage out of most of the European national newspapers, but there were certain journals, particularly business-related gossip-rags, who would undoubtedly regard it a scoop to find the mysterious Thierry Levant bedding a wealthy young Englishwoman.

'Perhaps so. Perhaps not. My people are checking him now. But he doesn't appear to be familiar, and certainly isn't carrying any significant amount of camera equipment as far as we can tell. Is it possible that your husband is having you trailed?'

Lucy found herself laughing aloud, but she knew that the chuckle carried a nervous edge which Thierry could not fail to notice.

'You must certainly be having problems in your marriage Lucy,' he said then, and Lucy had to quell the urge to tell him to mind his own business. But how could she? After what they had done together these past days, after the resurgence of the warm memories she carried so close – how could she pretend that he wasn't right?

'We are having problems, yes. That's why I came to see you,' she said, her eyes on the surface of the cooling coffee. The relief of honesty surged inside her.

Thierry's eyes flashed with grey rage, and he stood up smartly, ready to speak, but pursed his lips and turned from her.

'If you'd rather I didn't, I won't,' Lucy began, but he turned, and the fury was still obvious on his face as he leaned on the table and nodded gravely several times before carefully measuring his words. He spoke quietly, almost rhythmically, but the undertone was menacing.

'I am not a marriage counsellor. Your friend, yes, lover, yes, but I will never be just a shoulder for you to cry on. You could have been my wife. I could have been your husband. If we should have ever discussed anyone's marriage problems, they should have been our own.'

He stood erect again, his eyes suddenly moist. Lucy sighed and pushed the cup and saucer away from her.

'I need help. I'm not expecting you to give me advice. But you might know someone, you must know someone,' she said, and her voice was so empty, so despairing, that there was no questioning the sincerity of her request.

'What sort of problems can you have with your perfect man?' Thierry said sarcastically as he turned away from her and crossed to the sofa, lighting a cigarette before sitting. 'After all, wasn't it the wedding of the year, the match made in Heaven, the merger the business sections raved about for weeks? What was it now? Ah yes, he rowed for his country in the Olympics, his father owned the largest chain of supermarkets in the country, his mother was a movie star . . . For Christ's sake Lucy, the script was written and you read yourself into it like a starving showgirl. Only, you're no showgirl, and you've never tasted starvation in your life. You knew full well what you were getting into, and now, when something goes wrong, you run back to uncle Thierry. Well you have no right. If I had known that was why you came here, I would never have . . .'

He stopped, looked down at the coffee table before him, then leaned forward and stabbed the cigarette into the slate tray.

'You wouldn't have made love to me?' Lucy asked.

He smiled ruefully, shaking his head.

'No. I would have. I would always want to make love to you Lucy. Always, and you know it. Always, I want you. Always.'

Lucy crossed to him and he shifted slightly to allow her access as she sat beside him. She slid down and encircled his chest with her arms, drawing him close, savouring his smell, his warmth. He relaxed and sat back, allowing her to settle against him.

'So I suppose I must listen, and you must tell,' he said then, and Lucy sighed again. She didn't want to say anything more. Just being with him like this was enough. If only it could be like this with Don.

'I suppose so,' she said, and then she told him everything.

'Just check that everything is working.'

That was the only instruction Minami had issued, but Naomi was delighted – it meant she had pretty much free rein. The couple had been captive in the room for almost thirty hours, and although fed and watered at four-hourly intervals, they had not been permitted to leave the room, nor have any conversation with any of the staff who attended to their cleansing and sustenance. And although their binding allowed enough leeway for them to touch fingertips, they had long abandoned doing so, preferring to curl up in their respective corners to ward off the chill of the bare room.

So Minami had finally ordered the couple separated. The girl was still upset, crying miserably as the girls took her to the bath.

It was still necessary to have the guards present. The man was simply too fearsome, even for Naomi, although she suspected that he would not misbehave now, with his mate out of sight. Not knowing where she was, he was in no position to protect her.

He had eyed Naomi warily as the men ordered him to undress, scarcely taking his eyes from hers as he peeled off the tight jeans and grimy, sweat-soaked T-shirt.

'You understand English?' he'd asked, quietly, inquisitive.

Naomi had nodded slightly, but remained otherwise motionless, maintaining her rigid standing position as she supervised his stripping.

'Why are you doing this?' he asked, now fully naked apart from the boxer shorts, standing little more than ten feet from her, the two guards facing him, their backs to Naomi.

'You do not ask questions,' Naomi stated coldy, and he raised his eyebrows, opened his palms, and shook his head.

'This is some pretty weird shit,' he said then, smiling, the bloody gap in his front teeth still prominent.

'You will be paid when this business is over,' Naomi said, straining to make the switch to thinking and speaking in English.

'Paid?' He laughed. 'Lady, you might find this a surprise, but I have a job, a good job, and I get paid well. I don't need your money, and neither does my fiancée.'

Fiancée? The word echoed inside Naomi's head. French, but also used in English. *Due to be wed*. Fiancée. She couldn't help herself smiling.

'If we asked you and your fiancée to come here, you would say no, so we take you here, then you cannot say no, but when you leave, you will say yes, you will be happy.'

The man raised his face to the ceiling and laughed aloud.

'You're damn right I'll be happy. I'm out for a drink with my lady, I say OK to a party, and the next thing I

81

know I'm trussed like a turkey and having my shins kicked by some mean mothers who don't like brothers. You're right, I will be well happy lady.'

Naomi smiled.

'Take off your underwear,' she said, and he shook his head, still smiling.

'Tell me about this payment,' he said, a futile effort to postpone the final indignity.

'I do not have details of your reward, but it will be generous,' she said as she raised a finger and pointed at his groin.

'Now, please,' she said, and he did as he was told, slowly drawing the mid-thigh trunks down.

She had to disguise her shock by taking a sharp intake of breath, but she could tell by the sparkle in his eyes that he knew full well that the length of flesh now visible between his thighs was something spectacular.

He kicked the pants away and stood, hands ridiculously clasped before the foot-long penis. The guards shuffled their feet, uncomfortable throat-clearing from one of them.

'What now?' the man asked, but there was a nervousness to his tone which encouraged Naomi.

'I must check that everything is working,' she said, and he frowned in response.

There was a momentary hesitation when she ordered the guards to leave. They were unsure, but Naomi had to take the chance that the man would display no violence, and when she shouted her instructions again, they left quickly, slowly closing the door as she neared the tall, naked man. The girls would return soon with his partner. But she reckoned she had at least twenty minutes with him. It was worth the risk.

'You're a good-looking woman,' he said, his eyes rimmed with fatigue and hangover.

Naomi stopped five feet from him. He remained motionless, his hands still clasped in front of his manhood.

'Is everything working?' she asked harshly.

'You've got to be more specific lady,' he said, briefly sucking at the raw gap between his teeth.

She stepped forward and swiped his hands from his groin. The cock was a dead weight, swaying lightly.

'Please lift it,' she said, and he looked down at himself, his eyes leaden with confusion.

Exasperated, Naomi reached down and grabbed the thickness mid-shaft, brusquely yanking it upwards so that his balls came into view, the upper half of the organ draping over her thumb. She lowered her face slightly to get a better view of his lower genitals.

'It's all working, lady,' he said then, the panic clear in his voice.

'You have to prove that everything is working,' she said as she stepped back, releasing the cock to swing back between the man's thighs.

She heard him sigh, muttering curses as she crossed to the door and opened it. The guards were there, and jerked nervously as the partition was opened.

'Tomoko,' she said before shutting the door.

She returned to the man. He had one palm at his balls, cupping them protectively, and his expression was removed, sad.

'The girl will come now, and you have to prove it,' she said, and he nodded, resigned.

Naomi watched his eyes as they traced a path down her body, along the exposed upper breasts enhanced by the rubber corset, the broad planes of smooth flesh between her thighs and hips neatly framed by the black rubber straps straining their presence through the tightness of the dress, the prominent mound of her pubis gleaming in the dim light.

'I guess I got no choice,' he said, and Naomi nodded as the door slid open again and Tomoko entered. She had been dressed since the shift started some two hours previously, and she would be ready for anything.

Tomoko was the smallest of all the staff, and, at only eighteen, she was one of the youngest girls Minami had ever allowed to work in the house. She had been recommended to Minami by a client who had seduced her at his workplace, and he was keen that Minami should know of the girl's oral prowess. Naomi had tried the girl with several regulars, received outstanding reports, and so Tomoko had been in the house ever since.

When she entered, Naomi kept her eyes on the man, and she saw the instant dilation of his pupils as Tomoko crossed towards them. When Naomi turned to see the girl, she understood his sudden, instinctive interest – Tomoko had been well dressed.

Her outfit was simple: the hip-length silk top was plain, shimmering purple in the dim light, the thin shoulder straps accentuating the fine slenderness of the girl's collarbones. Her shoulder-length hair had been raised and twisted into a rough bun, the pile carefully curled and arranged to look as if it had been done in a minute, but Naomi knew it would have taken the best part of an hour and would be solid with spray and scented gels. Her face was very lightly made-up to allow her naturally pale complexion to contrast against her large dark eyes, and Naomi felt a deep but undeniable twinge of envy at the girl's youth and simple, unaffected beauty. No stockings, no bra, and certainly no panties. Flat-soled cream canvas summer shoes completed the girlish outfit. She was unsmiling, her eyes cast to the ground as she slowly, almost fearfully, crossed the room towards Naomi, pausing just behind her, as if seeking the head girl's protection from the huge man.

Naomi beckoned to the girl to step nearer, which she did without complaint, but her head was still bowed, a slight tremble discernible about her clasped hands, and when Naomi issued an order to the girl, the reply was an almost inaudible whisper which Naomi asked her to repeat.

When the girl repeated her reply, Naomi lost her temper. The girl was refusing to do as she was told. She was afraid of the man, of his size, and didn't want to be damaged by him.

Naomi crossed to the wall behind the man and slid a door partially open. When she closed the door, she held a pair of thick-chained gleaming handcuffs, and these she applied to the man's wrists, joining his wrists behind him as he stared at the girl before him.

'Don't worry little friend. I won't hurt you. Not if it's down to me anyway,' the man said, but the girl did not remove her eyes from the tiles at his feet.

Naomi then ordered the girl again, and this time she did respond, fetching a bowl and towel from the steel table by the washbasin.

On her knees, the girl wrung out the towel, before wrapping it about the lower end of the man's cock, carefully stroking the warm fabric about the rim of his glans, teasing out the uncircumcised flesh to clean him fully. After rinsing the towel, she repeated the process, this time on his upper cock, lifting the heavy shaft with one hand to expose his thickly haired scrotum as she briefly wiped beneath. He parted his legs lightly to allow her to complete the cleansing, and then the girl returned to the sink where she carefully rinsed the bowl and dropped the used towel into a small swing-lid bin.

Naomi placed her open palm on the man's muscle-rippled belly and pushed him back nearer the wall, then raised the cuffs and looped the central link of the connecting chain over the end of the waist-high hook. She tapped his toes with the point of her boot, and he yelped slightly, unsure what she wanted, but when she repeated the action, he drew his left foot back to the wall, his torso suddenly shifting, his arms starting to take the strain as he realised he was required to move the other foot as well. When he drew back his right, the hook strained, the creak of the wall betraying the sheer weight of him. Naomi knew that the hook was solid, but he was clearly not so confident, and struggled to stay upright, his back arched.

Another sharp toe-poke to the side of his foot, and he brought his ankles together. Now his scrotum was trapped between his legs, and Naomi burrowed briefly before drawing the heavy sac from between the massive thighs. She raised her hand behind his neck and exerted a steady pressure. The shoulders stressed and stretched, and he allowed his upper body to lean forward, all weight now on the hooked wrists.

'Now we will find out if everything is working,' Naomi said, and she issued a rapid set of orders to the girl, who stepped cautiously in front of the man before slowly reaching out her thin arms towards the huge cock.

The small hands were deceptively strong, and the man winced at the power of the grip as she clenched the fingers of both hands about the base of his dick, then pulled it down, simultaneously lowering herself to her knees.

Naomi shifted her position to better check what Tomoko was doing. The girl had already had to be spoken to regarding her shoddy ropework earlier in the week, and her insolent reluctance to do as she was told was further reason for Naomi to keep a very close eye on her.

But now she did as she was told. She did not slacken her tight grip as she swung the thickened end of the cock towards her mouth. The man was looking down, breath held, his expression betraying dread and astonishment as the girl gasped her breath across his glans, raising the swollen bulb to hover in front of her mouth, but not allowing the skin to make contact.

Suddenly, she released her grip, but held the cock in place as the blood raced to fill him. He lengthened, his cockhead visibly pulsing with the infusion, but the girl simply moved her head back so that her opened lips, though mere millimetres from him, still made no contact. Again she tightened the grip about the thick base of him, her fingers closing off the main vein which was straining to supply his erection, and again she breathed over him, even allowing the peak of his helmet to enter her mouth without touching lips or tongue.

The man raised his head and groaned; he was feeling it now. Naomi clenched her thighs together as the familiar cramp of need struck again. She would have to have it, and soon, but the enforced pain of delay was all part of the treat. He looked at Naomi, the gappy grin, the glaze of lust over his eyes.

Naomi tapped her toe against the tile, and Tomoko released him again. The sudden tumescence took even the girl by surprise as the cock was filled, straining against Tomoko's grip as veins throbbed into view and the tissue stretched to its maximum length, thick ridges supporting the gnarled, snake-like vein running along his length.

Tomoko stood up again, and had to bend only slightly from the waist to bring her mouth over the end of him. It was impressive enough that she managed to get his cockhead into her mouth at all, but what she did with her tongue made him cry aloud, for she poked it into the eye of his penis, and with both hands twisting the end of his length, but in opposite directions, the pain competed with the pleasure for dominance of his senses.

Naomi stepped closer and lowered her hand to locate his balls. The testes were swollen, his ridged scrotum grasping them tightly together. Naomi worked her gloved fingers into the soft flesh, gathered the sensitive orbs into her palm, and slowly brought her thumb and forefinger together to complete a circle about the loose skin, his balls now filling her palm. She twisted her fist as Tomoko began to work more deliberately on his cockhead, her head moving up and down in a steady rhythm, both hands now massaging him firmly.

Naomi pulled further down on the sac, and the groan which came from him was low, and trembling with fear. Naomi looked down to see that his cock looked enormous, the length of him exaggerated further now that she was exerting such pressure on the skin. It gleamed darkly where Tomoko's hands had worked in her saliva, and the younger girl was intensifying her strokes and taking more of him into her face with each movement as Naomi tugged at his balls in time with her younger colleague's efforts. He heaved, hauling himself back, but Tomoko, with her throat full of him, simply shifted forward, and Naomi did not let go either, gripping him harder, yanking his scrotum upwards. At a tap of Naomi's boot, Tomoko swiftly moved back, allowing the man's cock to bob back to it's natural fullness, the erection as complete as it could be. Naomi released the testes, and he slumped forward once again, fresh sweat erupting all over his face and torso as he gasped and groaned in relief.

Naomi gestured Tomoko further back, then allowed herself the first full feel of the magnificent erection. She gently palmed his bulging glans, marvelling at the velvety wet smoothness of him, then drew her forefinger down along the thick vein which seemed to be holding the whole thing together. His eyes were closed now, a thin dribble of saliva nearing his chin. He had to be very close, and she felt a sudden impulse simply to hike up the rubber skirt and masturbate herself with his organ, to bring him off over her swollen lips there and then. But that would be too easy. The door slid again behind them, and she saw his eyes flicker open for an instant, then clamp shut again as if denying what they told him.

Naomi flicked at his balls with one hand while softly massaging his length with the other. Tomoko helped the girls to bring in the female, who was still resisting.

They had bathed and creamed her, greased her hair away from her face and removed her underwear so that she was now totally naked apart from the simple black linen gag which helped muffle her sobs.

Her colleagues followed the instructions as fast as Naomi could issue them, and they soon had the girl in front of her man, back to him, her naked behind a full foot below his groin, his cock pointing at the ceiling. It would be difficult, but he was so close that it wouldn't take long.

Naomi grasped his cock at the base, steadying it as the four girls raised the female. With one girl assigned to each limb, they lifted the dark-haired girl up, palms under her buttocks and thighs, other hands steadying her shoulders and waist as they poised her above the straining cock.

The man was grinding his teeth, but whether it was from rage or frustration Naomi could not tell. She followed the man's eyes down to where the distended and freshly shaved pussy of his girl was being parted and probed by eager fingers. Naomi tightened her fist and drew her clenched grip up the cock, pushing the helmet to a darker crimson which contrasted dramatically with the girl's pale pinkness. The girls lowered the torso further again, and Naomi saw with satisfaction that the female had started to jerk of her own accord, obviously keen to get it over with. Naomi, with her rubbered fingers now firmly encircling the solid helmet, made a rough circle on the parted labia with the cockhead, fanning the reddened flesh. He grunted, urging Naomi on.

'Please, please,' he gasped, and Naomi brought her palm to the small of the girl's back, then slapped once by way of a signal.

The girls then released their grip, and the prisoner was steadied only at the shoulders as she was left impaled on the cock. Naomi too released her grip on the man, and stood back to watch the shock and pain fill the girl's face as she slid down, a high scream filling the gag as her buttocks met his groin and she could go no further.

The man bucked and writhed, his feet still together, heels against the wall, his eyes wide and rolling as the girl struggled to find some support for her feet. She brought her legs back to wrap about his thighs, and he parted his legs as far as he was able, to lend her some relief.

He continued to fuck desperately, her body connected to his, so that the thrusts only brought him deeper, perpetuating her pain. He grimaced, and Naomi could hear the come building in his quickening groans, so when she ordered the girls to remove the female, they did so just in time. His cock sprung upwards again, shining with fresh fluid, and Naomi brought her right hand up and down him with a speed and firmness which made him cry aloud as the orgasm sparked and he started to thrust into Naomi's tight hand.

When the ejaculation started, Naomi released her grip so that the seed could flow unhindered, but continued to stroke her fingers along the underside of his jerking cock, and she watched carefully as the come spurted from him, only fully removing her hand from him when she was satisfied that he was beginning to wilt.

The girl, still sobbing, was removed, and Naomi had the guards brought back in before she unhitched the chain of the cuffs from the hook.

'Everything is working,' she said, smiling.

The man, eyes coated with fatigue and humiliation, slumped into the corner and buried his face in his cuffed hands.

* * *

Thierry led. The corridor was surprisingly narrow and low-ceilinged, and Lucy formed the distinct impression of being underground. Quite far underground. Although the air had a superficially dry heat about it, even a slight brush against the whitewashed wall sent a shiver through her. It was as though the building had somehow been hewn from the icy rock of the mountain which grew up behind the bay.

After a five-minute walk during which they turned corners so many times that they must surely have completed several circles, they came to a dead-end. The wall buttressing the corridor was raw black stone, damp and glossy. The door Thierry knocked sounded to be made of metal, and when it was opened, the ear-grating screech of metal on stone confirmed her suspicion. Thierry entered, beckoning Lucy.

The cell was about twenty feet square, windowless and dim. A panel in the centre of the ceiling allowed a weak blue strip light to illuminate the space immediately below it, but could not reach the corners of the room. There was a hardbacked chair, a crumpled sleeping bag on the floor, a small square table with an empty ashtray, and that was all.

Thierry's bodyguard, Stefan, moved slowly to the far left corner and dragged the man into the light. Lucy felt herself back off, as if instinctively retreating towards the door, but Thierry's arm steadied her.

Stefan drew the man nearer so that he was directly beneath the light panel. He was of medium height, broad and dark skinned, crew-cut straight hair. Lucy pondered his nationality. He was either mulatto, or very tanned. Thierry stepped nearer the man, then indicated the chair. The man stared at Thierry, but Thierry simply continued to point, holding the man's gaze for the several seconds it took for superiority to be established.

When Thierry turned again to Lucy, she caught the excitement in his eyes. Perhaps this was all taking him back to his own early days, in the factories and wharfside back rooms of Marseilles, where he had conducted so much of his early business.

'My dear, I want you to take your time, because we certainly have plenty of it, and so does this young man here. I want to you study his face very carefully and tell me if you have ever seen him before.'

Lucy stepped forward. The man was looking at the table, directly at the centre of it. His eyes were dark and clear and very wide awake, but he seemed to be removing himself from the scene as if by some form of meditation. Lucy recognised that, if he was indeed a spy, he would probably be trained in methods of resisting interrogation, and that even now he would likely be in an advanced state of self-hypnosis.

'No, I've never seen this man before in my life,' Lucy said quietly as Thierry joined her at the table-side.

'Won't you even tell us your real name?' asked Thierry with a smile in his voice.

The man's stare did not deviate from the point at the centre of the table beyond the rim of the ashtray. Thierry leaned forward and moved the ashtray so that it moved across the man's focal point. His pupils did not flicker an iota.

'Charles Allan. That's the name you used to register at the chalet. That's the name on your passport. But you're not really Charles Allan are you? You don't look like a chartered accountant. You look too honest.'

Thierry allowed himself a laugh. The man didn't blink, his facial musculature remaining relaxed, steady.

Lucy double-checked. No. She'd never seen him. He reminded her of a young De Niro – the prematurely lined face, the intensity of his brow and eyes. He was surely no more than 35 or so. How did these men get into these jobs?

She realised that Thierry had moved back to the door and was waiting for her. As she moved, the man looked up sharply, his eyes fixed on hers. He glanced at her, searching her face, and she saw the recognition register. She may not have clapped eyes on him in her life, but he surely knew her and no mistake. There was no pleading in his expression, no attempt to communicate, no anger or fear – it was a simple visual check, like sweeping a barcode over a laser. Just as suddenly as he had looked up, he returned his gaze to the centre of the table, and Lucy could almost hear the click of his attention being switched back off. She felt the shiver shoot from her ankles to the base of her spine. The room was bloody freezing, and yet the man looked comfortable. He was weird.

The briefing took place next door. Thierry's excitement had, if anything, bolstered since leaving the cell. He was as animated as she'd ever seen him, pacing the room with the coffee in one hand and a cigarette in the other.

'This is perfect, Lucy. Don't you see? This man is just what you need.'

Lucy warmed her hands about the mug and frowned at him. He was talking in riddles again.

He downed the remainder of the coffee and dropped the plastic beaker into the bin by the sink. The small utility room was normally used by the hotel cleaners and waiting staff, but Thierry seemed not to be distracted by the unsalubrious surroundings, his mind on weightier matters. He drew up a plastic chair in front of Lucy, sat, then clapped his hands quietly together as he lectured her.

'Some men are powerful, Lucy. Like me. I'm powerful because I am heartless and grim by nature. That's me, and I don't care, because I know now it's too late to change me, and I've seen enough men like me to know that I probably cannot be changed. But most men are not like me. Most men are weak, and they are weak because they are decent. Like that man in here. He may be a killer for all I know, and maybe he is, but there are plenty of killers who are decent men at heart. And it's the heart I'm talking about Lucy. That's what I tried to explain to you years ago, and what I'm still trying to get through to you. You have no idea of your power over men. No idea whatever. Men have fought wars over women like you, and I understand why. Sometimes there comes a woman in front of you who you know you would kill and lie and cheat for, and you would not worry about making excuses or trying to justify it to yourself or anyone else. No, sometimes you would kill just for a look from that woman, and do even worse for a smile. You have that kind of power, Lucy. You've always had it. Now, you can prove it. Prove it to yourself, and you'll be a long way to solving your problems with your husband. I know what I'm talking about. This is the perfect opportunity to draw out the power you have, to see it for yourself.'

Lucy shut her eyes and shook her head. What the hell did he want her to do? He read her expression.

'Take that man and break him. He is yours to do with as you wish. He is here to spy on you, and me. We don't know why, and we won't know unless we tear it from him. We can do it one of two ways. We can do it my way, which will involve prolonged periods of physical torture and unimaginable pain, or we can do it your way.'

'Which is?' Lucy asked.

'That is up to you,' Thierry smiled as he sat back and used open palms to indicate Lucy's body.

'This is insane,' Lucy protested.

Thierry stood up, lifted the plastic chair, and carefully stacked it atop a pile of its partners.

He pointed at the wall through which Lucy could imagine the man still staring at the table.

'He will talk,' Thierry said, 'that much is certain. Stefan is getting tired, and when he gets tired he gets very irritable. That young man is a fine physical specimen. It would be such a shame to have to cripple him.'

Lucy felt the disgust well in her guts, but the nausea was worsened with the underlying realisation that she had always known Thierry was, if not capable of exercising such brutality, certainly very capable of ordering it. He was not joking.

Thierry had never been sadistic with Lucy. Rough at times, yes, but he'd never subjected her to pain beyond what had been mutually agreed. He had pushed her as far as the corporal punishment side of things went, pushed her at times to limits she thought she could not endure, but always she had come through, and she knew it was thanks to the trust she placed in him. She knew deep-down that he never would or could hurt her. But others? It was

93

chilling to contemplate what he had already inflicted on those who had crossed him. And to see the nervous excitement of Thierry now, it was clear that the prospects facing the man next door were stimulating him.

Now he was leaning against the wall, peering up at the low ceiling. It was as though he was thinking aloud more than speaking to her.

'He will succumb. I would say certainly. But if he doesn't, well, if he doesn't . . .'

He looked over at Lucy, and she tried to work out what he was pondering. The idea of releasing the fearsome Stefan on anyone was frightening enough in itself, but to be so close to it, to be a part of this scheming, was sickening.

'If he doesn't succumb my dear, I might well offer him a job. Any man with self-will enough to resist you is a man I could use in any number of ways. Whichever way this works out, I feel this is a most useful development. But first things first. You just find out who he is and why he is here. Beyond that, I have no interest in his business.'

The idea that the man might be hurt was appalling, but the notion that she was expected to somehow seduce him seemed fantastically inappropriate. The man was a prisoner, and she and Thierry were very probably breaking several laws by keeping him here against his will. To rape him into the bargain – For wasn't that what Thierry was advocating? – would surely catapult their offences into the categories deserving of custodial sentences. And yet, there was an absurd logic to it. If she did seduce the man, and he later complained to the authorities, who would believe him? He was taking part in a sado-masochistic game and was well aware of the rules before they began. It was feasible – indeed, it might even explain the alleged imprisonment. Lucy's guts churned at the realisation that she was actually relishing the prospect. But to practicalities.

'And how will you guarantee my safety?' Lucy asked in her very best business tone. Thierry laughed aloud.

'That's my girl! Stefan!'

* * *

Don simply could not come. It wasn't that little Charlene wasn't doing her level best – in fact, truth be told, Don found her rather too demanding, and knew he was struggling.

In the club, he hadn't really had the opportunity to assess her body. She was short, perhaps only five two in her bare feet, but her shape was that of a voluptuous fifties starlet: broad hips, pinched waist and full, heavy breasts, finely boned shoulders and a lithe, long neck, her hair tightly curled, dark and sprinkled with nightclub glitter. With the make-up, careful but dense, like an actress, it was impossible to tell her age, but Don guessed by the tight peachiness of her buttocks and velvety smoothness of her feet and hands that she was certainly not twenty.

And she was wild. Don had experienced enough agency girls to know which were capable actresses and which were more involved with their work. This Charlene was undoubtedly doing the job expected of her, but she did it with a palpable relish and vigour which almost alarmed him. As soon as they'd closed the door of the suite, she'd dropped to her knees, extracted his penis and subjected him to a tooth and nail assault which had made him cry out, and it was with some difficulty that he had managed to disengage her from him long enough to fling her on the bed.

It was she who'd torn the shirt off him, tearing the material in the process. He'd almost lost his temper then, enraged that this whore should be calling the shots, but she'd drawn down the shoulder straps of her dress to reveal her engorged brown nipples atop the jutting fullness of the breasts, and pulled his face on to her with a demand to suck her. He'd done so, and she'd bucked and writhed while pulling at his belt, then pushing the trousers off him with her feet. And then he was on his back and her pussy was being ground against his face, the hot smoothness of her riding him as one hand pulled the back of his hair, fingers digging into his scalp, her other hand frantically pulling at his cock.

And then the turn, again orchestrated at her convenience, when she'd flipped about to take him in her mouth and her shaved lips were poised above his face, twitching and beckoning his tongue as she took him deeper and deeper, every downward thrust of her mouth accompanied by a deep, desperate grunt of need. So he'd done it – it was something he'd always avoided with Lucy as he thought she'd find it obscene, but with this one he could do it, especially when she wanted it so much, and he'd plunged his tongue in between her puffed lips as far as he could, the nub of her clitoris grazing his chin as he grasped her smooth tight buttocks and drew them hard against his face. Charlene had bucked against him harder then, and it was all he could do to breathe in between the lengthy invasions of her pussy, his tongue lapping the walls of her insides, savouring the musky saltiness of her juices. But her own efforts more than once forced him to pull his face away for breath, when she had found the rhythm and length of him and was feeding him deep into her throat, so deep that he had to suspend his breath, suspend all noise and motion to savour what was happening. He felt her teeth gently close about the base of his cock, then draw back up the full length of him, sporadically biting as if measuring him in centimetres with her teeth, and the hard tonguing of his glans and cock-eye. Then her mouth was open wide again as she drew him fully along the hot smoothness of her throat once more.

And he should have come. More than once. Perhaps sensing that he couldn't concentrate on servicing her when she was so close to bringing him off with her mouth, she'd swung her hips over and away and settled her torso beside him as she continued the blow-job, shifting further down the bed so that he could see her, drawing her right leg up towards herself to form a pyramid with her legs, one of her hands reaching down to pull at her own clitoris as she continued to grip his balls with the other, her head still working up and down him as she stared at him, defying him not to come there and then.

She'd closed her teeth about his head and sucked on it like a lollipop, her cheeks drawing in, her eyes still fixed on him, her hand gripping him at the base so hard that he could feel the blood swell and strain in every vessel, and she'd released him then with an audible pop, drawn her tongue up the full length of him once more, and begged him to come.

'Do it on my face. Come on, spunk on me darling, do it, come on,' and then she licked at the spot below his cock-eye like a cat at milk, her tongue rasping the sensitive skin, and he threw his head back, eyes spinning, and felt the come well within him.

But he couldn't. It wasn't up to her. He couldn't allow her to do it. He was in charge. He decided when he came.

So he'd pulled her face away, got off the bed, and made her crouch on all fours, her arse raised and waving before him as he viewed her. She had her face buried in her crossed arms, her shoulders, waist and buttocks weaving and tracing the course of her lust as she moaned, her arsehole pulsing, her pussy lips, red, parted and spasming.

'You really want this don't you?' he asked, and she moaned deeper and longer in reply.

'Do it anywhere you want. Do anything you want. That's what you paid for, so that's what you get. You want to fuck me, fuck me, fist me, beat me. Do what you want, mister. I don't fucking care, just do it, but please, please, whatever you're going to do, do it soon.'

Her fingers suddenly appeared at her pussy, drawing her lips together tight between her middle fingers, then drawing up the cleft of her cheeks deep and hard, her inner flesh glistening under the pressure.

'Get your hand back down and don't do that again,' Don ordered.

She did as she was told, but her groaning took on the quality of a cry, a yearning.

Don gently traced his fingers about the curve of her hips, at the point where her thighs creased, her arse gently bucking upwards in search of him. He pulled her closer to the edge of the bed so that he could remain standing, and allowed his semi-rigid cock to slide beneath her sex. She gasped in satisfaction as his length grazed her bud, jiggling her hips slightly to get maximum effect from the friction, but Don pulled back and gently bucked his groin so that his cock rose and rested between her cheeks.

She was well lubricated there, in the smoothness along the junction of both openings, and she clenched her cheeks in an effort to hold, perhaps guide him nearer. He grasped himself and engorged his penis as fully as he could. She was getting more restless, her head shifting, her hands now knotted behind her head as she whined into the sheets.

Don gripped his cock as tight as he could bear – his cockhead was obscenely purple and knotted with bruised tissue. He placed it carefully against her pussy lips, and she jerked back instinctively but so violently that he almost disappeared inside her. He drew his cock back once again, leaned forward, and gripped her hair.

'Don't move again,' he said, and she shrieked into the bed.

One hand still gripping her hair tight, her own hands clawed over his, he placed his cock at her little anus. He weighed up the size of himself against the tight brown hole. It was wet, it was moving, and when he gingerly grazed the rim of her anus it pulsed full, like an awakening eye.

'You want it up the arse don't you, you little slut?' Don said then, smiling, and she groaned that she did.

He traced a circle about her brown hole, rimming his pre-come about her as she moved again, much slower than before, but now with a determination which he could sense in every part of her as she concentrated on what was about to happen.

Don drew himself back again, grabbed her hips, and stroked his cock up over her anus in a quickening series of motions which started her bucking again.

'Sorry my dear,' he said, the laugh barely concealed, 'but I have to see it, I really have to see it. You can get your arse fucked all right, but it won't be me doing it.'

Don turned and walked away from her, leaving her squatting.

He didn't even knock the door. Martin was on his back, the little blonde atop him, the two of them kissing as she slowly writhed against Martin's erection. By the look of her, they hadn't even fucked yet.

'Martin,' Don said, as if popping his head around the office door, 'so sorry to interrupt but I need you two in here for a minute.'

Don couldn't help laughing aloud when the blonde, alarmed, threw herself off Martin, and his friend's astonished, reddened eyes focussed on him.

'What? What the fuck do you mean, you need us in –'

Don closed the door again and returned to where little Charlene had thrown herself on to her back and was frantically fingering herself.

'Just a minute my dear, just a minute,' Don cautioned, but she didn't seem to hear, continuing to eagerly probe at her arse and pussy with short stabs of her fingers.

Martin came storming in, his face flustered and disbelieving.

'What the hell are you playing at? Can't you even . . .'

Don, smiling, raised a forefinger to his lips and gestured with his free hand to the bed. He watched as Martin took in the sight of Charlene, arse raised high, her stockings racked and wrinkled above the knees, three fingers of one hand rabidly fingering her pussy, the thumb of the other buried in her arse, both arms flexing as she fucked herself, oblivious to the two men watching her.

Martin stood, jaw open, as Helen appeared at the door. She was clearly tipsy, and not obviously upset at being interrupted. The blonde registered mild shock at the sight before her, but quickly recovered and brought her hand down to Martin's flaccid cock.

'Where now?' she giggled.

Martin pulled her towards him, his hand about her waist, in a gesture which Don found at once curiously moving and absurd.

'You wouldn't desert a friend in his hour of need would you?' asked Don as he moved back towards the bed, but Martin's frown suggested that he might very well have done so had Helen not already started to mount the bed.

'This little lady wants to do something very naughty,' Don said, and he could tell now by Martin's eyes that the initial shock of being disturbed had been overriden by stimulation at the wantonness of what writhed before him on the bed. Charlene, her face buried in the sheets, was hurting herself with the ferocity of her fingering, and Don watched as Martin neared the bed, his short, thick cock already rising again.

Helen's movement roused Charlene, who turned, lay on her back, and brought her legs open. Now was Don's moment to direct, as he knew Martin would let him, would need him to.

So they were soon as Don wanted them to be: Helen and Charlene both concentrated on Martin for a few minutes, taking turns to blow him as he stood, knees trembling, across the bed from his boss. Don stood watching, mentally framing the picture, wishing he had his video equipment to hand. It was a good one, what with the softish red light and the open view. Charlene had some initial difficulty with the girth of Martin's penis, and as she struggled to get him into her throat, Helen was sucking on his balls, gently pulling them down with her mouth as he struggled to stay on his feet, his head rolling as if in the grip of seasickness.

And then Helen, with her delicate cream stockings and frilly garter belt, with her long slender legs and tarty ankle boots and her pink bottom and long straight blonde wispy hair, her gleaming smile and smeared lipstick, was happy, more than happy to lie across the bed as Charlene arranged herself on top, carefully following Don's directions. He told the brunette to move a little further up, get her hands under Helen's thighs and her own thighs spread high and wide above the blonde's face. And Martin was standing unsteadily, his face a mix of anger and helplessness as the girls did what they were told.

And with it arranged just so, Don then instructed Martin to bugger Charlene. The brunette was already licking at her colleague with long, hard strokes of her tongue, and Helen was raising her head to nibble at Charlene, and Martin shifted closer to the bed, his cock, stubby and hard, jutting from his profuse pubes.

'You'd better give her it in the pussy first to get yourself wet,' said Don, as if the hapless Martin needed instructions on everything, but Don was providing the commentary more for his own entertainment, and the effect he could see it was having on Charlene, her face buried in Helen's sex.

Martin had to mount the bed to get close enough to have any contact with Charlene, and as he did so the mattress heaved up with his weight, bringing Charlene's head conveniently close for Don to grab her and direct her to his cock.

Martin took Charlene gently, as he surely did with every woman, scared to hurt them with his girth, and indeed, Don noticed Charlene bite on him as Martin's member was pushed into her. She groaned as the thickness was embedded in her pussy, and stayed still, waiting for Martin to start fucking. But he didn't. He simply grabbed Charlene's behind and pulled her harder on to him, not withdrawing at all, but using his grip to yank her against him. She pulled away from Don, her mouth still open and eyes shut as she accustomed herself to the thickness now stuck fully inside her. Helen was squealing with delight beneath them, and Don could only guess that she was still attempting to pleasure Charlene's bud despite the motion.

'Get her arse ready,' said Don, and Martin withdrew, rubbing his length between Charlene's cheeks as Don had done a few minutes previously.

'Think you can take it?' asked Don, Charlene staring up at him, her eyes dark with pain and lust.

Without replying, Charlene reached a hand behind her, and she fumbled at Martin's glans before stretching further back to encircle her fingers about him. Don saw the dread register in her eyes as she looked back to him and momentarily hesitated before nodding, her teeth clenched, a low moan in her throat.

'Do her,' commanded Don, and Martin, his own face now grim and determined, shifted further up the bed, raising himself to ease the entry.

Don brought Charlene's mouth back over his own pulsing dick as Martin started to force himself into her. Helen was bucking and shifting dramatically, presumably having difficulty reaching Charlene now that she'd shifted her hips slightly higher, but Don was concerned only with his own position, and it was perfect. He could see Martin's cock slowly but surely distending Charlene's ring, and he could see her mouth working ever further along his own cock as he made an effort to control his own breathing. If she could keep taking him as deep as that at any kind of rhythm, he would blow. But not before Martin had hurt her. He wanted to see it, feel it in her as he came.

Martin, perhaps eager to get it over with, raised himself further, used one hand to steady himself against Charlene's behind, and used the other to help push his dick inside the girl. Don felt her muffled scream reverberate through his groin as Martin's cockhead suddenly slid inside the reddened ring, and Martin immediately pushed to fill her, stretching her further.

'Fuck her!' Don shouted, his own teeth gritting, but he managed to keep his eyes open long enough to see Martin withdraw, then sink himself fully, Charlene's buttocks briefly flattening against the hairy groin as it slapped against her, then back again, and home again, and again, The power of the thrusts was forcing her throat more full of Don, and he tried to push it all in one last time as the come rumbled and coursed within him, exploding down the girl's throat as he gripped her hair with both hands and pulled her fully against him, his balls slapping against her jaw as she screamed again, her arse full of thickness and her throat full of more.

Don staggered back, his cock catching briefly on Charlene's teeth as he withdrew and collapsed on to the carpet. He was aware of Martin grunting in the background, and Charlene crying for him to stop, but that didn't matter any more, and when he looked up to see that Charlene had rolled over to the top of the bed and Martin was methodically wanking the last of his come on to the silent Helen's face, Don wished only that he had thought to bring the fucking cameras.

Maybe it was two hours later, maybe more. The girls had gone, sore of arse and weary of mouth, but they'd be well-paid for their efforts and so sleep had come easily to Don.

But obviously not to Martin.

The light was flicked on as Don struggled to make sense of where he was. Martin had come through the door adjoining their apartments and was clearly not the happiest of men.

Don sat up, screwing his eyes against the light.

'Martin, what the hell –'

'Shut the fuck up and listen to me, you self-centred prick,' Martin slurred. He must have got back on the sauce after the girls left, probably down in one of the late bars, for he was fully clothed, if a tad dishevelled.

'Why?' Martin asked, arms spread in supplication, his face the very picture of wounded pride.

'Why what?' Don replied, the impatience clear.

Martin stepped closer to Don's bed. Don sat further up. Martin pointed at him

'Why do you have to fuck up everything? I mean, you're not content just to fuck up your own life, you have to do it to other folk as well.'

Don closed his eyes and wished he was having a nightmare, but when he opened them again Martin was still there, only closer.

'I'm afraid you'll have to be a little more specific,' Don said.

'Tonight. Why couldn't you just leave us alone? You knew I liked her. Why did you have to ruin it?'

Don smiled and lay back.

'If I remember rightly, you enjoyed yourself enough to shoot your load all over that girl's face. I suppose you're going to tell me now that you faked it.'

Martin threw something imaginary at Don's face as he struggled to find the words he wanted.

'Always! Every fucking time, you can't let anyone . . . it doesn't . . .' Martin whirled away, hands grasping his own hair, and when he turned again his eyes were closed and he was breathing deeply, as if what he was about to say had been rehearsed.

'You have probably lost your wife, Don. I know you won't believe that, you won't even want to hear it, but whether you like it or not, I am your friend. I've been a good friend to you for a long time, a much longer time than most folk would have put up with you, and I'm telling you, as a friend, I'm telling you that you deserve to lose her. You can dress up your lies and your betrayal as some sort of modern marriage, some sort of understanding that the both of you have, but I'm telling you if no one else will, I'm telling you to your face that your wife has gone, and barring some sort of a miracle, she's gone for good. There are so many men in the world who could make a better job of loving her than you've done. I should know. I am one.'

Don stared at Martin, but didn't know what to do, what expression to wear, what voice to use now.

'What do you know about it?' Don asked then, his voice quiet and serious.

Martin turned and walked to the open door, flicking off the light as he reached it. The light from his own room silhouetted him, a hunched, portly, sad shape.

'I know that she's in Reykjavik with Thierry Levant. That's what I know,' Martin said quietly, and although there was no malice in the voice, neither was there sympathy.

And then the door closed, and Don lay motionless, staring at the slivers of light outlining the door frame, his mind whirling with rage and grief, and he stayed awake until it was light.

Six

Lucy looked herself up and down in the tall mirror. She felt uncomfortable, not only because of the clothes she was now wearing, but because of the room itself, a small changing room offshooting one of the complex's larger lounges. It was a room reserved for performing artistes, mostly minor cabaret acts, and there was a rather sad mirror framed with dust-coated coloured light bulbs in one corner, racks of cellophane-covered costumes lining one wall, a grimy sink and perfunctory work unit against the other wall, upon which was ranged a sordid mixture of old make-up containers and tubes, a kettle, scattered tea bags and coffee sachets, all with a fine powdering of dried milk.

Thierry had secured the costume from God only knows where, and Lucy frowned at herself as she tugged and smoothed it. The skirt was calf-length, blue-black rubber, and very tight at the thighs; the blouse was good quality silk, white, high-buttoning, with a Victorian-style lace detail at the collar; the cream stockings beneath the skirt were also silk, and authentically Victorian in style, thick and warm, firmly connected to the corset via six belts with firmly fastening clips. The shoes, or perhaps they would be better described as boots, were very tight, intricately laced and sensibly heeled.

She smoothed her palms down over her chest. Her breasts felt absurdly high within the tight, constricting corset, but the effect was pleasantly flattering, as if she was possessed of more than she actually had. The heels, although modest, also lent a certain elevation to her behind, and she could see, as she turned sideways, that her posterior was pronounced within the sheer rubber sheathing.

She had arranged her hair, with some difficulty, into a French bun, using several plastic cocktail sticks to secure the pile of tightly wound locks. Her hair did look good, and with it away from her face – unusual for Lucy – she could appreciate for herself the fine line of her own jaw and cheekbones against the dingy backdrop which was the wall opposite the mirror. She had been sparing with the make-up, careful only to pronounce her already dark eyes with a touch of mascara on the lashes, a smearing of rouge on her lips to emphasise the fullness of her mouth. Uncomfortable, yes, but she knew she looked good. Whether or not she looked good *enough* remained to be seen, and when Stefan knocked, then entered and asked if she was ready, she took only a second or two before replying that yes, she was.

The man was still in the chair, still at the small square table, just as Lucy had seen him some three hours previously. His head was bowed, his hands tied with a short length of electrical wire behind the back of the chair. He seemed to be asleep as Lucy crossed the few yards towards him, but when she drew the chair opposite him from beneath the table, he shifted slightly, his head still bowed.

'Do you hear me?' Lucy asked, but he remained staring at the floor beneath his thighs, his eyelids moving, but nothing else.

'My name is Lucy, but I suppose you already know that. I'm here to talk to you. And you have to talk to me. Do you understand?'

He didn't move. His eyelids slowly closed, but otherwise there was no movement at all bar a slight rippling of his shoulder muscles beneath the thin grey T-shirt.

'You do understand English don't you?' Lucy asked then, and he remained motionless. So she asked him the same question, in German, in French, in Dutch. At the last he smiled, barely perceivable from Lucy's viewpoint, no more than a brief crinkle on his brow, but she noted it and asked, in Dutch, if he was familiar with Monsieur Levant.

The man looked up, his eyes red-rimmed and heavy with sleep denied. He said nothing, but his eyes told Lucy that he knew full well the situation he was in. He was fearful, certainly, but there was a resignation about him which at once impressed and confused her.

'Did you come here looking for me?' she asked then, and his eyes shot back to the floor.

Lucy slowly moved her downturned palms across the table towards him and he breathed in deeply, as if preparing himself against some imagined assault, his brow furrowing. Stefan coughed in the background, and Lucy herself puffed aloud.

She saw her own hands as if for the first time: the fingers, long and thin, nails gleaming scarlet under the merciless blue strip light. She spread her fingers, touched both thumb-tips together as she addressed him.

'You can tell me, and everything will be all right,' she said then, and she was surprised at how soft her voice was, considering what she knew she was about to do to him if he didn't. He raised his head and stared directly into Lucy's eyes, and she felt herself at once melt, then harden into something brutal, inhuman, as he spoke.

'My name is Ryan, Ryan Villiers, and I am here on business,' he said, low and confident and with a lilt which Lucy immediately recognised as Irish.

She stood up, the chair making an unpleasantly grating sound against the thick old linoleum. The heels of the stumpy, tight ankle boots reverberated around the small room. Stefan coughed again from his dark corner.

Lucy moved behind the man. His smell rose to her as she brought her hands gently upon his shoulders. It was sharp, almost citric, an aroma of dirt and fear.

'Ryan?' she said, rolling the word slowly, savouring it. 'Ryan Villiers? That's a nice name. Very nice.'

She brought one hand up to his scalp. His hair wasn't even long enough to get a grip of. She smoothed her palm across the velvety darkness, then cupped his right ear with

107

her fingers, toying with it. She folded the ear roughly in half, then squeezed. He jerked slightly, an almost dog-like whine emerging as she tightened her fingers, making her hand into a fist.

'Very nice indeed. But is it real? Maybe it's too nice to be real,' Lucy said, and then she released her grip and stepped to his left, looking down at him as he continued his stubborn scan of the floor beneath the table.

'You're going to talk to me Ryan, Ryan Villiers. You're going to tell me everything, aren't you?' she asked, bowing her head so that she was speaking into his ear. He stayed still.

Lucy stood upright and took her right palm across his neck, her fingers slapping against the lightly haired nape, the dark muscles coated with sweat.

'Won't you!' she shouted then as she brought her left palm across the same area, and he cowered lower, a low grunt of defiance his only reply.

Lucy moved back to her chair opposite him, but moved the seat in, under the table, indicating that she didn't intend to use it again. Villiers shut his eyes, as if praying. Lucy deliberately stepped outside the area of light bestowed by the inadequate strip on the ceiling, and drew her palms down over her thighs. The thick rubber was certainly adequate protection against the chill air of the room, but the feel of it against the skin above her stocking-tops was infuriating. She wanted to remove it, and as she paused in the dark corner across from where she knew the Neanderthal-looking Stefan was watching every move, she couldn't help but realise that she wanted to comfort the wretch in the chair. But that could not be. Any contact with him would have to be punishment for him. She struggled with her inclination – the poor bastard was probably some second-rate aspiring Sam Spade who'd blundered into something he hadn't the first clue how to negotiate. That she should now be forced into the situation of having to torture him – for what else could it be called? – was absurd, and yet she knew now that it had gone so far that it could not be stopped. And besides, there was always the small matter of who had actually sent him, and why.

Lucy wagged a forefinger towards the opposite corner of the room, and Stefan crossed, lumbering, his massive frame starkly lit from above as he passed Villiers, who seemed to shrink momentarily into his own shoulders, as if expecting a blow.

As Lucy gestured instructions to Stefan, she maintained a close watch on Villiers, and she was sure she saw him shift slightly, as if directing his unmolested ear in an effort to glean some clue as to what was about to happen next.

But he couldn't have guessed that Stefan would lift him from the chair like a toddler from a high chair, then carry him to the wall at the darkest end of the room. Villiers did not resist as Stefan made him face the wall, then released the handcuffs, brought them in front of Villiers' groin, and reapplied them. Then, with a quick movement which elicited a grunt from the Irishman, Stefan brought the clasped arms high above his head and looped the chain of the handcuffs over the metal hook set in the ratcheting bar. Using the lever to the right of the simple device, Stefan levered the bar higher, and with it went Villiers' wrists. When the man was on tiptoe, his chest grazing the wall, Lucy indicated enough, and Stefan, now sweating enough to have darkened the armpits of his already dark-blue shirt, moved back into the shadows of the nearest corner.

Lucy walked slowly across to survey the man. It would be quite impossible for him to remove himself from the hook, unless he found strength enough to leap and somehow flip the chain over the curved end of the thick steel and, even then, he would have his hands still bound and Stefan to contend with. No – he would stay put as long as Lucy wanted him there, and she was already forming an idea of what she wanted to do with him.

But of course, there was still the interrogation. She would have to make sure to remember to get at least some information – Thierry would expect something.

So she returned to the basics, asked him his name again. He stated the name as before. He rattled off a date which would make him, if her arithmetic was right, twenty-eight. She asked him to state the birthday backwards, which he managed, and then down to the real questions.

'Who sent you here, Ryan?' she asked as pleasantly as possible.

The man grunted and shifted. It had to be painful, being on tiptoe like that. His calves and feet would surely start to cramp with the strain and, if he sought respite by suspending his weight from the handcuff chain, it wouldn't be long before the steel biting into his wrists would force him back on to his toes.

'You know I can't tell you that,' he said then, and there was a weakness there in his voice, a definite crack, possibly brought on by fatigue. His forehead was resting on the smooth dark plaster as he spoke, his torso shaking with the strain of the unnatural position.

Lucy beckoned Stefan over and indicated with signs what she wanted. Stefan lifted the man off the hook, turned him around, then replaced him, reached for the lever, and racked it up one more notch. Villiers' head was tightly wedged between his raised arms, his shoulder muscles further cramping the possible movement of his head, and he was staring now, staring right into Lucy with an intense anger she'd rarely seen in men. Don would lose his temper easily, tantrum and gesture, and Thierry had always been the silent, morose type who would stew a grievance for days or weeks before, without warning of any kind, releasing his rage in an explosive outburst of verbal and physical violence against the object of his annoyance. But this man's anger was there, stark and real, right there on his face, and Lucy could tell it was the real thing. He wasn't acting, he wasn't striking a pose. At that very moment he hated Lucy, and she could feel it as surely as she could smell it.

'What have I done to you?' Lucy asked then, quiet and curious as she stepped closer.

Stefan moved with Lucy, step for step. Villiers could have raised his feet against Lucy with ease. But his only movement was to try to raise himself further against the

110

wall, as if using his shoulders in a vain effort to grip the plasterwork. He screwed his eyes shut and moaned, a long, piercing moan. It had to be the start of the cramps, probably in his legs. He hadn't slept now for, what, twenty hours since Stefan and the boys had burst into his room, and he'd been given only some watery orange juice and stale sandwiches to keep him going. He must be very tired indeed.

Lucy indicated to Stefan that she wanted the lever adjusted, but when Stefan, obviously sympathising with the man's plight, ratcheted it down a notch, Lucy angrily ordered it racked back up, but twice. Villiers' eyelids peeled back in their sockets as his anger peaked, and he released a roar of frustration which, when it died, became his answer.

'What have I done to you? Nothing! Nothing! I was sent to watch you, not do anything. Not do anything at all. Watching, that's all,' he said then, his eyes closing.

Lucy stepped as close as she had been to the man. Even with her heeled boots on, she was still having to look up at him, at his face, perhaps tanned in natural light, squashed between his arms, twisted with pain, his chest moving faster now that his movement was so constricted. Lucy raised her right hand and drew her forefinger lightly down his furrowed brow, then down the line of his once-broken nose, across his tightened, grimacing lips, and finally flicked the drop of sweat off the light dimple at the centre of his jawline.

'That's right. You haven't done anthing to me, Ryan. But I'm going to do something to you unless you start talking. I'm going to do something very naughty to you, something which will hurt you in more ways than one. Are you understanding me?'

Villiers attempted to spit, but he must have been so dry that he couldn't muster enough fluid. But the motion was anticipated by both Lucy and Stefan. Lucy stepped back and moved her head aside, whereas Stefan took the less evasive action of stepping from the darkness and, with one great swoop of his hand, tearing Villiers' T-shirt off, then punching him in the guts with a force which made Lucy wince and turn.

When Lucy looked back again, Villiers had drawn his knees up almost to his waist, his entire weight straining on the handcuff chain which now creaked and squeaked against the hook as the victim twisted his torso in silent agony. The ridged musculature of his belly and sides twitched and strained as he buckled, trying to writhe away the pain of the blow. Lucy composed herself before continuing.

'This isn't a game, Mr Villiers, as Stefan would tell you if he had any command of English. By the way, I should have introduced you two earlier this evening, but there's still plenty of time for you to get to know each other.'

Villiers' eyes opened, and were fixed at some imaginary point high above the room, above the complex itself, perhaps even on the stars. Lucy turned her back and walked slowly back to the table beneath the light. She turned the chair which Villiers had occupied, so that it faced him. He was perhaps twelve feet away, but she could make out his shape well enough. She sat down, smoothed the thick rubber of the skirt as she crossed her legs, then gently wagged the toe of her airborne boot at the ground as she spoke, one hand calmly cupping the other in her lap.

'Stefan was born in Brazil, Mister Villiers. Rio, to be exact,' she said, as if addressing a classroom.

Villers was groaning again as he strained to reach the floor with his toes. Lucy discreetly indicated that he be relieved, and Stefan quickly ratcheted down two notches, allowing the Irishman relief as the balls of both feet found firmness.

'Interesting fact you may or may not know about Rio. Fifty per cent of the men are bisexual. Did you know that?'

Villiers' eyes opened and briefly glanced towards Stefan.

'Astonishing, but true,' Lucy continued. 'It must be all that naked flesh on show, they simply can't resist it. Then again, Stefan was only born in Rio. He was actually brought up on Andros. Do you know it at all?'

Villiers grunted a negative.

'It's an island. A Greek island. Quite a normal little island. Stefan loved it though, didn't you, dear?'

Stefan remained motionless, staring at Villiers.

'Stefan's proudest claim is that he has fucked every living creature on the island. Hens, ducks, goats, sheep, you name it. Stefan isn't that fussy. In fact, the only animal on the island that Stefan didn't manage to acquaint himself with was a snake, and that was only because he couldn't locate an appropriate orifice. Isn't that right, Stefan?'

The huge man turned his head, like a dog in response to a high-pitched whistle.

'Stefan, snake? Good, eh?' Lucy said, as if to an idiot.

Stefan's laugh was low and, under any other circumstances, infectious, and he nodded enthusiastically as he replied, 'Stefan make love everything, snake no good!'

Villiers released a whine which seemed to crawl about the darkened walls, and then he spoke.

'Look, this is all a terrible misunderstanding. I was sent to check that you were safe and sound. That's all. I didn't know this character Levant was here. I'd never heard of him until yesterday.'

'So, for the umpteenth time, Ryan, who sent you?'

'I don't fucking know! The client is English, some big shot in the city. I honestly don't know who it is. I was told to find you, watch you, keep a note of what you did, who you saw, where you went next. That was it.'

'And you were given no instructions regarding Mr Levant?' she asked.

'Like I just said, I'd never even heard of him. Who the fuck is he anyway?'

Lucy stood, straightened her skirt, then adjusted her blouse. It was getting chilly. Time to warm up.

'It's such a pity you didn't do your homework before coming here, Mr Villiers, because I'm placed in the difficult position of having to test your apparent ignorance. If you really don't know who Mr Levant is, then that may be the saving of you. But if you do . . .'

Lucy tutted and shook her head as she neared him. He was genuinely scared now, his breathing laboured.

113

'There's really only one way to find out,' Lucy said, her arms crossed as she scanned the man from the feet up.

'Stefan want to eat snake?' Lucy asked. Again, the man's head snapped towards her at the mention of his name. She repeated the absurd question with a side-nod to Villiers, and Stefan beamed a boyish grin as he quickly unbuckled Villier's belt, tore the trousers open at the waist and roughly drew them down the man's stocky, well-muscled legs.

'Stefan has had a long day, Mr Villiers. It's about time he had some recreation. You don't mind do you?'

Villiers screwed his eyes shut, raised his face to the ceiling and howled.

'We are approximately seventy feet underground, and the relevant staff have been informed that some of the special guests are having a fun night, a sort of game you understand, dungeons and maidens sort of idea. So, scream all you like Ryan. Believe me, no one will bat an eye.'

Stefan tore the waistband of the boxer shorts and whipped the long, ragged strip of material from between Villiers' legs, causing additional anguish, and then the bodyguard's hand was pulling at the man's cock, testing it for length, genuinely curious to see it.

Lucy returned to her seat and resumed her position. She felt a glow of arousal as Villiers' cock became visible. It looked long and thin as Stefan tugged down on it like a milkmaid, and Lucy could see Ryan's thigh muscles cramp and seize, no doubt due to him resisting the urge to kick Stefan away from him. And then Stefan was pulling upwards, perhaps hoping for some indication of an erection, but Villiers' cock remained stubbornly flaccid, so Stefan pulled and tugged all the harder, the man's slack scrotum and prominent testes bouncing up and down with the vigour of the action.

'Please stop him!' Villiers cried, and now he really was begging.

'I'm sorry,' Lucy replied, as if apologising for a misdialled phone number, 'but when you throw a dog a bone it's really not fair to take it back. Stefan will have to be

114

satisfied to some degree. My advice would be to relax and enjoy it.'

Villiers brought his head back against the wall with an audible thud as Stefan bent over and started sucking on the cockhead which was protruding from his fierce grip.

Stefan slurped and grunted as he sucked, now feeding the man's penis into his mouth, playing roughly with the tightening testicles as Villiers arched and writhed, perhaps hoping to locate a crack in the wall through which he could will himself.

Lucy tightened her thighs, the straps of the suspenders edging insistently at her flesh, stinging her buttocks. She wanted to be where Stefan was, but she had to maintain this detachment, if only for a little while longer. She took a deep breath, and felt the silk of the blouse cool on her upper breasts.

Villiers gasped and looked down to where Stefan had brought the reluctant member to semi-erection and was steadily working the shaft in and out of his mouth with apparent relish, grunting deeply when the in strokes brought Villiers' glans to the head of his throat, his other hand now playing with the balls as though they were die he was about to cast.

'Everything. I'll tell you everything you want to know, anything at all. Just stop him. Please!' whimpered Villiers, the tears no doubt genuine, but Stefan had managed to rouse the man's member to an impressive degree, and was now able to let go of the cock as it stood upright, clearly visible.

Lucy felt herself contract involuntarily. She would have to get this over with quickly, before she lost control. Ordering Stefan from the room wasn't really an option, but she would glean what pleasure she could from the scenario.

Stefan had aroused himself to the extent that he was having to rub himself through his suit trousers, and Lucy had to call his name a couple of times before he snapped to attention, his lips glistening in the dimness.

It only took a minute or so to remove Villiers from the wall, snap off the handcuffs and reapply them behind the man's back, and then Stefan bid him lie on the floor. He whimpered all the while, as Lucy walked slowly about the pair, supervising.

Villiers, with his dignity all but removed, seemed now to have regained some composure, and had stopped sobbing. His eyes followed Lucy's as she paced about him, the steady, dull click of her heels echoing about the room, the rubber skirt swishing almost silently against her stockinged legs as she moved.

'Who do you work for?' Lucy asked then, and he answered in a level, calm voice, no doubt aiming for utter conviction.

'Eyestar Limited. Industrial espionage. I've been with them three years.'

Stefan had removed his jacket and carefully framed it over the back of the chair Villiers had occupied.

'Have you been eavesdropping on us?' Lucy asked then.

'No. I would have, if I'd been able to get access to your room, or his.'

'Where's your equipment? We found none at your room.'

'It'll be at the airport. I never carry it with me,' he replied, his eyes wide and following her.

'Good. We can check that easily enough.'

Stefan left his shirt on, but his trousers were already about his ankles, and Villiers started to jerk again, his anxiety building.

'Please, please, don't let him –' he stuttered.

'Don't worry Mr Villiers. Stefan won't do anything without my permission. I won't let him fuck you. But he's been such a good boy today that I'm sure you'd agree he deserves a little bit of relief. And aren't you grateful to him for looking after you all day?' Lucy said, and she didn't even try to conceal the wicked enjoyment she was now experiencing.

Villiers shook his head in disbelief at Lucy as Stefan straddled him, the trunk-like legs on either side of his waist, the hairy arse high above, the mess of flesh and hair which was his genitals growing and shifting in the dimness.

116

'Stefan eat snake?' Lucy said then as she drew the chair up beside Villiers' head.

Stefan laughed again as he dropped to his knees, his hands already working on Villiers once more.

'Yeah. Stefan eat snake. Good. Man eat Stefan snake. Good!'

And then Villiers' cried out as Stefan stretched out his legs as if to do a press-up, wiggled his huge hips and dangled his swelling cock over the spy's face.

Lucy shifted the chair a little further back so she could still see the man's expression as the stubby, sweaty cock was pushed on to his face.

'Come now, Ryan, you know it makes sense. The sooner you get it over with, the sooner you can have a drink and a little nap. You'll be laughing about it all this time tomorrow.'

The man's eyes snapped open for a split second, and the rage and fury was sparkling bright as he opened his mouth and screamed. Stefan stopped the cry by stabbing his dick into the man's mouth, and then it was all happening. Villiers gagged several times as the motion was established, but Stefan was already methodically working at a beat he was replicating on Villiers' own privates. The effect was curiously balletic, as if the two men had suddenly become one and were gradually morphing into a single creature.

Villiers' eyes were shut, and he'd clearly decided that Lucy's advice was probably correct: the sooner it was over, the better.

Lucy felt her breathing increase, and it was becoming more difficult to conceal her arousal. She gasped aloud when Stefan's cock momentarily emerged from the man's mouth and hovered above it. Villiers' mouth remained open, his eyes shut as Stefan shifted his body slightly, and Lucy felt a screaming urge to hike the skirt up and pay some attention to herself.

Stefan lowered himself on to the man's face again, and this time, it was clear that the bodyguard was on the home straight, his small hard penis gliding in and out of Villiers' mouth with increasing speed, the large, wrinkled scrotum

117

slapping on to the man's nose and eyes as the strokes deepened. And Villiers too must have been nearing relief, for Stefan's arms were now working harder, his head bobbing up and down furiously as he tried to complete the job.

Lucy slipped off the chair, crouched, both feet still on the floor, and steadied herself with one hand on Stefan's trembling, bucking thigh. She smoothed her hand down the crack of Stefan's arse, a revolting crevice of hair and sweat. The stench of the men filled her nostrils with an acrid nausea, but it also bolstered her abandon as she gripped Stefan's cock and began roughly wanking it.

'Come on, Stefan,' she said, teeth gritted, and she saw Villiers' eyes open briefly in between strokes.

Stefan, perhaps confused at hearing his name, or wondering where the hand had come from, looked round quickly, and when he saw Lucy he smiled.

'Stefan finish?' Lucy smirked at the bodyguard as she squeezed on his hardness, drawing the wet shaft down towards Villiers again.

'Let's finish you off,' Lucy said quietly to Stefan so Villiers could hear. The spy was exhausted, his face slack and resigned, his mouth still agape, a low moan deep in his throat as Lucy, still rubbing steadily, pulled the shining member back towards him.

The huge man resumed with vigour, and Lucy released her grip, simply stroking Villiers' face as Stefan built towards his climax with a series of long, purposeful strokes deep into the man's throat. It seemed that Villiers too must be coming, for his eyes had screwed shut and he was groaning rhythmically. A reciprocal grunt of surprise from Stefan seemed to confirm the spy's completion, for then Stefan fucked so hard that Lucy winced for Villiers. She had wanted to watch Stefan come on the man's face, but interrupting the giant now was probably not the best of ideas, so she simply sat back and watched as the strokes became stabs, the grunts became loud, joyous cries, and Stefan buried his cock to the hilt in Villiers' face and released himself down the man's throat in a series of painfully grinding thrusts.

Lucy brought her palm to her groin and pushed down hard. A mini-orgasm pulsed through her, and she could feel the cool dampness of herself against the rubber skirt.

As Stefan pulled himself from the man's face and got to his knees, dazed but smiling, Lucy felt a surge of pity for Villiers. He was motionless, his own engorged cock lying across the crease of his thigh, an apologetic dribble of come and spittle forming a small pool on his hip.

Stefan, gasping with relief, shook some drops of sperm from his penis just as if he were finishing a pee, and Villiers didn't even register the final indignity of the drops spattering on to his belly and chest.

But it was too late to feel sorry, and above all else, Lucy was horny. And horny was the right word for it. Not frisky, or in the mood for a bit of slap and tickle. She was horny, pure and simple, and she wanted to be fucked, but it wasn't going to happen with this poor wretch.

She stood up. A tell-tale trickle of coldness on her inner thigh told her that her arousal had become liquid. Lucy needed fucking. Right now.

Don spread the briefing notes across the desk and scanned them again. It was straightforward. The minister would stay only long enough to hear the usual assurances that the developments in the Northeast would bring such and such a number of jobs, bolster business confidence levels in the area, further the image of the company as a progressive, eco-friendly firm, blah blah fucking blah.

Martin had boiled down the essence of the arguments, as usual, on to three sheets, the salient points emboldened, some underlined according to importance. They'd done this, what, a dozen times together? And yet, with the words and statistics staring him in the face, Don felt strangely removed from the whole business. It wasn't just Martin's outburst in the hotel, nor even the fact that Lucy was still, technically, missing. It was that he had no control whatsoever over what was happening. Lucy could stay away for as long as she liked, but the fact that she'd ended up in the same part of the world as Levant was deeply worrying.

She'd never hidden her love for the enigmatic magnate, and he'd even viewed the relationship as something of a bonus in their early days: if she'd been shagging someone as powerful as him then she had to have plenty of clout, and even Don's own father had encouraged him to use Lucy to try and get closer to Levant. Don had tried, on numerous occasions, to engineer a casual meeting, but Lucy had always ruled out any contact between the two point-blank – it was one of the very few issues in their life which Don had not been able to sway to his advantage, and he knew that it was pointless trying. Lucy loved the man, nothing surer, but Don also knew that Levant had married, now had children, and the chances of Lucy allowing herself to be used as a mistress were slim indeed. He was sure of it.

The door opened and Martin entered, straightening his tie.

'Are you ready for them?' Martin asked.

Don stood up.

'Yeah. Let's get it over with. Incidentally, any word yet about our man in Iceland?'

Martin shook his head.

'Nothing. He's either walked off the job or he's in trouble. Either way, there's no point sending anyone else. Levant has some of the best personal security money can buy. And some of the nastiest. Let's just hope that Levant didn't actually get his hands on the lad, cos if he did, and he finds out who sent him, we might be looking for personal security as well.'

Don grimaced and swallowed before sitting down again. He hadn't followed it through quite that far, but, as usual, Martin was probably right in his thinking – Levant was not the sort to take kindly to being spied upon, but very much the sort, if rumours were to be believed, to exact revenge upon those who crossed him, be the intrusion personal or business-related.

'Are you sure you're ready for this?' Martin asked.

Don shifted the papers back into a single pile and stared at it.

'How many of them?' he asked, the fluorescent statistics seeming to hover above the top sheet.

'The minister, three of his favourite pen-pushers, and that Daly chap from Mallhouse.'

'Daly? Oh Christ,' Don groaned.

It was impossible to meet anyone with any clout now without also having to deal with these people. Daly had already built himself something of a reputation as a brilliant manipulator of news and was highly valued by the Cabinet.

'Well?' Martin asked yet again.

Don stood up and checked his own tie.

'Let's do it then,' he said, and he felt his guts lurch and twist within him. Something was terribly wrong, and he hadn't a clue what it might be. He had never felt like this before a meeting, regardless of how important the company might be. This should be routine.

But, as he followed Martin out of his office to head for the conference suite on the top floor, he realised that his knees were stiff, his wrists seemed to be locked, and his eyes were suddenly sensitive, even to the diffuse light streaming through the blinds behind him in the office. Either he was in for a cold, or he was terrified.

Don had to wipe a thin film of sweat from his brow and cheeks before they entered the suite. The layout was pretty much as he expected. Minister Jack Falley was helping himself to the iced water as the three stooges, all familiar faces, hung about and around him like crows around a corpse. And there, wearing an insultingly inappropriate black polo neck under a brilliant white jacket, was Daly.

Don advanced to the minister, shook hands warmly and bid him take a seat.

The chat flowed easily. Jack Falley was nothing if not a gentleman, and he seemed to take particular care to ask after Lucy, and her father and mother, as well as dropping in a faintly risqué reference to the fact that he and Lucy still hadn't had any children.

Daly kept quiet, and Martin shadowed the spin-doctor carefully, making sure that he sat between him and the minister.

There had been three previous meetings with Falley to get Home Office approval for the out-of-town developments, but Don knew, as soon as the formalities started, that this one was going to be different. It wasn't anything particular that was said, but Falley's manner – the sixty-something seemed ill at ease, as if suffering indigestion, and Don could see that the man's discomfiture was also being noted, with apparent understanding, by Bill Daly.

Don quickly ran through the main contractual obligations he undertook on behalf of the company, then, as Martin confirmed those actions which had already been taken, he weighed up Bill Daly. The man was absurdly young – perhaps in his early twenties – but already had the ear of the Prime Minister himself. He was Fleet Street's main route to the heart of the most up-to-date government thinking on just about everything, it seemed, from famine to flu outbreaks, and it was an open secret that his services had already been secured for the forthcoming election. He was the whizz-kid that Don had once been, the name on everyone's lips, the most desirable bachelor in town and the best mate in any careerist's wildest dreams. An easy man to hate, thought Don, as Martin wound up the dryness of the planning permission approval dates and passed copies to all present.

Don felt time slow, then grind to a halt, as the minister, the three suited stooges and wunderkind Daly all stared at the standard forms, stamped and approved by the council who had been such perfect hosts just two nights before. It was as if Martin had passed them all a pornographic photograph, and all were imagining that they alone had a copy. No one said a word. It was now, right now, in every other meeting, that Falley had simply passed the forms back to Martin and asked for the HO release papers to be presented so that approval could be granted and they could all get on with having a decent lunch.

But Falley simply laid the form flat, smoothed his palm over it as if removing dust, and cleared his throat. Don glanced at Martin, whose eyes showed the confusion and dread Don was feeling. It was Daly who spoke, his voice shattering the silence as spectacularly as if a brick had just been hurled through the window.

'It's going to be difficult to pass this one,' said Daly, and Don could see excitement in the young man's eyes as he met them and held the confident stare.

Don heard a waver in his voice as he replied, 'Really? Why is that?' addressing his question pointedly at Jack Falley.

Falley sat back in his seat, and the clearing of his throat became a racked, loaded cough. Whatever was bothering him was certainly enough to prevent him saying anything, and Daly seemed to take this as a cue.

'The problem, Mr Langford, is the –' Daly blurted loudly as Falley's coughing fit reached a peak.

'I wasn't speaking to you,' Don heard himself say, his finger pointing directly at Daly over the table. Don was aware of Martin shifting in his chair beside Falley as the older man recovered and leaned forward again, readjusting his specs as he made an effort to intervene.

'Don, please don't get yourself upset over this, but we really do have some serious concerns, and, well, it's not easy to say, in fact, it's . . .' Falley stuttered and stopped, wiped his nose.

Daly, looking totally unfazed by Don's interruption, now tapped his pen against a manicured fingertip as he carried on, 'I've advised the Minister that these developments are best postponed for the moment.'

Don sat back, smiled at Daly, and felt whatever colour remained in his face quickly drain to his thumping heart.

'You advised Jack Falley to postpone these developments?' Don laughed, but even Martin was struggling to smile as Don launched the words across the table.

'Five years of planning applications, God knows how much spent on feasibility studies, market analyses, traffic flow projections, you name it, not to mention the endless hours of toadying to anal retentives like the three monkeys here, and the whole thing is now up in the air because you, *you* advised the minister against it?'

'That's right,' Daly smiled back. The younger man was flushed with the thrill of the confrontation.

123

'Would you like to share the reasons with us?' Don smiled, top lip sticking to dry teeth.

'Not particularly, given your attitude,' Daly replied.

Falley tapped the table as he glanced across at the spin-doctor, as if reprimanding him. He probably just wanted Daly to do the explaining to save him the unpleasant task.

Daly took a deep breath, as one might do before entering a room full of decay.

'Public opinion, for the moment, is firmly against the continuance of this sort of development,' he said, frowning for the first time.

Don glanced across to Martin, who himself looked agape. That couldn't be the only reason.

'And?' Don persisted.

'The government wants to promote a greener image right now, and this would be taken by many protest groups as a volte-face.'

Don shook his head. It was bollocks. Valid reasons, perhaps, but they'd always been successfully negotiated in the past. There had to be something else.

'What's going on here?' Don asked, and his voice had lowered almost to a whisper.

Falley suddenly looked up at Don, and there was something approaching sympathy in the older man's expression.

'I want to speak to Don alone,' said Jack Falley. The three mandarins instantly rose from their seats and made for the door without comment or hesitation. Daly stayed put, but for the first time, looked uncomfortable. Falley was staring across at the window, past Daly, apparently ignoring him.

'Minister, I strongly advise against speaking without –'

Falley raised a hand slowly.

'I've had enough of your advice for one day, you little shit. Now get out and make yourself scarce.'

Daly reeled back in the chair. Falley turned and stared at him, and the young man rose and left, his face reddened and lowered. Falley waited as Martin also rose after a nod from Don, and then the two men were alone.

Falley beckoned Don to move closer, and when the older man started to impart what he had to say in a hoarse whisper, Don's spine was raked by an icy finger – the minister thought they might be under surveillance, here, in Don's own offices?

'Listen son, I don't have much time. Frankly, you are not the man to be seen with at the moment.'

Don's mind raced as Falley cleared his throat yet again.

'That little wanker Daly has dirt on you. What it is, I don't know exactly, and even if I did, you know I couldn't and wouldn't say. But Lucy's father called me this morning. He's got wind of it as well. Something's landed in Daly's lap and he can't ignore it. The Northeast developments are off, and if I were you, I'd get out of the country before it all hits the fan. I don't know what it was you and that friend of yours got up to the other night, but Daly has you hook, line and sinker, and if Lucy's father is to be believed, so do at least two of the broadsheets. I'm only telling you this because Lucy's father is a friend, and whatever hurts you will inevitably hurt her. But be warned Don. Her father is not amused by what he's heard, and if what the little birdies have been telling me is correct, I'm not surprised.'

Don was frozen. The old man's skin seemed like that of an elephant, lined and heavy, and the faint aroma of stale tea on his breath was nauseating.

Falley stood, straightened his tie, and pushed the chair towards the table before extending his hand.

Don rose and took Falley's hand, and the man's brief grip was shockingly strong.

'Good luck,' Falley said, and then he was gone.

Don wandered, like some short-circuited automaton, over to the fireplace which had been removed, piece by piece, from his mother's mansion in Fulham after her death. He reached above it and took down his father's favourite golf club, the mashie used the day he'd won the seniors at Carnoustie.

And then he wrecked the room. By the time Martin burst in, Don had already smashed every mirror and

125

framed picture in the suite and had started on the furniture. And when Martin returned with the security guards from reception, Don was on his knees before the empty hearth, a glittering carpet of glass shards all about him – his head was buried in his hands, and he was rocking back and forth, sobbing like a child.

It had taken more than an hour to bind the naked man. Naomi had struggled to maintain her composure, her stern façade, as the three men strained and sweated. The captive writhed and kicked, trying to frustrate their efforts every step of the way.

But once his hands, ankles and knees had been secured with the rubber-coated twine, his efforts were wasted. Naomi could feel herself weaken at the sight of his back and leg muscles straining against the firm knots, and the moistness at her sex was now constant, but she knew that her moment would come, and this terrible waiting was an essential ingredient.

The tension of the ropework allowed him only to raise his head. Every other part of him was securely trussed so that his entire body could, if Naomi so wished, be rolled across the floor with comparative ease now that he had no purchase with foot or hand to oppose such an action. He was utterly helpless.

The girl, on the other hand, had been left comparatively free to move, her hands lightly tied behind her back as she sat on the fabric-covered blanket box. She was still completely naked. The captives were facing one another, and although they had been maintaining fairly regular eye contact, it always seemed to end with the girl sobbing, and so they had ceased the silent communication.

Naomi checked her watch – three hours had passed since it had been confirmed that everything was working and now the man was starting to crack, muttering to himself, his eyes searching the tiled floor for something. The door slid open, and the men entered bang on time, two of the girls directly behind.

The men pushed the man on to his side, and quickly rubbed down his limbs, digging their strong, short fingers deep into his flesh. The relief on his face was pitiful.

The girls fussed about the bound female, rubbing eucalyptus balm into her shoulders and thighs, smoothing her bare feet with cooling cream, cupping their small hands to gently massage her little breasts, carefully drawing the long-toothed comb through her bobbed, jet-black hair.

Naomi savoured yet another brief glimpse of the man's penis as he was rolled on to his back. It was trapped between his belly and legs, and she could see little more than his helmet, but that alone was enough to make her almost weep with desire – it was like a plum, even in its deflated state.

She remembered the cock in her hands, and was imagining the thickness working against her womb, when the sudden shuffle behind alarmed her and she turned to see Minami beckoning.

'It is time,' said Minami, and Naomi nodded, eager for the green light to be confirmed. And Minami related her orders slowly, carefully. The man was not to be touched. Not a finger of any female was to be placed upon him. The men would continue to relieve his muscles every hour, and when the seven hours was complete, he was to be unbound, walked, fed, then bound for another seven hours. And so it would go on.

But the girl? Minami detailed what was to be done to her. Naomi absorbed the directions in silence, unquestioning. The girl was to be used every alternate hour, and it was imperative that the man be made to witness what was happening to her. If he struggled, or appeared to be finding relief through movement of his muscles, he was to be flogged by Naomi herself. He must not be allowed to ejaculate, not one drop. The preparation was to begin immediately, and would continue until the strangers arrived, with a three-hour sleep break after two seven-hour sessions. It might be within the next few hours, it might be two days, but the regime had to be strictly adhered to.

Naomi remained bowing as Minami made her slow shuffling way down the corridor, then returned to the room determined – despite the powerful urges sweeping through her – to follow the orders to the letter.

Seven

Lucy realised why Stefan had experienced trouble describing Thierry's whereabouts. The concealed entrance Stefan led her to when they emerged from the car was natural, a curious cleft of jutting rock forming a perfect barrier to eyes prying from the roadside, and behind the promontory of granite, a sudden, sharp descent into what appeared to be a cave.

Stefan considerately flicked on a small pencil torch and passed it back to Lucy as they made their way down the well-worn track between the rocks. Stefan clearly knew the route very well, but Lucy had to take great care not to trip over the sharp stones.

Their steps echoed about what had to be a high-ceilinged cave, and the sound of them was mingled with the trickle of water, a deep babbling somewhere further ahead, and single drips, closer, splashing on to cold rock. It was a frightening, eerie place, and Lucy stayed as close as she could to Stefan.

All at once, the treacherous path became a true level concrete platform, and within seconds, Stefan had located and opened a small but thick metal door which made even Lucy stoop in order to pass through.

The sudden glare of light after the darkness sent spots swimming before her eyes as she waited for Stefan to shut and bolt the door. Then he started off down the corridor. The lurid puce walls, with similarly nauseating pink industrial linoleum flooring, through the long narrow entrance put Lucy in mind of a hospital, a government building of some kind, with its soulless, dusty dryness.

But when they emerged from the elevator, in which the buttons were worn blank with usage, she guessed that they had descended further, and the transformation when the door slid open was remarkable.

Soft lights of varying warm hues lit the apartment, which was a huge, open-plan living-area. There was no sign of Thierry, but Lucy fancied that she could smell him, that he was near.

Stefan descended the three broad steps and crossed, only turning briefly to make sure that Lucy had kept up. When he opened the door beside what appeared to be a kitchen, she fully expected to see Thierry waiting for her, but what lay before her was an empty bedroom.

'Miss Lucy, please,' said Stefan, indicating that she should enter.

'Where's Thierry?' she asked, and she was aware that a note of mild panic had introduced itself.

'Monsieur Levant busy now. Miss Lucy sleep,' Stefan replied, and she wasn't sure if that was a hint of an order in the bodyguard's voice.

She stared at him for what felt like a long time, but he did not elaborate.

'OK,' she said, suddenly weary, 'OK, Miss Lucy sleep.'

The room was small and plainly furnished, the bed freshly made-up, the sheets cool and new, and despite her longing for Thierry, despite the myriad of questions she now had for him, she was soon asleep.

Lucy knew she was dreaming, but there was a quality of solidity about the scene and the faces, the smells and sounds surrounding her.

She wasn't familiar with the room at all, but she knew that it was abroad – not Iceland, not Geneva, but further away. Ryan was there, just behind her, watching her, and Stefan was outside the door to protect them both from unwelcome intruders. The room was oppressively warm, and the scent of unfamiliar food was mixed with the heavier, sweet aroma of perfumed flesh.

129

The girl hanging from the chains was gagged with a broad rubber band over which she had clamped her clean white teeth, and the rubber hood she wore was secured about her neck with a studded belt. The thick black strap which bound her wrists was connected to the chain above, bolted to the ceiling. The leather corset was painfully tight at the waist, causing the girl's hips to flare unnaturally, and her heavy breasts, oiled and gleaming in the dim green light, seemed absurdly full, perhaps silicone-enhanced, her nipples tight points of hard arousal.

The man tethered opposite the chained woman was also clad in a tight suit, but his, in brilliantly shiny petrol-blue rubber, was a complete body-suit with attached full-face mask – there seemed no obvious means of breathing bar a tiny slit in the centre of the face, a flap which was rapidly moving in time with the captive's heaving chest. The only other opening in the suit was at his crotch, where his penis, semi-erect, appeared surreally pale, almost white against the dark rubber. He was attached to the pole, which ran from floor to ceiling, with two sets of cuffs, one binding his hands, the other his ankles. His head was raised slightly, as if he were trying to hear what was going on.

Lucy turned to Ryan. He was bare apart from leather trousers, and she beckoned him towards the couple. Lucy looked down to see that she too was wearing a costume, but it could hardly have been more unlike the garb the others wore – the velvet suit was just like Phillipa's, deep burgundy, the beautiful court shoes were softest leather, high heeled. Her stockings were purest silk, white and glimmering. Without any reflection to check, she knew she had been carefully made-up in fifties style, with thick, heavy make-up, especially about her eyes, and the slight discomfiture on the scalp brought the realisation that she was wearing a hat of some sort, a pill-box affair with a thin net veil covering her face. Her body felt incredibly restricted and she supposed that she was wearing a corset of some kind – the unusual elevation of her chest suggested that the firm support bearing her breasts was also ribbed and tightly fastened.

Lucy's movement felt strained, almost slow-motion, and this strangeness of movement seemed to be repeated in the actions of the others – Ryan, now at her side, was suddenly between the bound couple, staring at the woman as she gently swung her torso to relieve the tension on her raised arms. Lucy ordered Ryan to do something, she wasn't sure what, and he moved to the side, allowing Lucy space to get to the girl.

The girl's face was perfectly framed by the hood, and Lucy saw herself in the dark, defiant eyes, the awry smirk, and even when Lucy brought her hand – white cotton gloved – across the girl's face, the captive did little more than shake her head slightly before pursing her lips and blowing a sarcastic kiss.

Lucy turned to see that Ryan was on his knees and had the penis of the bound man in his hand, squeezing it, checking it closely, and the man himself was jerking his hips as if in reflex, obviously in need of relief.

Again, words came from her mouth, but Lucy could not hear them. The pole-bound man clearly could, for he jerked his torso back from Ryan, fearful, and the gasp from the woman behind told Lucy that she was indeed now in charge of this scenario. Ryan stood, his hand still gripped tightly about the captive's cock, and as he did so, he unbuckled his own belt. The lowering of the thick zip seemed to be the only sound in the room as Lucy turned again to the female, now cowed, her eyes hooded and wary.

Lifting the breasts, the warmth came only gradually through the white cotton, but Lucy massaged firmly, avoiding the nipples as the woman writhed, her head thrown back, deep groans rumbling in her chest. The woman had parted her legs as far as she could considering that she was practically on heeled tip-toe already, but there was room enough for Lucy to step forward and work her skirted hips against the thrusting pussy, hairless and gleaming with oil.

'Filthy bitch,' said the girl, and Lucy did not respond, but leaned down and took a hard nipple between her teeth and gently bit. The girl gasped aloud and slumped on the chain in a vain effort to remove the sensitive bud from Lucy's mouth, but Lucy stayed exactly where she was, and the severe tugging on the girl's nipple forced her to return to her original position. Lucy licked long and hard into the large brown softness about the firm small nipple, swirling her tongue circularly, probing into the tenderness as the woman started to pant. The scent of her was warm and sweet, the smell of entrapment and frustrated passion, and when Lucy turned to the other nipple, not biting or nibbling, but sucking long and hard, as if at a miniature cock, the girl seemed to pass into a faint of sorts, slumping heavily, forcing Lucy to lean further down to keep the nipple in her mouth.

Lucy brought herself upright and looked down to see that the woman's pussy lips were parted, the brown labia like little wings between her legs, and Lucy brought her right hand up slowly, merely brushing the cool cotton over the shaved crotch before allowing her palm to close in, her fingers to massage deeper, down towards the well of the frustration. She maintained the grip on the woman's sex as she turned to see that Ryan, now squatting, had his own cock in his hand and was rubbing it frantically as his head bobbed over the captive's erection. Lucy tapped Ryan on the shoulder, ordered him to move, and soon she had him with his trousers at his ankles, the engorged, saliva-coated cock of the pole-man stuck inside his rectum as he leaned forward to suck on the female slave's breasts.

Lucy was still constrained in the outfit, her breasts aching for release, her pussy cramping with the need for fingers, cock and tongue. And yet, she seemed able to maintain the detachment, stood patiently, her heeled feet parted as far as the tight skirt would allow as she teased the woman's bud, only occasionally allowing a cottoned finger to slip into the hotness of her gaping sex as Ryan sucked ever harder on the scented breasts.

Slapping Ryan's arse as it was fucked by the man seemed to signal the impending climax, and it was Ryan himself who started to buck faster then, the rubbered man responding immediately with a series of toe-stretching thrusts which had him straining against the pole so that the cuffs ground noisily against the metal, and Lucy brought her hand beneath Ryan, gripping his erection as the orgasm started to sieze the girl, her cries intensifying as Ryan pulled and sucked ferociously, working his fingers vigorously into her chest flesh as he clamped his teeth hard about her right nipple, his fingers imitating the pressure on her left.

They all seemed to come simultaneously, Ryan bucking and gasping as Lucy worked her clenched fist along his member, the suited man moaning inside his hood as he emptied himself into Ryan's backside, and the girl herself reaching a breathless, soundless peak as Lucy's gloved fingers fucked deep into her pussy, Ryan's mouth and fingers still working hard on her besieged nipples.

Lucy alone didn't come, and she felt herself float back from the scenario, her legs encased within the stockings, her pussy trapped within the tight panties, her breasts imprisoned by the girdle and straps, ankles arched, toes squeezed and pointed, face caked beneath the powder, lips coated with sweet ruby fat. And even if she had been able to get her gloved hands to her aching pussy, it would not have been enough.

If it was possible to have a mind orgasm, she had it, and her senses fluxed and reeled and fused, and the room vanished, the costume was torn from her. Her legs were suddenly apart, her pussy available and open to her, and she brought both hands down, briefly smoothed her inner thighs and pubis to make sure that all was as it should be, then pulled on her pulsing bud no more than half a dozen times before the come surged through her like an electric shock, leaving her arched and rigid before relief washed in like the tide, and she started to wake.

And when she woke she was still alone. The room was uncomfortably warm, and she had kicked off the covers in her sleep. She scanned around for a clock, but there was nothing to indicate the time, and with no natural light she couldn't even guess what time it was. She rose, drew one of Thierry's shirts over her head, and gingerly opened the bedroom door. The open-plan suite was empty, a long, low fish tank bubbling brightly along a far wall, diffuse light from an ante-room spreading across the scattered furniture.

She found herself almost tip-toeing across the heated floor, as if she was about to spy on a friend, or make a furtive midnight raid on the fridge.

There was no sound, no sign of life at all. She used the toilet and, feeling strangely chilled, returned to the bedroom. Her clothes were neatly piled on a chair by the sliding mirrored door which led to the wardrobes. She hadn't left them like that. She sniffed them and realised they had been washed.

She dressed quickly, shunning the shower. She wanted to get out, a sudden desire for fresh air and sunlight gripping her as well as a maddening urge to find out what time it was, what day it was.

In the kitchen, a frustratingly simple arrangement of steel boxes and units, she eventually located the refrigerator and found orange juice; a cupboard yielded peppered biscuits and some dark, fruity bread. She ate and drank as she toured the strange apartment.

Thierry had always kept the bulk of his art collection in Amsterdam, happy to lend it to various institutions and galleries on condition that they cared for it properly. But he'd clearly brought some of his favourites here, to this strange underground place. And they were good. A Rembrandt sketch here, Durer woodcuts plainly framed, dimly lit. Much of the work she didn't recognise, especially the small statuettes which appeared to be Egyptian, perhaps long ago raided from tombs.

But there was an austerity about the place which at once unsettled and saddened Lucy. This great man she'd loved for so long, but who would never be her partner, this enigmatic, sometimes frightening man who undoubtedly loved her – he seemed, through these works, to be expressing some great loneliness which she couldn't describe yet innately understood. He loved beauty, wanted to have it all about him. But none of it felt like his. The apartment, impressive though it was, did not feel like a home. It felt like what it was: a refuge, a bunker which protected him from the real world.

She felt suddenly depressed and confused. Perhaps it had been a mistake to come here. She had probably just upset him. And yet their lovemaking had been so intense, so rewarding for both of them. Surely it could not be wrong to love someone so much, so genuinely?

But she knew she was denying too much. Whether she liked to forget it or not, Mrs Levant was a reality. She was undoubtedly beautiful, probably very intelligent. It would be astonishing if she wasn't. And there was more she was denying. Don. Her man – her husband.

She slumped into the reclining armchair and briefly scanned her options. She should go back soon, but she felt that nothing had yet been resolved. Don had sent a man to look for her. So what? He may well have done so before, but she'd never noticed – after all, it was Thierry's security who had noted and apprehended the man. Was Don's action one of love, or merely suspicion? Was he anxious to secure her protection, or simply his own reputation? She felt that there was such a distance between them now, that these questions could not be asked, let alone answered. She didn't trust him enough. And yet, what to do about it? Walk away?

She thought of Don, their early relationship. She had loved him then, and still did now. No doubt about it. Despite any logical arguments she made to herself about leaving him as a bad lot, an irredeemably selfish child, she knew she could never stop loving him.

But did he really love her, and love her as much? That was what she wanted to know, and this trip, thus far, had not provided any possibility of finding that out.

A movement and shifting somewhere made her sit up, and when she stood, a shadow on a far wall indicated that someone was moving down the short corridor. She felt a sudden blast of icy fear, and when the shadow thickened and shortened and became a figure and she could see that the figure was Stefan, she almost cried out with relief.

The big man was shaved and had changed into a lurid blue silk suit which made him appear like some nightclub turn. He looked grim, even a little sad. He stood at the top of the three broad steps which led down from the corridor and beckoned her.

'Miss Lucy, come.'

Lucy met the man's eyes and saw a mixture of fear and disgust. He was unhappy about something, and he was not doing a good job of disguising it.

As she followed him down the corridor leading from Thierry's underground living-room, she tried to ask Stefan, in Spanish, then in Dutch, what was wrong, but he would not say anything other than that she should follow, so she did.

The room to which he led her was tiny in comparison to the open-plan area. It was square, perhaps a little bigger than the bedroom, and the walls were about as long as they were tall, so that Lucy felt as if she had walked into a huge cube. The windowless walls were uniformly lined with loaded bookshelves, and against the right-hand wall there was a portal with no door, which led into another room which Lucy could see was the same size as the one she was in. It too was full of shelves, all packed with books and magazines and sheaves of papers. And on the far wall of that room too, another door, and another room, and so it seemed to continue. It had to be a trick of some kind, a *trompe l'oeil* masterpiece of mirrors and hyper-realistic draughtsmanship.

But when Stefan led her through the first of the connecting rooms, then the next, she realised to her astonishment that it was real. It had to have been a depository at one point, for the shelving was old, perhaps not antique, but certainly not brand new. And the iron, runner-bound stepladders which hung in every room were certainly rusted in parts, their old rubber wheels reminiscent of hospital trolleys.

After seven or eight rooms, Lucy had lost count, and even when turning round to try and see how many rooms they had passed through, she found that it was impossible to determine as the rooms were very slightly longer on one side, and although she could see through four or five of the doorways they had passed, the first of the entrances had been incrementally obscured by the door frames of the others.

It seemed that the rooms would go on forever, perhaps in a huge circle which would end up in the room they had first entered, but then, without any warning, they entered a room which was just as broad as the others, and also had a door which led to another section of the library, but this room was immensely long, also shelved to the ceiling all the way, and with an additional bookcase, also ceiling-height, running down it's centre.

Stefan coughed as they turned left sharply and made their way along between the walls of books, evenly spaced lamps, slung low from the ceiling, passing over them every five yards or so.

Lucy saw Thierry before she heard him.

He was standing at the end of the room, still forty, perhaps fifty, feet away, and she stepped up the pace, passing Stefan as they neared. But Thierry did not extend a hand, or even a smile as she approached. She slowed, instinct telling her something was badly wrong. Thierry avoided her eyes, then moved away towards the computer console in the recess at the end of the room.

This area was, compared to the rest of the library, almost cosy. The ceiling had been lowered to little higher than Thierry's height, and a low curving pine wall waist-high, enclosed the area, which was dominated by a long black desk upon which the computer terminal sat.

Thierry bid her sit beside his, and he donned his specs before talking. He looked grim, almost perplexed, and was breathing slowly, audibly.

'Stefan told me what happened,' said Thierry, and Lucy waited, eager to find out what was causing the sullen, heavy atmosphere.

'It seems that this Mr Villiers is harmless. An amateur. The usual story I'm afraid. A young man with some experience of the armed forces finds himself hungry for excitement, joins any outfit which might offer it in some shape or form. He's lucky he joined an agency. So many of these men become mercenaries, end up dead in parts of the world no one knows exist.'

He removed his specs, frowned at them, then carefully circled on the offending spot with a portion of his thin cotton sweater nipped between his fingers.

'Do you remember Willem?' he asked then, smiling, and Lucy struggled to place the name. 'Willem, the good-looking young guy, great skier. Remember, he was in charge of foreign acccounts when you started with me.'

The man's face flew back into her mind after so many years. Yes, she did remember, and yes, he was a startlingly handsome guy, a personable and popular head of department whom Lucy had never worked under, but who caused all sorts of excited gossip among the girls in the staff restaurant. Lucy nodded her recollection at Thierry, and he replaced his specs.

'That boy had such a bright future. When he said he was resigning, I offered him everything within reason, even a place on the board if he committed to another ten years, but he was adamant. An offer, that's what he said, a good offer. Do you know what it was?'

Lucy shook her head.

'He had a friend who worked freelance for a group of rebels in East Africa. Willem liked the sound of it, so he joined his friend. He didn't want the money, it was the excitement, the challenge. So he went missing. This was long after the coup attempt had failed. His mother contacted me. I sent some of our people to trace him. It took them three months, but they eventually came back with his papers, stinking of death. The pro-government militia had taken him with six others, staked them out in the open for all the townfolk to see, then opened their abdomens with bayonets and left them to the dogs and pigs. That's how he died. Eaten alive by animals with people watching, powerless to help.'

Lucy's guts churned, and Thierry obviously noted her pallor change.

'I'm sorry, my dear, I don't intend to upset you at all. But you see, some men will pursue thrills and excitement to such a degree that they bring death to themselves. I have seen so many friends do it. They overreach, on a whim, an impulse, only to find that beneath them is air, empty space, and then they fall. One after another, they do it. So many men who should be great men, comfortable, happy men, they reach too far and end up in their graves. That's what happened to poor Willem. His mother died of a broken heart, his father shortly after her. It wasn't only himself he threw into the grave.'

Lucy found anger supplanting her nausea.

'Why are you telling me this, Thierry?' she said, and the tone of her voice drew a warning glance from him as he turned to the console and flicked the screen into life.

'Your husband has a very good security system protecting his files. It took us much longer than it ought to have done to access them, but we learned from it and will know better next time. I don't know if you are aware of the sort of material he keeps in his office, but this is only a fraction of the bank we first opened.'

He fiddled with the mouse, and the screen suddenly shifted to a video of a chained, leather-bound redheaded girl being orally attended to by a peroxide blonde in a pale green rubber nurse's outfit. The quality was good, the picture clear, but the zooming-in, the crude sidestepping to better capture the blonde's face burying itself into the hairs of the bound girl, was obvious and amateur. Upon an unheard direction, the blonde girl pulled away from between the redhead's legs and stared up at the camera, her tongue tracing an obscene circle about her smeared lipstick, her eyes half-shut in fake ecstasy, and Lucy could now see that the blonde's hand was fully inside the other girl's backside. Lucy felt the colour flush back to her face, memories of that recent night with Phillipa. They hadn't done anything quite as disgusting as that, but the crassness of the image still embarrassed her.

Thierry used the mouse to fast-forward the footage, and it shifted and broke and slowed and reformed and Lucy felt her eyes shut involuntarily as the face of her husband appeared, and his cock was buried in the blonde's arse and the redhead was licking the blonde, and the blonde was fisting the redhead, and then Don was out and manically wanking himself over the two girls. Lucy rose from her seat and turned to leave, her footing unsteady. She grabbed the broad ridge of the low wooden divider and stood staring at the corridor of books, Stefan beside her, Thierry sniffing behind her.

'Would you like to see any more of this?' Thierry asked, so matter of factly that she almost screamed with rage as she turned back to face him.

'No, I would not. Would you like me to?' she asked then, and she noted that his eyes briefly found the floor, something like shame glazing them before he stood up.

'If *I* didn't show you this, who would?' he asked then, and Lucy felt tears well, her chest quavering.

'Your husband!' Thierry barked.

Lucy felt her legs quiver. She returned to the seat and shielded her eyes from the brilliant colours pulsing and shifting onscreen. It had shifted to another place, perhaps another time, two young brunettes dressed as French maids, long black stockinged legs entwined, pussies grinding together, a juddering stream of sperm, in slow-motion, spattering over their conjoined labia and bellies as they gaped and writhed theatrically.

Lucy raised her hand to her already closed eyes and made an effort to get rid of the tears she knew he had noticed.

'Please turn it off,' she said, and he did.

She sniffed. Thierry sighed. Stefan shifted uncomfortably behind them.

'I know you have a very difficult decision to make, but you cannot make it without knowledge of this, this ...'

Thierry stopped, unable to find a word. Lucy cleared her eyes and looked up at him. He looked shattered, perhaps just as angry as her.

He leaned forward in the seat and took one of her hands. She laid the other above his and he caressed her fingers, staring at them, frowning.

'Whatever you want to do, I will help,' he said then, and when he raised his eyes to meet hers, she knew he meant anything.

Have Don killed? It wasn't out of the question for him, and she knew it. A mosquito in his bedroom would cost him more in lost sleep than ordering the assassination of a man like Don. If there was any way of making sure that he would be undetected, he would probably be happy to do it himself.

Lucy brought his hands up to her face and kissed them, then held them to her cheek. If only things had been just a little different. She summoned a smile, then sniffed and drew her loose hair behind her ears.

'How much of this stuff is there?' she asked, and Thierry didn't have to reboot the monitor to tell her.

'There are three separate banks of files which are similar in length, all contain approximately two hours of footage, and if this is typical, it has all been roughly edited. This is the first, the others are still being downloaded. We can only assume that they contain more of the same.'

Lucy swallowed hard, then clasped her hands.

'Let me see it, from the beginning,' she said.

Thierry winced.

'Please. As you said, I have a right to know. Well, I want to see who he's been fucking behind my back. I want to see their faces as well as his. He always told me it was best that he let off steam now and then, that he had special needs in that department. Well, if the expression on his face there was anything to go by, the special needs he has concern him being in charge and having as much fun as he can afford. Let me see the rest of it, Thierry. Please.'

Thierry had already rebooted the file.

Stefan brought iced drinks for them as they sat and watched the endless array of uniformed, luridly made-up girls being dominated by Don. He was always the centre of attention, always his cock, his expression, his come, his directions being obeyed, and always, always, two girls having to perform various acts on one another before he made as photogenic a climax as possible, usually over their kissing faces.

141

Lucy was transfixed by the shifting, sometimes stuttering images. It was as if she were seeing Don for the first time. Objectively, rationally, she saw a healthy, tanned young man enjoying himself imaginatively, but with a certain undercurrent of violence which disturbed her. Emotionally, she saw only betrayal and the red haze of a blinding anger. It was as though he had simply carried on where he left off when the lads in the first fifteen of 1993 had gone their separate ways – it was sheer indulgence on his part.

But there was also the jealousy. He was enjoying it all too much – this wasn't the desperate behaviour of a man who had to unburden odious urges to spare his wife unpleasantness – it was prima facie evidence of simple adultery, and it made her blood boil. And his performances were so vigorous, so involved. She couldn't recall him ever grabbing her by the hair, stuffing his cock into her mouth as he came. He'd never even asked her if she'd ever dreamed of being urinated upon. Not that she had, but the occasional evidence of his prowess in that department had been particularly arousing, and she couldn't help wondering what it must be like.

Only once did she ask Thierry to freeze the material, and when she did so, it was clear that her older lover had been daydreaming, pondering other matters. But he did as she asked, and Lucy shifted her chair closer to the monitor.

The lighting was good, but the girl's face was not visible. Don was sitting on the carpet in front of the sofa, his back resting agsinst it. His face was obscured by the body of the girl sitting on his lap, his cock firmly lodged inside her as she rotated her hips. The dark line of a condom's elasticated base was visibly nipping into Don's shaft. The girl was wearing a short, pale-blue skirt which had been brought up about her waist, and her panties, also light blue, had been pulled to the side to allow him entry. Her top, a plain, tight white T-shirt, had also been drawn up, and there was no sign of any bra. From the movement of the girl's body and arms, it seemed that Don must be sucking at her chest.

But it was the girl's hair that triggered recognition in Lucy. The straight, coppery locks with faint golden streaks. She had seen that style before, vaguely recalled admiring it but dismissing it as too girlish for herself.

Even a careful scan of the visible furniture was not helpful – none was familiar. But it was Don for sure. The picture quality was good enough to make out the light brown scar above his right knee, and she would recognise his hands in any event. And those hands were groping eagerly at the girl's behind, lightly rubbing at his own balls as the girl quickened her strokes, bucking faster, the circular motion maintained as she buried her head into his shoulder. The tell-tale jerks of the girl's buttocks signalled her climax, and from the sudden wilting of Don's cock, still inside her, it seemed that they had found satisfaction mutually – something she'd never ever managed with Don. As the girl raised herself clear of him, and the flagging, rubber-sheathed cock flopped heavily on to his thigh, the girl briefly turned to retrieve a small towel from the end of the sofa.

Thierry froze the moment, as requested, and Lucy's tired mind raced to match the face with a name, a place.

And then she had it. She remembered seeing the girl in passing, perhaps half a dozen times on the way up to Don's Fulham apartment. She was a neighbour. Her name was Kelly. She was an economics student. She lived in the apartment directly below theirs with her two chums. And she was only nineteen. Lucy excused herself. Stefan guided her to the small, functional toilet, and there she spent five minutes throwing up. The bastard.

Any thoughts she had entertained of abandoning the marriage were now dismissed. Before any divorce or separation, before any discussion or arbitration of any kind, she would have revenge. It need not be of the drastic variety which Thierry would undoubtedly favour, but retribution of her own devising, and executed by her. She would have him, one way or another, and he would know the depth of her rage. Feeling better now that her mind was made up, she washed her face and returned to the room.

After a further hour, the patterns of Don's dominance and preferences had been detected; after two hours, they had been confirmed; it was little more than halfway into the third hour when Lucy, drunk with enraged lust, threw herself on to Thierry and demanded to be taken to his room and fucked.

Don stopped halfway up the third flight of stairs to the girl's flat. He raised a hand to his temple and found that it was cold and clammy.

He shouldn't really. He should go home, but he knew he wouldn't stay home. He would be back out, wandering, roaming, and he would eventually end up here, or somewhere like here, so he might as well get it over with. Then he might find sleep.

The girl was different. The flat was the same – always the same – but the girl was definitely new. She welcomed him in, and he sensed that she was nervous.

She offered drink, he declined, asking for water. She was away too long to be pouring a glass of water. He scanned the framed posters on the walls of the cluttered, pink room. A real bordello, no getting away from it. It reminded him of his uni days, when he and the boys would come down to the city for weekends, ostensibly for rugby matches, in reality for their sex education, using their parents' maintenance cash to indulge their schoolboy fantasies.

Snatches of the early experiences passed, unbidden and unwelcome, across his mind's eye. The laughter of what he remembered as an old woman, leather-dressed and garishly painted with stage make-up, as he looked down at his flagging cock; the pain administered by that redheaded woman who'd reeked of gin and cheap perfume; the embarrassment of being thrown from a house, mid-session, after throwing up on a bed after an evening of heavy drinking.

She came back with the water, placed it carefully before him, and tried to sit beside him. He motioned her away. She offered a cigarette, again he declined.

'Sandra's off just now,' the girl said, but Don couldn't even remember who Sandra was. The blonde French maid? The scarlet-heeled German student? It didn't matter any more.

'What do you do?' Don heard himself ask. His hands were limp in his lap. He hadn't even removed the overcoat, though he was sure she must have offered to take it.

'I don't do anal, and I don't swallow,' she replied chirpily, as if relating details of her hobbies in a job interview.

Don closed his eyes and breathed in deeply. It was as if he could smell all of the previous encounters in that one breath: the reek of booze and air-freshener, carpet shampoo mixed with urine and the faint whiff of dung.

'I didn't mean that,' Don said with stilted patience, 'I meant what is it that you actually do, or want to do.'

The girl drew deeply on the cigarette and scanned the cornicing above the curtains, as if the answer might be written there.

'I'm getting singing lessons, and I've done a bit of acting here and there, some photo-shoots,' she said, her smile careful and clean.

She was presentable and polite, her accent marking her as Northern, probably suburban, from decent middle-class stock. Another one who'd headed for the big smoke, looking for a toe in the door, a shot at the big time.

Don surveyed her body. She wasn't slim. The armless blue-green velveteen dress showed her shoulders, but the neckline was high, her breasts beguilingly concealed. Her crossed legs were obviously stockinged, the sheer material shining softly, but he was surprised to see that her feet were unshod. High heeled courts, usually white, were normally *de rigueur* in this class of establishment.

There was something about her face which intrigued him. Her eyes were dark, very dark, and she might well have been wearing contacts which seemed to catch and magnify the available light, making them sparkle.

'Would you stand up?' Don asked, and she smiled closer, as if he'd lapsed into a foreign language.

Don took a deep breath. He wasn't even sure why he was asking her to do it, but he asked again, suddenly shy, feeling that he was somehow intruding, asking something unreasonable.

But she carefully stubbed out the cigarette and stood up. She clasped her heavily ringed hands, apparently awaiting instructions. She was trying to smile at him, unsure of her lipstick, and he caught her briefly flicking her tongue across her front teeth, wiping imagined gloss away. And were her hands trembling? She kept fingering her rings in turn, like prayer beads. She was trying so hard.

Don made a circle in the air with his forefinger, and she turned for him, slowly, carefully, glad to be doing something, and he took in the shape of her, the curve of her hips where the dress was cut to emphasise them. It was clearly an off-the-peg dress, probably cost thirty quid or less, but it suited her, the colour turquoise, sheening emerald on the folds. She kept one knee slightly bent at all times, throwing her hips at an angle which emphasised the firm planes of her buttocks. She turned to face him again, hands now clasped behind her back.

Don stared down at his own hands. They were not shaking, but they felt as if they were.

'May I take a shower?' he asked, still staring at his hands.

'Of course,' she replied.

He frowned at himself as she moved away. May I take a shower? He heard his own voice in his head asking the question. Since when had he ever asked a whore for anything in that manner? May I? He shook his head and leaned forward, took a cigarette from the girl's packet and used her lighter.

When she came back in, she was flushed, embarrassed.

'I can't get the shower to come on,' she said, grimacing.

Don got up, removed his overcoat, and followed her into the bathroom. It was the same set-up as he remembered from his last visit – six months ago perhaps – but the carpet was new. The glass-doored shower cubicle was the same. He leaned inside, reached across to the control panel and turned the main switch clockwise until a click was heard, then the dull distant puff of gas igniting, and the unit hummed into action.

He didn't draw his hand back quickly enough, and a spurt of water caught his forearm, spattering his jacket.

She grabbed his arm, whipped a small towel from the rail behind her, and pressed it over the dampness.

'It's all right,' he said, 'don't worry about that.'

'That's my fault. This isn't my place,' she said, 'so I don't really know where everything is, and –'

'It's all right,' he repeated, but his normal impatience seemed to have deserted him in the face of the girl's obvious anxiety to please.

'Look, why don't you just go and relax and I'll be in shortly,' he said, but her hands had gripped his forearm, and when she looked up to him, it was with real feeling in her eyes.

'I want to please you,' she said, and he slowly drew her hands from him and nodded.

'I know, but please, just let me, I just need to freshen up, then I'll be in. Go on now.'

She left. Don undressed and stepped into the steam-filled cubicle. There was no ledge on which to sit, so he leaned against the tiled wall, letting the hot water scatter across his head, run down his back.

The events of the day flitted through his mind, broken and crazily sequenced. Falley's face, Daly's smugness, Martin's obvious shock at the refusal. Perhaps it was all his own fault. Maybe he'd become lazy, complacent. He leaned on his crossed forearms and breathed in the steam, felt it sear his lungs, fill his stomach. He would have to get sorted out, get clean and fit again if he was going to take on these people, because surely, he would have to fight now. Blackmail? But who? Why wasn't hard to imagine – the recent articles in the business sections had been guessing at his wealth, and the most conservative estimate of his holdings and stocks arrived at a figure of ten billion dollars. He wasn't so sure himself, but Martin had confirmed that a total realisation of assets would probably be in the region of seven billion.

The hand on his waist was such a shock that he jerked upright and emitted a short gasp of surprise. He hadn't heard the door slide open, and she was already inside. Seeing his alarm, she muttered an apology and retreated, but he found her arm and drew her back in.

147

Naked, her hair pinned up but already wet from the shower spray, she was voluptuous, her skin silky smooth, chest pulsing arousal, her nipples prominent and dark. She raised her face, eyes closed, and he kissed her softly. She didn't respond, her lips open, and he felt the slackness in her body as he brought her closer. He breathed in the scent of her hair as the water soaked it – a familiar aroma, muted but strangely reminiscent of the outdoors, a half-forgotten holiday.

Her hands found the back of his neck and started to rub in long, hard strokes down the tensioned tendons, smoothing her thumbs against the points behind his ears. He stretched his head back and savoured her touch. Perhaps she'd trained in aromatherapy or something similar, because she certainly knew where to apply her fingers, how to locate stress in the muscles, and when her grip lowered to his waist and gently directed him to turn, he did so, leaning against the wall, the shower cascading directly on to him. Her fingers worked into his shoulders, pressing hard at times, hard enough that he tensed and arched his arms back, but then she would palm him calm and repeat the motion, pressing the accumulated tension away, and further down, into the columns of muscles about his spine, each stroke of her fingers seeming to absorb the pain of the day.

He lost any sense of time as she worked her way surely down to his legs, both of her hands kneading his thighs, his calves, and finally even the complex architecture of his ankles. He could feel his knees weaken with the debilitating effect of the relaxation combined with the steam.

She dried him there, in the bathroom, quickly and firmly, the towels pre-warmed, compounding the now pleasant fatigue.

He could have slept right there, on the bathroom floor, but she led him to the bedroom and left him with a towel to finish drying his hair. He pulled the collar of the thick towelling robe she had given him close about his neck, and rubbed languidly at his short hair.

Looking at his reflection in the mirrored wardrobe, he contrasted the face with that in photos and videos of years recently past, and knew that he was in a bad way: the darkness below his eyes, the sternness of his expression and the puffiness about his jawline confirmed a growing physical resemblance to the father he'd sworn never to emulate.

He'd lain back and passed into a light sleep, for when he awoke, the girl was back, lying beside him, her hand palming his stomach.

'How long was I out?' he asked.

'About half an hour,' she replied, and Don sat up, remotely aware that he should feel some vague annoyance at being allowed to slumber when she was being paid.

In the reflection he saw himself, tousled and frowning, and beside him, also sitting upright, the girl was wearing a plain white bra and matching panties. He watched her in the mirror as she put her face to his neck and gently kissed. He breathed in deeply. There it was again, that smell, distinct one second, gone the next.

He stood up and removed the robe, and he was about to remount the bed when her head was at his cock, one hand gently cupping his scrotum as the other peeled back his foreskin and gently squeezed him to fill his glans.

Don watched her in the mirror, lapping at the underside of his dick, her hand raising him so that she could trace a line down his length with her tongue tip, and her eyes were shut when she opened her mouth and carefully, slowly brought him into the warmth of her.

He watched himself standing, one hand on her head, stroking her hair as she fed his cock into her, sucking gently. He stiffened quickly, his member thickening where it was visible between her hand and mouth.

A silver string of saliva slung from her mouth to his dick as he gently removed her and lay her down. She kept a hand on him, stroking long and hard now. He moved on top of her, his eyes riveted on hers. She was, he had to admit it, beautiful. As far as he could tell she had donned no more make-up after the shower, and he could see now that she didn't need it – her complexion was perfect, the blush of genuine arousal on her cheeks, the tell-tale glow on her upper chest, her blood-filled lips parted to allow only a glimmer of the white teeth, lightly gritted. She wanted him. She really did want him, and he felt himself harden further as he cupped one hand about her waist, another behind her head, and kissed her.

He'd never kissed a whore, not like this. She bucked her body beneath him as he probed her mouth, wrenching her lips against his, and she struggled to get her legs apart as he wound his fingers into her slightly damp hair and gripped as if he feared she might suddenly slip away.

She moaned when his cock-tip nudged her sex lips, and he felt her whole body shudder with sudden restraint. He drew his face away and looked quizzically at her.

'We have to, you know, I have to use a . . .'

Don was momentarily lost, and when she drew the small foil packet from beneath the pillow, he thought at first it might be a drug of some kind, then realised with relief that it was a condom.

'You don't mind do you?' she asked, and Don said not at all.

'Can I put it on?' she asked, smiling cheekily. Don smiled and nodded as she wriggled down the bed beneath him.

He rolled on to his back as she tore open the packet and fiddled with the black rubber. Her face was a picture of concentration as she carefully placed the slippy condom on his cock-head and squeezed him hard to stiffen him further. But he'd wilted slightly with the interruption, so she removed the still rolled condom, cupped it in her palm and sucked on him again, stroking his shaft faster than before, her saliva helping to ease the friction between skin and skin. He lay back and enjoyed the sensation of the tight fingers about him, the warm tongue and nibble of her teeth along his hardness. And then she stopped, and the frantic fumbling told him she was attempting to sheathe him again.

He looked down just in time to see her fingers draw fully down him, and as they did, they unrolled the fine black rubber. She carefully adjusted the band at the condom's end about the thickness at his base, pulling his hair away where it might be trapped, and then she brought both hands to his rubber-encased cock and massaged it as she savoured it with her eyes, treating it gently, as if it were a prize of some sort. He was now rigid, his glans straining against the rubber, the thick veins of his cock highlighted within the casing. As he watched her squeeze and stroke him, the flush on her cheeks now glowing, her eyes wide, fingers eager, he wanted to sink himself into her, to draw her down on to him slowly, but she hadn't finished.

She took him again into her mouth, this time watching him closely as she rolled the bulb around it, forcing it to the door of her throat, then taking it out and biting gently into the blackness, and he felt his balls rise and tighten as she continued to stare at him.

'Are you ready?' she asked then, wiping her lips.

He drew her face towards him and she quickly moved up, throwing her self atop him. He brought his hand down to his erection and the sensation of her saliva, comparatively cool on the rubber, was like silk beneath his fingers.

Don drew his own hand up and down himself a couple of times, and then her hand was with his, also pulling, strengthening the fullness of him, and they pulled him into her together, her pushing her hips down, him jerking up to help the entry.

And she was tight. As tight as any girl he'd ever been with. She grabbed his hair with both hands. Don could smell her now as she resumed kissing him as only Lucy had ever kissed him; long and hard. Some passion within the girl had been aroused which was infectious, invigorating, and he responded, pulling her against his lips with a vigour which brought one of her teeth against his bottom lip, and the blood mixed sweetly as she brought her pelvis down against him and he felt, despite the numbing effect of the rubber, the heat of her sex pulse and grip about him as she sank on to his cock.

She threw her head back, hands still in his hair, and now bucked with an animal urgency which hurt. He brought his mouth to her nipples, sucking them deeply in turn, feeling the heaviness of the young, full breasts upon his face as she clasped him nearer, and still she pounded her sex on to his, forcing him deep with each full motion, making circular motions with her hips and drawing herself down his body so that his cock strained downwards, his stiffness keeping him inside her as she drew herself to the end of him before thrusting herself back on, tightening her muscles simultaneously to make each entry feel just like the first.

Driven by the girl's enthusiasm, he turned her over on to her back, all the while kissing her deeply, and dictated the pace for himself as she wrapped her legs about him, high, her calves crossing at his back, her openness raised fully for maximum depth. He thrust fully into her time and again, slowly at first, but then with greater urgency, and she threw her arms back behind her head, closed her eyes and screamed sidelong into the pillow as he raised her buttocks with both hands, his head deep in her hair, and that smell arose once again, that smell which seemed to taunt him, bolster him, and, with the memory still evasive but tangibly hovering in his mind, and with that smell invading his senses, and the frantic need of the girl below, he started to come. She clasped his buttocks, her fingernails digging deeply into his flesh as he started to jerk uncontrollably into her, and she cried out as his grunts told her he was finishing, her pussy tightening about him as she reached her own come, their bodies sticky with sweat as the peak passed and they slowed to the tender kiss which marked the start of a much-needed sleep.

Eight

Thierry was due to leave for South Africa that evening, and Lucy had found herself toying playfully with the notion that she could easily find a reason to go to Johannesburg – a fact-finding mission could always be justified.

But as she towelled herself dry after the sauna, she forced herself to realise that it was nothing more than a fantasy. Their lovemaking had been so complete, so secure and rewarding, that she'd slept soundly, not stirring at all until the lack of his arms about her had registered.

He would be busy somewhere, perhaps back at the console, cataloguing Don's guilt. Stefan was lounging in front of the television, watching his wrestling videos, and had already left a tray bearing breakfast for her in the bedroom.

Perhaps she could persuade Thierry to join her on a quick tour of the inland. She was sure he could secure the use of a helicopter for a couple of hours. Then again, perhaps a quiet, leisurely lunch by the lakeside would be more relaxing, give them a chance to speak before they went their separate ways. *Separate*. The word hurt her inside even as she thought it, but she knew that the ugliness of home and all it held would have to be faced, and she had never been one to turn from difficulties. Don would have to be dealt with, and if he didn't see sense, confess and apologise fully and sincerely, it was over. Simple as that.

Stefan had procured a small but tasteful selection of new clothes, all of which were functional, expensively labelled. She picked a pair of black leggings and donned the thick, hip-length Aran sweater. The thought occurred that Thierry may already have arranged an outing of some kind, but when she went through to the living area and asked Stefan, the big man acted as if he didn't understand her question, shrugging his massive shoulders and shaking the shaved head.

Lucy stared at him, glued to the cartoonish wrestlers like a gigantic toddler. Suddenly, she remembered the previous evening in the library, the traumatic encounter with proof of her husband's perversity.

'You told Thierry what Villiers said, didn't you?' she asked, smiling, and Stefan's brow wrinkled slightly before blanking as he looked up to her, the innocence of ignorance writ large.

'Thierry said you'd told him all about it. How could you have, unless you understood Villiers, unless you understood English?' Lucy persisted, fear edging the question.

The big man flicked off the television and stared at the remote control as if seeing it for the first time.

'Stefan no understand,' he said guiltily.

Lucy crossed to the armchair opposite the two-seater which he filled, and raised her brows at him, as a teacher might voicelessly reprimand an errant child.

He drew in a deep breath and exhaled it slowly.

'I am dumb to questions,' he said, 'I am dumb to everything, deaf to everything. It is the safest way for me. Monsieur Levant advised me so, and so I have done. And he is right. No one troubles me with questions. I am dumb in whatever language is appropriate.'

Lucy smiled. It was like talking to a completely different person. The façade of idiocy dropped, his face took on a troubled, slightly uneasy aspect.

'No matter,' Lucy said, not wanting to prolong the man's discomfiture. 'Where is Thierry now?'

Stefan shifted in the sofa, scratching at his neck. His jaw was set, the muscles at his temple twitching.

154

'Stefan, what's wrong? Where's Thierry?' Lucy asked, now standing, arms crossed.

'Monsieur Levant has gone,' he said flatly.

'Gone? Gone where? I thought he wasn't due to leave until this evening.'

Stefan nodded.

'Tonight he will fly to South Africa. But he had to go early. He didn't want to see you before he left. He said it would be better,' Stefan said, avoiding her gaze.

Lucy sat down again. Gone? No goodbye? Her insides seemed to be missing altogether, a painful void where her heart and guts should be.

Stefan stood, moved slowly to the corner where the brilliantly coloured fish hovered silently in their bubbling tank, and came back with a thick, padded envelope. He passed it to Lucy, then turned to leave, but paused at the stairs to the elevator just as Lucy was opening the flap.

'Stefan will be here until you have decided what you want to do,' he said, and then the door shifted open and he was gone.

She spilled the contents on to the two-seater. Three compact discs, a letter. Her hands were trembling as she unfolded the paper and read.

My dearest Lucy,

It is such a morning. A morning of a most painful day. I have just left you, beautiful in your sleeping. I am still damp with you, and I can smell you, in my hair, on my fingers, all about me is your smell and I am happy.

But it is over now. I have a wife and family to meet, and I must leave you now to your future, and to your difficulties. I have made some arrangements which will become clearer in due course. Please be assured that your husband will not be harmed physically, by me or any of my people. But, even as I write, there are problems developing for him which may or may not help you resolve your own.

I have spoken with Ryan Villiers, and he has accepted my offer of employment. He now belongs to you. If you choose to discharge him, that is your decision, but I would urge you to take him on the journey I have arranged.

At the airport there are tickets for you and Mr Villiers, and he has been given all relevant details for your arrival and subsequent safekeeping. The other item enclosed is vital, so keep it always with you, and you will know when it is to be used – without it your trip will be wasted.

The discs contain the accessed material we viewed. It may be useful.

Please be safe, and always remember that I loved you as no one else ever will. It was not to be, my dear Lucy, not in this lifetime, but perhaps there will be another, for both of us, and perhaps, in that next time, we will find one another again.

T.

Lucy sank back, raised her hands to her face, and sobbed miserably, tears spilling over her fingers. She read it again, sniffing, her whole body trembling, then reached the mention of the 'other' item enclosed. The discs? She lifted the envelope and shook it. Nothing, but when she palmed the cushioned paper envelope the lump became obvious, and she delved inside it, withdrawing a tiny green glass phial, securely stopped with a cork.

Lucy raised the bottle to the dimness of the lamp. Liquid, thick and murky inside, but something, long and thin, vegetablelike shifting within the darkness, and then she saw the dark-green glint, the curve became a shape, made sense, and she recognised the ring, the plain gold band she'd given to him all those years ago, still where she'd placed it, just under the second knuckle of his left hand's little finger.

She rushed to the toilet to throw up, and when she had finished, exhausted with the painful heaving and retching, she opened her palm to find the phial still there, as if, somehow, she was already following her mentor's final instructions.

Having slept, Don woke to find himself curled tightly about the girl, her back to him, the pair of them like spoons beneath the perfunctory duvet.

He had never ever fallen asleep with a prostitute. Not once. Passed out perhaps, but never slept. He lay awhile, watching the curtained bay-window change from deepest blue to amber, then gold as dawn rose upon the capital.

She stirred when he moved to go to the toilet, and so he stayed, drew her close, and she sighed in her sleep and shifted herself nearer. Her shoulder, exposed, was fringed with wisps of her curls, and he absently studied the natural wave of the hairs as they became defined and darkly golden with daybreak.

Thoughts of the office scattered, like windblown litter, across his mind, but with them came a tightening of his chest and a coldness on his brow. He pulled her closer, savouring the smoothness of her skin against him, the aroma of her now dry sweat. He closed his eyes and allowed the perfume of her hair to sweep over his memories, but still he could not locate the source. The maddening *déjà-vu* almost compelled him to wake her, to ask her what she was wearing, where she had been, but he resisted and lay, waiting, until she stretched and stirred and turned, and then he was ready for her, ready to make love again.

So the morning came and went, a mad tumble of sex and laughter and he allowed himself, for the first time since he could remember, to have fun – real fun. She spanked him theatrically, giggling, chastising him for imagined trans-gressions, and he howled and laughed, then tried to be serious, and she spanked him more, but the laughter erupted every time, and he grabbed her close and had to make no effort whatsoever to enjoy it.

It was only when the hands of the clock started to meet at noon that she became serious and started trying to apologise, but he saved her the effort by quickly showering and leaving.

But before he did, he did something which astonished him, even as he was doing it – he located his wallet, drew one of his cards from it, and handed it to her.

'If you'd like to see me again, please call. Anytime.'

She'd perused the card carefully, studying his name.

'Don,' she said, still staring at the small white rectangle. 'Yes. And, you?'

She made a face, as if shaking off some mask, then kissed him swiftly on the lips.

'Julie,' she said, sounding almost surprised.

He smiled and moved towards the door, but she held him back and engulfed him in one last, lung-draining kiss.

When Don emerged on to the glaringly bright street, the bodies whizzing by, the traffic blaring and screeching, the horror of the office yet to face, he felt like a sixteen-year-old who'd just kissed his favourite teacher.

He hailed a cab, laughing to himself, and then, as he replayed the fun in his head, Julie's face still clear in his mind, her scent and laughter still hovering about him like an aura, Don was driven into the office, and into the worst day of his professional life.

Stefan had driven them both to the airport, and the connecting flight to Heathrow had been awkward.

Villiers was quiet, and understandably so. That he had been imprisoned and assaulted by Lucy and Stefan was probably bad enough, but to now have to take orders from her as a matter of choice seemed somehow, she imagined, to compound the offence, make it all seem like part of some peculiarly cruel interview process.

Lucy concentrated on asking him about the trip ahead, but she felt that the basement episode hung between them like a lover's argument. He outlined, tight-lipped, what Thierry had told him, showed her the names of the places and people they would be looking for.

It had been hard not to register shock that they were going to Japan. Thierry, as far as Lucy was aware, had never developed his business interests in the East to the extent that he travelled there on anything like a regular basis, but she knew that he did have several friends there who had significant contacts. Perhaps it was one of them they were on their way to meet.

Whatever Thierry had arranged, it had obviously been done with his usual scrupulous attention to detail as well as his sometimes neurotic preoccupation with personal security, but the directions, although specific with regard to names and locations, were short on reasons. It irked Lucy that Thierry thought it necessary for her to be accompanied at all, but she trusted that he had thought it so.

On the flight to Osaka, Villiers opened up a little under Lucy's gentle questioning. With a thirteen-hour flight ahead of them, it was just as well, and he told her of his background, his abortive accountancy career, his stint as a nightclub doorman, security escort for a number of minor celebrities, all of which seemed to have led naturally to the job with the private investigation agency. But Thierry's offer had been impossible to refuse. Villiers hesitated slightly before confiding that he was to stay with Lucy as long as was required, but that as soon as she no longer had any use for him – be it next week or next year – he was to report to Thierry's Geneva headquarters for further assignments. It was, he claimed, a dream come true – he had escaped from the city, escaped from the selfish squawkings of soap-opera starlets, escaped the humdrum of the agency, and it was all, in a literally perverse way, thanks to Lucy. She should be sure of his loyalty.

When they did eventually land, after a flight which followed night around the globe, it was dawn in Osaka, and Villiers, who had slept much more than the slightly fazed Lucy, took control as they passed through Customs and Immigration. They were not married, no, but they were partners. They had come to Japan on business. Villiers supplied the address of the company they were working with. Business would only take a couple of days, but they wanted to take the opportunity to view the autumn leaves in the Southern islands, and would be touring the ancient capital, Kyoto.

The official, a curiously grumpy little woman, seemed unhappy with Villiers' passport and took it away to a windowed office where the pair watched a group of light-blue-shirted men stare at it, discussing something, tilting their heads in uncertainty, then checking the document against something on a desk. When the woman came back, she was still as grumpy, but the passport was stamped and they proceeded to the search of their baggage, where Lucy could only stand in mute fear as her hand luggage was carefully picked through.

The phial was in a little zipped pouch containing basic make-up essentials. The officer actually removed the bag at one point, opened it and carefully withdrew a fistful of facial scrub tubes, mascara brushes and sundries. Lucy could see the phial within his grip, its green glint like an alarm beacon screaming to the whole world, but he was looking inside the bag itself, running his fingers along the cushioned lining, and then he replaced the contents, returned it to her bag and wished her a happy stay in Japan.

'Happy' wasn't the word which sprang to mind as the taxi crawled through the early morning smog. Ryan had passed the uniformed driver the address, but neither he nor Lucy had the faintest idea where it was. In the city, presumably, for the driver headed along the motorway ever closer to the distant office buildings slowly materialising through the haze as the column of traffic ground its way into a thickening rush hour.

Lucy stole a look at Ryan as he stared out of the window at the cityscape. He was quiet, calm, in a way which somehow assured her, and she was glad he was there. But was he to be trusted? She couldn't imagine that Thierry would dream of assigning a bodyguard to her unless he was utterly convinced of the man's character, but how could he possibly know this man? Perhaps he had used his web of contacts to find out about him. But that still didn't account for such a decision – what if the man decided to avenge the humiliation which had been visited upon him by Lucy and Stefan? He was powerfully built and looked to be in excellent shape – if he wanted to exact physical revenge, he would surely be able to do so without great difficulty.

Lucy felt herself twinge at the memory of the spy bound, on his back, the expression of resigned horror on his face as he was face-fucked by the monstrous Stefan. He wouldn't forget that in a hurry, Lucy thought. He might even be thinking about it right now, planning some unspeakable retribution as he gazed absently through the smog.

On an impulse, perhaps irrational, perhaps due to jet-lag and general confusion, Lucy placed a palm on Ryan's leg. He turned to her, his eyes red-rimmed with fatigue, his complexion sallow and dry.

'About the other night,' she said, and he stared at her with what she imagined to be a mixture of embarrassment and sheer hatred.

'I'm sorry. It just sort of, well, it was what I was told to do,' she said, unable to hold the burning eye contact.

'You were just following orders, right?' he replied, and the sarcasm wasn't overstresed, but certainly there.

'Something like that,' Lucy replied, but her sense of shame and regret was evident in her tone.

'Don't worry about it,' he said then, almost cheerful, and Lucy looked up to find him smiling ruefully.

'My folks sent me to the priest training school when I was twelve,' he said, his eyes full and open, 'and I got a lot worse there, believe me. An awful lot worse.'

Lucy froze, stared at the head of the driver in front of her. There was nothing she could say. But then his hand was on hers, and he squeezed it to get her attention. He was smiling again, but now positively, almost gratefully.

'But I never ever had anyone as beautiful as you in there,' he said, chuckling, and Lucy could only smile and strive to conceal the tears of pity.

Don was surprised to see Martin standing at the reception desk when he entered the building, and when the concierge nodded and Martin turned and saw his boss, it was clear that the aide was a little more than surprised to see him.

'Where the fuck have you been?' demanded Martin, with such ferocity that Don had momentarily to remind himself that he was in charge of the building, the company, and that Martin was his assistant, but he didn't frown or retort, he simply held his arms out, as if readying himself for a search.

Martin placed an arm on Don's shoulder and guided him towards the door behind reception, the small room where the concierge made his tea – a dingy cupboard which doubled as a first aid point for the ground floor. As they neared the reception desk, a young woman, smart bob-haircut and expensive waxed jacket, sprang from the recess reserved for waiting clients, and headed for them, a notepad in hand. Martin raised a palm to her and she stopped, pen poised as Don attempted to remove Martin's hand.

'Mr Langford, I'm from the *New Standard*, and I'd just like to ask you about the—'

The concierge closed the door behind them as Martin bundled Don into the room.

'I've been trying to get you since ten last night,' he gasped in an unnecessary whisper.

'I was busy,' Don replied, smiling.

Martin took a step back and sniffed.

'You've been at it again,' he said, his face crunched with disgust.

'So?' Don replied, eyes wide.

'Are you still pissed?' asked Martin.

'What do you mean, still pissed? I wasn't pissed at all. I spent the night with a new friend.' Don laughed, his own tone of outrage somehow hilarious to him.

Martin looked to the ceiling, released a grunt of exasperation, and turned full circle before facing Don again, his hands clasped, as if in prayer.

'Fuck the new friend,' Martin said, low and even as he glared at Don. 'The press have been on to us all morning, that bitch out there is just the first of many. Some mob in the States bought out Zilco and Hardlenza before opening here, the shares in Lenworsch have rocketed, and we're expecting a bid before three o'clock. Something is badly wrong, and unless I'm much mistaken, it's to do with this Manchester shit.'

Don was still worrying about what to do about Martin saying 'fuck the new friend' when the assistant raised both palms in readiness for delivery of the worst.

'Some Swiss outfit has secured Franzi,' he said, his voice trembling, and Don snapped awake.

Franzi held thirty per cent of the supermarket chain. Don knew the family, they'd known the old man well. Surely not.

'They've sold, which means that this new crowd now has fifty-three per cent.'

Don felt himself tilt backwards and it was Martin who quickly moved to guide him to the chair below him as he gripped a shelf and sat.

'Xavier?' Don asked, his mind now shifting back into work mode.

'No, Harlewws or something like that. They were a sub of Geromes but belong to this consortium. We still don't know who's actually in charge. But they're moving fast and have the cash to back it up. Don, the whole thing is up in the fucking air. You have to consider selling. Right now. And I mean, now.'

Don palmed his cheeks and drew his hands down his chest. He felt suddenly filthy, putrid.

'You'll have to be ready for the press, and Bowden is upstairs waiting. He wouldn't be dissuaded. He didn't believe you weren't here.'

Don felt his guts liquidise. Major Bowden? Lucy's father? What the fuck did he want? It was like being inside the tiniest of Russian dolls, hearing the other, larger dolls being clipped shut, sheathed about you. Somehow, the face of that girl, Julie, seemed to hover still in his mind, like a promise of something better, and as Don got to his feet and straightened his collar, smoothed his fingers through his hair, he thought of her, of her smile, of her laugh conjoined with his. He wanted her back, right now.

Martin had both hands on Don's shoulders and was staring hard at him.

'You can do this. You have to do this shit,' Martin said, and then Don felt his head turn sharply and heard the crack as Martin slapped his left cheek, a full-palm, meaningful smack, but Don wasn't quite sure what Martin was talking about, why he had slapped him, why no pain registered.

'Yeah. OK. I can do it,' Don replied, 'I always have done it, and I always will. I'm Langford. I'm the man. I can do any fucking thing I want. I'm the man.' But even as he said it, he felt a laugh erupt from somewhere deep within him, and he knew, as he was being led from the small room, with Martin's hands carefully, considerately, guiding him, that he was surely going mad.

Naomi flicked the switch which allowed the one-way mirror to shimmer into transparency. The black man was standing with his back to her, against what, to him, was a long mirror.

Not that he would be able to sense the nature of the material behind him, for he was bound from head to toe in plastic film with only slits cut at the eyes and nose allowing him to take in air and the sight before him. But he would probably be grateful to be on his feet after the hours curled up. His arms, raised high above him, were shackled, the cuffs chained to the hook on the low roof above, and even the arms had been carefully, tightly bound in the seemingly endless strip of film. With his back pressed against the window, Naomi could make out the swirling descent of sweat along his spine, his chest heaving as he fought for air.

Before him, his girl had been tied to a waist-high bench which supported her back, and only her back; her hips were clear of the bench-end, her head also had no support apart from the girl holding it, and what they were doing to her was unusual, even in Naomi's experience.

The three girls chosen for the task were the best on the books, all experienced, in their own free time, with foreigners. Their costumes had been chosen by Naomi from her own collection, the outfits she reserved for her outside work. Minami-san had granted permission.

So there was the Nurse, brilliant white starched tunic with green cross, white silk underwear and white ankle boots; the Schoolgirl with standard Japanese naval-style uniform, pigtails and rosy cheeks; the Mistress, with an outfit similar to Naomi's – black leather basque, seamed black stockings and tottering heels.

164

With the girl on her back, the Nurse had already straddled her face, and was slowly working her lightly haired pussy across it. The girl's mouth was defiantly shut, her eyes screwed closed as if in pain.

And it might well be pain, for the Mistress had already fed most of the strap-on inside her pussy as she yanked at the prominent clitoris. The Schoolgirl was concentrating on the girl's breasts, taking each nipple in turn, sucking hard enough to bring a flush of redness to the peaks of the small tits.

The man was straining, and Naomi could almost feel his frustration through the window. The angle of her viewpoint meant that his cock was not visible to her, but she could imagine that he must be dripping by now.

On a command from Mistress, the Schoolgirl rose, crossed to the table, and selected the small, flesh-coloured strap-on. She donned it quickly, tightening the strap to find a secure fit, stroking it lightly in her palm as she returned. The Nurse then removed her sex from the girl's face, reached below the bench and unclipped the restraints which held the girl's wrists to the support. The girl, eyes still shut, brought her palms to her nipples, covering them, her fingers shaking.

A moan emerged from the man. It was a low, animal moan which grew to become a suppressed roar, and as if registering the warning, the girl glanced back to see the Nurse return, now also wearing a strap-on. And it was frightening. It was black, as thick as Naomi's wrist, and almost a foot long.

The Mistress instructed the other girls, and they obeyed quickly, raising the girl to stand while the Schoolgirl took her place and lay down on the bench, facing up. The girl tottered, weary with dread, as the Mistress pointed down at the Schoolgirl who now had both hands braced about the base of the smaller flesh-coloured plastic cock.

Her understanding of basic Japanese was good enough that the girl understood she was to sit on the thing. She shook her head. The Mistress advanced a step and brought her hand smartly across the girl's face. Again she shook, tears welling. The Mistress commanded the Nurse to bend the girl over. With her hands braced against the end of the bench, her head only inches from the swaying fleshy tool below her, the girl was forced to part her legs. Naomi wondered what the man would make of this view of his girl's sex – he had probably never viewed her like this, with this detachment.

The Nurse squeezed the pink cream directly on to the flesh below the girl's coccyx, then stepped forward and used the black dildo's head to smear the viscous fluid down over the distended sex in one, smooth movement which made the girl's cheeks twitch. Mistress commanded the girl to stand up and face her as the Nurse squeezed some more cream on to the end of the Schoolgirl's cock.

The Schoolgirl was still massaging the lotion on to her artificial dick when the Mistress barked at the girl to sit down and the girl, now flushed with what might be mild arousal, carefully backed towards the bench, her bare legs having to straddle the lightly oiled thighs of the Schoolgirl.

Again the Mistress shrieked her insistence that the girl sit down, and now, resigned to her predicament, the girl decided to co-operate, looking down between her own legs to locate the end of the tool. She smoothed her own palm over the little bulb and the upper thickness of the tool as if briefly assessing the length she was about to take, then, with her eyes shut once more, her bottom lip nipped between her teeth, a frown wrinkling her brow, she sank slowly on to the dildo, her mouth opening wide to release an audible gasp as she settled on to the Schoolgirl.

Mistress stepped forward and brought her hand under the girl's throat, slowly pushing her backwards until she realised she was expected to lie down. As soon as she did so, the Schoolgirl's hands came up to caress her breasts, tweaking at the hardened nipples as she started to work the cock in and out, short, steady jabs which had the girl clenching her teeth. Mistress paced to the other end of the bench and tapped her dildo on the girl's forehead. When she opened her eyes, she needed no instruction, and craned backwards, mouth open to receive it.

As Mistress cupped the girl's head, allowing her to suck on the tool, she commanded the Nurse to come forward. She was ready, stepping between the legs of the Schoolgirl and the captive. Nurse worked her own hand along the brutal length of the dark rubber tool – it was coated with cream so that the ribbons of fluid took on the appearance of white veins – while feeding three fingers of her other hand into the lubed cleft. With the girl's arse already full, this would be a tight fit.

Mistress, perhaps impatient, ordered Nurse to get a move on, and so she did, circling the massive bulb against the engorged labia several times before stepping forward, bringing the tool into the girl with a slow, excruciating relentlessness, until it was buried up to the rubber shield.

The girl struggled wildly, thrashing her head from side to side as Nurse started to work the monstrous weapon in and out. Mistress angrily grabbed the dark bobbed hair with both hands and brought the dildo back down over the girl's mouth. Tears streaming, the girl opened her mouth again, leaning ever further back so that the tool could be fully inserted.

Mistress was enjoying herself, Naomi could see that. It wasn't her job to enjoy it, so she would have to have a word with her later.

But in the meantime, she'd better let them get on with it. The man had calmed again, but was rocking gently within the limits of the small space he had. She would get her chance yet.

Minami-san entered the anteroom and stood beside Naomi, silent, watching as Mistress withdrew her strap-on from the girl's throat and ordered the turn-over.

It was swift, and accompanied by much screaming when the girl realised what was about to happen. Naomi felt herself stir slightly. The earlier frig had helped, but her frustration was beginning to mount again as she watched the girl being forced to lie on top of the Schoolgirl, this time face down, with the little flesh-coloured cock already stuck in her pussy. Her hands were brought down below the bench and clamped again, and they had to be, for this time, as Nurse stepped forward to start feeding the giant black dick into her arse, the girl went berserk, kicking and screaming. Mistress had a job steadying her face long enough to get the dildo back into the captive's mouth, but when she did she forced it long and deep, silencing the screams as Nurse, with palms spreading the arse cheeks as far as they would go, slowly buried the final few inches of the vicious tool inside the woman's rectum.

Minami-san grunted her disgust and left. Naomi felt slightly sorry for the girl, especially as she displayed no obvious affection for anal penetration. Still, she would have a rest and something to eat soon. Only another three hours to go.

The smoggy morning mist had melted under the autumn sun, and now great cartoonish white clouds drifted over Osaka as Lucy sniffed at the dish in front of her.

They'd ordered coffees and pastries, and sat outside the diner. It was a garish building, pink and yellow, a kitsch imitation of an American drive-thru burger joint, and not the type of place Lucy would ever have selected of her own accord, but at least the coffee was good and strong.

Ryan had double-checked the address of the diner with the staff, and they had, after lengthy consultation among themselves, agreed that yes, this was the same address as the one he had on the piece of paper.

'How will we know?' Lucy asked, but Ryan was no wiser than her, and shrugged to confirm it.

Someone would be watching. The bodies piled past on the pavement, the traffic snailed along, the bodies changing with almost incredible speed at the tables surrounding them as the office girls and salarymen bolted their lunches and headed back to work.

And when the approach did come, it was so swift and overwhelming that Lucy felt entirely useless, as though there was nothing at all she could do to affect the outcome.

The men were, despite their casual clothes and easy demeanour, utterly menacing. The three of them had walked directly up to the table and seated themselves without invitation, and Lucy was vaguely aware that two other men standing at the low-walled entrance to the diner were colleagues of the three. It was difficult to guess the age of the man who spoke, but he seemed a little older than the others, who looked to be in their late twenties.

'Mrs Langford, I think,' he said, smiling as he removed his sunglasses.

'That's right,' she replied unsmilingly, 'and you are?'

'And you are Ryan Villiers,' the man continued, ignoring Lucy altogether.

Ryan nodded, his hand frozen about his coffee cup, his eyes darting from one man to the next, weighing them up.

'You must be a very powerful woman,' said the man after ordering coffee for him and his companions.

Lucy did not answer, but raised her eyebrows and waited for an explanation.

'We will take you to see another important woman. That is our order. But I think maybe you have something to give me first.'

Lucy looked at Ryan, and he produced the slip of paper on which he had written the address of the diner, and the name 'Minami-san'.

The man scanned the paper, then returned it to Ryan, smiling.

'That is accurate, but not what I want to see.'

Lucy suddenly remembered the phial, Thierry's finger. She located it quickly and offered it to the man. He stared at Lucy, ignoring the little bottle, then nodded at the bottle which was lifted by one of his colleagues.

The curiosity on Ryan's face was plain as one of the younger men made a litle blanket of some tissues on the table, used a tiny penknife to quickly strip the seal from the cork, then used his teeth to open it.

'Very careful,' said the leader, still smiling, as the younger man up-ended the bottle on to the tissues, allowing the liquid to drain. When he lifted the bottle, the severed digit tottered briefly on its meaty end before toppling wetly on to the pinkish paper.

Lucy felt her guts tighten, the nausea sweeping over her. Ryan's eyes were wide, his complexion suddenly drained.

169

The young man, seemingly oblivious to passing customers and staff, cleaned the little finger, then passed it to the other, who had produced a small lap-top, the screen raised.

'If you need to eat, please do so before we go,' said the older man, but Lucy raised an open palm to indicate that there was no need.

The leader waited until the check was pronounced positive, then the men got up and stood silently as Ryan drained his cup and Lucy put her jacket on. Within minutes they were in the back of a black stretch Mercedes, being driven at speed further towards the city centre.

Major Bowden was an unhappy man, and Don could do little other than sit and take it.

'I got a call this morning,' growled the Major as he paced before Don's fireplace, the suite otherwise empty. Martin would be hovering about, but Don had to go through this alone. It was, after all, a family matter.

'Thierry Levant is an old friend,' said the Major as he returned to where Don was slumped behind his desk, his eyes aimlessly scanning the items on the shiny surface.

Thierry Levant. Don had been right. That bastard was to blame for all this. Martin's earlier words about the hostile take-over suddenly resurfaced – a Swiss company? It had to be him.

'Thierry informed me that Lucy just spent a few days with him. He didn't go into any elaborate detail, but he assured me that she is well, and is on her way to Japan.'

Don looked up to meet the Major's livid stare. Japan?

'You look as surprised as I was,' said the Major then, managing a smile, but nothing could disguise the anger. And he was, despite his seventy-three years, still a physically daunting prospect, the moustache and military mien further compounding the building atmosphere of dread and certain violence.

'But the difference between you and me is that Lucy is my daughter. She is a free agent as far as I'm concerned, and can do with her life as she pleases. You, however, are her husband, and you have a responsibility for her safety and security. How can it be, I wonder, that she has ended up on the other side of the globe without your knowing of it?'

Don looked up again, but it was simply impossible to hold that raging stare for long.

'I think our personal lives are just that,' Don started to say, but the sudden shifting of Bowden and the thunderous crack of his walking stick on the desk-top forced silence.

'Listen to me, you excuse for a man,' Bowden spat the words, flecks of froth forming at the corners of his mouth.

'The grapevine is an amazing thing. A little birdy tells me that you've lost the two Northeast Freshfield developments, and certain parties have photographic evidence of wrongdoing on your part. I don't know any details, but I know enough about you to be able to guess that it probably involves young women who are, shall we say, ladies of the night. I've known for years, Langford. It's bad enough that you fuck about, but to let it affect the company in the way it has is inexcusable. My shares have already been sold, and I've recommended everyone I know to cash up and get out. By market's end today you'll have lost the company, and you know it. I didn't particularly like your father, but at least he knew his priorities, and always covered his tracks well. You, on the other hand, are too concerned with your own pleasure to be concerned with the security of others, your own wife included. Five years you've been wed. There should have been children by now. My daughter should be happy and settled. Instead, she's travelling the world on a whim. It looks very much to me as if she has run away, and I warn you now, and I warn you well: if she does not come home, safe and sound, and soon, then I will solve her problem once and for all.'

The Major raised the heavy blackwood stick and tapped the end lightly under Don's chin.

'Do I make myself understood?' the old man growled.

Don took just a fraction too long to respond, and the stick was brought across his left cheekbone with such force that Don toppled from the chair in an instinctive effort to

171

absorb some of the blow. He got up, warily, his hands
raised against the next strike, but it didn't come. Bowden
was already at the door.

Nine

The men had left Lucy and Ryan in the small, dull room, but Lucy was pretty sure that at least a couple of them would be standing outside the door. The aggressive manner of the men had not manifested itself in any violence towards either her or Ryan, but he observed that they were probably local gang members. The younger ones in particular had a swaggering confidence about them which seemed typical of the sort.

There was little to look at in the plainly walled, tatami-matted room. The window was concealed behind a cream roller-blind, and although the light managed to struggle into the square ground-floor apartment, the atmosphere was stubbornly old and chilly, with a heavy smell of damp dust.

Ryan seemed withdrawn, almost worried, and Lucy was about to ask him what he thought about the whole situation when the door slid open and a tiny old woman entered, a strikingly beautiful, broad-shouldered woman close behind. The two wore traditional Japanese kimonos, staid, grey-blue wraparound robes with thick felt collars and heavy hems. Lucy had the impression that the younger woman had to be wearing something else beneath her gown – her waist was impossibly thin, and her breasts seemed unnaturally high within it.

The little, bright-eyed woman stood, looking at Lucy, as the younger woman gestured that Lucy and Ryan should rise. They did so, and it was Ryan who bowed first, long and deep. Lucy copied his movement as the younger woman drew across a low table and indicated that they should sit.

Lucy struggled to remember any basic etiquette. She had been schooled in fundamental oriental conventions while at finishing school, but the details had long since evaporated. No matter – as long as she was polite and patient, the two essentials, everything should be all right.

The little woman sat opposite Lucy, and continued to stare hard at her as a young girl entered with tea and proceeded to set the table. The old woman reached across the table. Her fingers were shaking.

'Lucy,' she said slowly, stressing the two syllables individually, like two different words.

Lucy nodded, smiled and extended her hand, and the old woman grasped it with both of hers and closed her eyes. Lucy felt a strange and sudden heat flow through her, from crown to toe. She attributed it to a rush of blood – the crouched position was uncomfortable – but when it became a chill, this time from toe to head, to be followed by an equally swift resurgence of heat as the woman drew her hands away, Lucy sensed that the woman was somehow checking her, assessing her.

The old woman said something to her younger colleague, and when this woman spoke, it was clear, careful English with a strong American accent.

'Minami-san says that you are welcome, and you must be very tired.'

Lucy nodded her appreciation, and insisted that she was not tired at all.

Ryan was not spoken to, nor looked at by either woman as Minami spoke again, Naomi translating simultaneously.

'You have something from your husband?'

Lucy thought, frowned, and shook her head. This seemed to cause a certain problem, for when Minami spoke again, it was with a low note of impatience.

'You have something which your husband gave you?'

Lucy glanced down at her hand. Her wedding ring. It seemed now to be such a worthless, pointless piece of jewellery, but yes, he had given it to her that day, in front of all their family and friends. She removed it, with a little difficulty, and passed it to the younger woman, who declined to touch it. Minami-san carefully accepted it and folded it tightly in her palm as the girl re-entered with tea and poured it.

It did not cross Lucy's mind to ask what Minami-san wanted with the ring. She would be using it to form a picture of Don. That much seemed normal enough, superstitious perhaps, but in a predictable, almost natural way. Lucy didn't believe in such nonsense, and never had, but for now she would believe anything.

Ryan asked a question. The expression on the face of the younger woman was so shocked, so offended, that Lucy was wondering what on earth he had said when the woman called, the door opened, and the two men who had sat in the back of the car with them reappeared, and waited for Ryan to stand before brusquely shouldering him from the room.

The old woman stared at Lucy throughout Ryan's expulsion, as though it simply wasn't happening.

'What did he say?' Lucy asked, worried that Ryan might also have landed her in trouble.

'I don't know,' said the younger woman, 'but he should not have spoken at all. He is your slave, is he not?'

Lucy's mind raced. Slave? She hadn't thought of it like that, but by the tone of the woman's enquiry it was clear what answer was expected.

'Yes, that's right,' she said, assuming an expression of worry, 'he is my slave.'

'He is strong?' asked the young woman.

Lucy pondered the question carefully. In what way Ryan's physical strength was important was not clear, but perhaps it was strength of another kind that was being referred to.

'I think so,' she replied, but the uncertainty was there to hear.

Minami moved her hand across the table, palm down. Lucy opened hers to receive back the ring. It felt cold.

The old woman was smiling broadly now, almost chuckling as she spoke to Lucy. Naomi translated as well as she could, but Lucy kept her eyes on Minami. It was a strange sensation, watching the old woman speak, but hearing the words translated, almost like watching a foreign movie with subtitles, and she could not square the obvious amusement in the old woman's eyes and voice with the gravity of what she was actually saying.

'Your husband is very powerful, very rich. Today his money is dropping down like blossom from the trees, but still he thinks he is very powerful. Always, with you, he was being powerful, but that is because he is afraid of you. You are the powerful side of your marriage, so you must show him the power you have. It is very simple. You love him very much, and he also loves you very much. But he loves his power too much to show you all of his love, so you must make him weaker. If you go to him now you will find him very weak and afraid, so it will be the good time to show him the extent of your power.'

Naomi stopped. Minami-san finished her tea. Lucy tried to grapple with what had been said. It chimed too closely with the reality of the situation to be pure guesswork, but the reference to Don's money dropping away was mystifying.

Minami coughed, then quickly uttered a string of sentences before rising and bowing and making her way out. Naomi frowned, trying to complete the translation which was clearly giving her difficulty.

Lucy tried the tea. It was virtually tasteless, some dark broad leaves shifting at the bottom of the cup.

'The husband is worth this trouble?' Naomi asked.

Lucy smiled, and wondered if he was.

'We have the possibility for you to practise before you must go,' she said then, but Lucy could tell that the woman was holding back, probably not giving an accurate translation of what sounded very much like a command from the old woman.

'What do you mean?' asked Lucy, and Naomi hummed a little before answering.

'What is that expression? My English is so bad, but we have the possibility for you to let your steam out.'

Lucy laughed, then apologised.

'I know what you mean. Let off steam?' she added, and the woman also managed a smile.

'Yes. Come now, and I will show you where you can let off your steam.'

Martin looked as bad as Don felt. With his hair stuck to his brow, his tie drawn from his throat as if he had attempted suicide by hanging but changed his mind, the aide who had stuck with him for so long now appeared to be ready to jump ship.

With his face still swelling, an ugly crimson welt across his cheek already starting to colour purple at the edges, Don was ignoring the headache as best he could. Martin was only intensifying it.

'Your dad is desperate to speak to you. You have to call him,' Martin gushed, like a worried brother.

Don hadn't the energy to raise his voice, but he attempted to convey whatever remained of his dwindling authority.

'I have to? I don't have to do anything. This will happen regardless of what I do. So, Daddy's going to lose a few bucks, the company will be out of the family's hands. He'll probably disinherit me. That would be typically dramatic. Point is, I don't give a fuck any more.'

Don opened the top right-hand drawer of his desk and withdrew his personal cheque book. He used it so seldom that he had to stare at the format of the slip before writing his name and the seven digits. Martin continued to babble, as if loaded with speed.

'The press are in numbers down there. The police are there as well, they don't like the obstruction outside. Cameras, the works. What are you going to say? At least give me a statement for them, please! Don!'

Don tore the cheque from the book and held it out to Martin. The aide took it, and stared at it, frowning, then laughed.

'What the hell is this?' he asked, a hysterical giggle building.

'It's exactly what it appears to be. It's a cheque for two million quid. And if I was you Martin, I'd nip off down to your local branch and deposit it toot sweet. There's certainly enough there. Don't worry, it won't bounce. But I wouldn't leave it too long.'

Martin slumped into the chair across the desk from Don.

'So that's it? You're quitting?'

Don stared at the little framed photo of him and Lucy in Austria, what, five, six years ago? Skiing. Klosters. Her face, glowing with love and happiness, his arms about her as they hugged, snow-specked and laughing and about to wed, everything to look forward to, the world in their hands. When had he lost her? How had it happened?

'Quitting this? Yes. I'm not the hard man I thought I was. I'm very tired. Very tired indeed.'

Don lowered his head and thought of this man opposite, the friend who had stuck with him for so long, accepted his rudeness and arrogance on a daily basis, and he felt the tears of guilt and regret welling.

'There's one more thing I'd like you to do for me before we go our separate ways,' Don said, his voice cracking, and when he looked up to Martin, the older man was white, chin trembling.

'Get me out of here,' Don pleaded, the first of the tears trippling on to his bruised cheek.

'Where to?' Martin asked quietly.

Don paused for several seconds. Where to? Right now, there was only one place he wanted to be, only one person he wanted to see.

Julie was just about to leave the apartment. Don had caught her just in time. She looked fantastic. In the freshness of daylight, with her clean, pinned-back hair and light, sparkling make-up, she could have been an office junior, a student teacher heading to work. She was astonished to see him.

178

'Please don't ask me what it's all about,' he'd insisted, 'but I want you to come with me. A break. A holiday. Call it what you like, but I want you to come with me.'

She'd smiled and blushed and stammered something about having to be somewhere, sometime, but he wasn't hearing it.

'Money isn't a problem. Nothing is a problem. I just want you with me. Please.'

'It's too soon,' she'd replied, 'too, too fast.'

But there was the hesitation he was looking for, the uncertainty, and he moved then to make her mind up for her, and within minutes she was in the car and they were heading for the slip road which would take them to the airport.

The bath had been an experience. Lucy had been reluctant to enter it at first, certain it was hot enough to scald her, but the girls had persuaded her by example, dipping their legs into the waist-high tub to prove that the water was not boiling.

And they had made sure she stayed there for what seemed like an hour or more, only her head protruding from the water. It was a curious sensation, to bathe sitting up, but eventually she'd relaxed, rested her head against the thick rim of the tub, and allowed herself to doze, the steam seeming to soak into her senses.

The girls moved with a silent purposefulness which at once impressed and unsettled Lucy. They had clearly been told to expect her, and knew exactly what they were supposed to be doing, for when they summoned Lucy to leave the hot tub, they had positioned themselves just so.

As soon as Lucy was out, she was directed to the shower cubicle, starkly white tiled with a ceiling-high sliding door. Lucy felt the weakness in her limbs, the trembling of her knees as she entered the recess. Her breath came in short, shallow gasps. Sleep would be good now.

But the shock of the cold water dismissed the comfortable notion of rest – the fierce, fine jets came from above and below, from the narrow sides of the unit, and with a force which made Lucy shriek. The door was firmly shut, as she found when she tried to escape, and she thought she heard a high giggle above the pounding of the water on her flesh. She drew her hands over her nipples, trying to protect them from the painfully cold water, but the stinging on her thighs and back was even worse, and she tried to palm the shock away, frantically turning and twisting. A click then sudden silence, and the jets stopped, becoming feeble spurts from the hundreds of pinprick holes spaced about the unit. Lucy tried the door again. Still firmly shut, and she squealed in fear as another click and sudden rush signalled the return of the water. This time it was not cold, but bearably warm, and she consoled herself, savouring the warmth, easing her stony nipples back to normality.

When the warm water also died, and the door slid open, Lucy stepped out. She had never felt so awake. The light-headedness was not unpleasant, but seemed to remove her somewhat from herself. It was as if she had never been so aware of her own body, of her own movements, the way her flesh shifted and settled according to even the slightest of influences from within or without.

And, lying on the bench, the girls expertly massaging her, Lucy started to imagine what had happened to Ryan. Her mind seemed to be conjuring fantastic rather than fatalistic possibilities, and the voices in her head seemed to become real, as if she was directly experiencing whatever he was. The grunts she remembered coming from him down in the basement when Stefan was playing with him seemed to return, muffled and tinged with panic. But the sounds also involved those of females in ecstasy and pain, moaning in strange tongues, begging, pleading for less or more of whatever they were receiving, and another male presence, muted, but throatily enraged, protesting.

It was a reverie she could have painted in her own mind, but when she opened her eyes, the girls beckoning her to rise from the bench, she realised that the sounds were real, and were being fed into the room via some sound system she could not see. She stood up, still naked, and looked to the corners of the room, up at the ceiling, where tiny black discs might indeed be speakers.

And as the girls led her to the reclining chair, Lucy did start to paint the scene in her mind. Ryan was certainly there, but there was definitely another man involved. The most detached voice, strident and female, seemed to be directing proceedings, and the cries of pain corresponded with her orders.

Lucy closed her eyes and in the weird contortions of flesh and face which her mind was producing in response to the sounds, she could see Don, naked and bound, helpless. How he could intrude on this scenario was unthinkable, but she could almost smell him, see his eyes pleading. As if she would show him any mercy or compassion. She wouldn't be in this place if it wasn't for him.

The girls had parted Lucy's legs gently, warm fingers smoothing her thighs across, palms on her shoulders urging her to slip further down the almost horizontal lounger, and when she felt the restraints clip about her ankles, she did not resist. They were going to shave her.

Somehow, she knew that it was going to happen, but resistance was futile and, knowing that it was, she found a welling excitement at the prospect.

Her response must have been visible, for when she opened her eyes, one of the girls smiled, drawing a cupped palm slowly up Lucy's pubis, asking her something in Japanese. Lucy groaned and shook her head, and the girl smiled and asked it again as the other brought over the thick porcelain bowl containing the lather.

Lucy reclined fully and let it happen. The closer girl used her fingers to spread Lucy's sex this way and that as the other girl applied the cool, smooth thickness. The sensation was instantaneous and painful, a surge of heat throughout her pelvis and upper thighs which made her bite her lip, but as soon as the razor started to remove her hair along with the foam, the pain receded into a throbbing pulse of heat which seemed to centre on her clitoris, now surely engorged and visible.

181

The chair was being manipulated. Lucy lost her sense of balance as the tilting projections holding her bound legs were raised and parted further so that the fullness of her pussy and arse was exposed, and then the fingers were there again, smoothing the heat-inducing foam down across her anus, and again, the fierceness of the heat was followed by the welcome strokes of the razor. Her inner sex was clamping, and with her breath now issuing in short, audible gasps, her arousal was impossible to conceal. This seemed to amuse the girls, laughter in their voices as they briefly poked at Lucy's swollen lips, examining her clit, gently pulling at it as if it was strange to them. And when they applied the fine jet of warm water to finally cleanse her sex, Lucy almost came. The girls worked quickly, too quickly for Lucy to find the relief she knew would easily come, but then the towelled palms were stroking her, each swipe of the towel seeming to absorb some of the maddening heat.

And when they made her stand, working quickly over her body with the lotion, she held on to the rim of the small washbasin, fearing she might topple otherwise. On her nipples they rubbed a thick, aromatic gel which seemed to harden quickly into a rubbery skin, transparent, but with a strawberry glaze to it which gave her bold, prominent nipples the glittering appearance of sugared fruits.

It was as if she were now a beast, a prized animal being prepared for exhibition. The girls had probably done this a thousand times before, for their work seemed to follow a definite pattern, a sequence, and Lucy found their nonchalance almost unbearably stimulating. Their apparent indifference to her arousal was somehow challenging, insulting, and she wanted to grasp them by the hair and grind their faces against her sex, make them taste the result of their attentions, especially the shorter of the two, who appeared so innocent, so wide-eyed and amused by the whole business – how sweet it would be to bring that bitch to her knees and force her to lick at the tingling bareness between her legs.

Lucy glanced at herself in the mirror, and caught the tell-tale dilation of arousal in her own eyes. She was almost furious with lust, and didn't care who knew it. Perhaps it was the depilation, or the shower, or the strange hot foam, but whatever it was, she wanted now to release her renewed energy brutally, painfully, and when the girls brought her to the wardrobe and indicated that the choice was hers, she knew instantly what she wanted to wear.

The rough suede boots, flared behind the thigh, were higher-heeled than any footwear Lucy had experienced, and she felt her denuded sex more keenly than ever, the smoothness somehow strange and new, her pelvis contorted with the added height. The brilliant blue rubber basque had full-length arms with gloves attached, and her fingers felt like someone else's, tight and small and new. The hood, likewise, was extremely tight, and her hair, painfully knotted and wound atop her scalp, had been so flattened by the tight rubber that she could well have been imagined bald. Her make-up was so thick, so densely applied, that she felt her face to be a mask, her lips unreal with the thick gloss, her eyes almost cartoonishly large and dark. And her skin, where it was exposed, felt invigorated, tingling with the after-effects of the showers and the lotions, sheening smoothly in the dim light.

Minami was in the ante room, viewing her girls at work, and Lucy's entrance seemed not to disturb her stern supervision. The old woman simply turned, scanned Lucy from bottom to top, then resumed watching. It was left to Naomi to speak.

'Your slave is strong,' she said, the approval clear in her voice as she beckoned Lucy closer.

The view astonished her, but brought the heat back to her sex, her lust bolstered now to an intensity so unbearable that it was painful to have to wait any longer. Ryan was face-up on the bench, his cock sheathed in what appeared to be a form of condom which also covered his testicles and, below the lurid pinkness of the rubber, she could see that some kind of thong had been tied about his scrotum and shaft. She could not see his face – the Nurse was astride it, working herself along his chin and mouth with quick, short grinding movements which were obviously doing it for her. And her colleague, the Schoolgirl, straddled one of his thighs, her hand closed about his cock, working slowly up and down as she kissed her colleague deeply.

Another girl, a small, Western-looking girl with dark hair and a plain white bra on, was crouched over a woman who appeared to be clad mostly in black leather and rubber. The kneeling woman, whose face Lucy could not see, had her arse raised high, her legs tightly together as the girl strained to manipulate the dildo she was wearing, clearly not very adept with the tool, but determined enough to have buried half of its length inside the woman's pussy. And what a dildo it was – sheer blackness at least as thick as Lucy's wrist, working wetly in and out as the girl's thighs shuddered with the exertion. The same, disembodied soundtrack continued, coming from somewhere behind Lucy as Naomi spoke.

'The girls know you are in charge. They will wait for you to tell them. You must be strong with them, and also with your own slave. But most of all, you must be strong with him.'

Naomi pointed to the extreme left of the window, and Lucy was shocked to realise that there was a body, almost leaning against the frame, a body which had been sheathed entirely in clear plastic film and was virtually still.

Before Naomi continued, she looked quickly behind her. Lucy followed the woman's backward glance to where Minami seemed absorbed in her own thoughts, absently scanning the room as if wondering how to decorate it.

'Please, if you want me to, I can take very special care of this man here,' Naomi said, and Lucy could see the desire sparkle in the woman's eyes.

'Yes, Lucy said, I understand. Now, please, let's get on with it.'

The hotel was perfect. The owner, a small man in his sixties, had registered visible shock at the state of Don's

face, but declined to pass comment on the now lurid
bruising.

Mr and Mrs Whalley. He'd used his mother's maiden
name, and it had felt strange. But denying his own name
was now surely part of the plan he had to formulate, and
quickly. The press had even managed to tail them from
Julie's apartment to the airport, but since arriving at
Glasgow there had been no obvious attention.

Julie seemed to be in a state of shock, unsure of
everything, docile to the point of dumbness. He kept her
close, insisting that she take his arm, even on the ascent to
the suite he'd booked for the next week.

She removed her jacket and went to the kitchen to make
them some tea. He told her not to bother, to call down for
it, and to order some food as well. Sandwiches would do
for now.

He moved to the panoramic window and scanned the
distant islands, deepening purple in the dusk. It had to be
safe here, if only for a few days. The name had come to
him from years ago, a recommendation from an older
business associate who regularly used it as a rendezvous
with his mistress. It was three hours drive from Glasgow,
and with it being off-season, the place was virtually empty.
And it had been a good idea to have Julie hire the car in
her name.

Time now, and space; space to gather his broken
thoughts and work out his next move. The pessimism of
the afternoon had given way to a brooding determination
not to let the bastards get him. Thierry Levant was
involved – of that he was certain. Lucy's father might also
have contributed, and his prompt selling of stock had
certainly done Don no favours. And then there was Lucy
herself. To what extent did she know what was happening
to him? Had she actually helped orchestrate his downfall?

The questions tumbled and collided in his mind, but
there would be time enough to work it all out. For now,
he wanted to relax, enjoy this beautiful place, this stunning
young woman with whom he suspected he had already
fallen in love. Perhaps it would be a fresh start. Perhaps he

could learn from what had gone wrong and take advantage of the lessons. Perhaps.

Her arms were about his waist from behind, and he gently palmed his hands over hers as they enjoyed the shifting clouds, blazing orange and gold against the darkening blue as the sun sank beyond the glowing sea. He felt an urge to smash the window, to make the scene real, feel the wind and the smell of the coast. As it was, it was like a postcard, too perfect, too picturesque.

'Too good to be true,' he said, and she tightened her grip, oblivious to the sneaking fear which lay behind the statement.

He turned and drew her close, breathing in her hair, her skin.

'Why me?' she asked, looking up at him.

He asked himself the same question, and smiled. Why indeed? But the answer, though he knew he knew it, was not to be discussed, not to be faced. Not yet.

He disengaged himself from her embrace and crossed to the drinks cabinet. The selection of spirits was comprehensive, if heavily slanted towards locally distilled malts, all in miniature bottles. Easier to tally the bill, he thought as he withdrew two double measures of Islay.

He raised one towards her and she smiled, shaking her head.

'I'll wait for the tea, thanks,' she said.

He emptied one miniature into a heavy tumbler and added half of the little bottle of spring water.

'Julie,' he asked, having to search for her name, 'tell me something.'

She was seated by the window, the sunset casting golden highlights on her curls. She was really quite gorgeous, no doubt about it, and she smiled and cocked her head, waiting.

'If you could have anything in the world, anything at all, what would it be?' he asked.

The girl stared at the carpet, frowned, then looked to the distant red glow where the sun had been. She hummed, as if ready to start singing, then looked back to him, her eyes bright.

'I would have a son,' she said.

Don crossed to join her on the sofa, and she was again staring at the gloaming as he swirled the drink, watching the bronzed whorls where water mixed with whisky.

'You wouldn't want a lovely big house somewhere idyllic like this? You wouldn't want a million in the bank? Exotic holidays?' he smiled, trying hard not to make his cynicism too obvious.

She turned to him, her smile broader than before.

'Oh yes, I'd want all those things, who knows, maybe even more. But I'd wish for a son, because I know that if I was ever going to have a child, things would have to be just right before I did. I would have to be happy. Maybe it would be holidays and a big house, maybe not. I don't know. All I know is that I won't have any children until I'm happy, and that'll mean the father will have to be happy too.'

Don took a lengthy sip from the glass, her words echoing inside him. Her tone was so confident, her manner so optimistic. Perhaps it would happen for her. Could it happen with him? He felt ready to make promises, the same promises he had made to Lucy.

'Why did you come with me?' he asked, and her expression became loaded, sad, and she looked away to where the sunset had suddenly become the dying of a light, the end of a fire.

'Because you needed me,' she said, and then she looked at him and lowered her head to his shoulder.

'There's so much you don't know,' he said, 'and so much I can't tell you. But whatever happens, I want you to know now that you saved me last night. I don't know what I might have done.'

She tightened a hand on his arm as she moved closer.

'But I know what you did do,' she said.

He placed the glass on the table, reclined on the sofa and drew her atop him, and as the darkness fell over the view like the dropping of a curtain, they made love, right there and then, and ignored the rapping on the door as the sandwiches and tea arrived.

* * *

The room was already heavy with the scents of sex. Lucy followed Naomi inside, and before she had even crossed the threshold, Naomi had barked a shrill, unintelligible series of instructions, and the girls had disentangled themselves from their positions and dropped to their knees.

Lucy measured her steps carefully. She was still getting used to the boots, to the sensation of being very nearly six feet tall, but it was exhilarating. She had always taken the orders – from Thierry, from Don. But now, she would give the orders, and she knew that the scenario had been constructed expressly for her to do so. The sheer excitement of the possibilities made her shudder as she took in what lay before her.

The Nurse, Mistress and Schoolgirl had all knelt side by side, in between the bench – on which Ryan was tethered – and the huge clingfilm-bound man. The little dark-haired girl was also on her knees behind the three Japanese girls, and was obviously exhausted. Naomi strode forward, faced Lucy, and knelt down in front of her colleagues.

'Please, Miss Lucy, you must say now what you want us to do,' Naomi said, her face almost touching the tiled floor.

Lucy did not answer, but paced slowly across to the bench where Ryan lay, a film of sweat covering his naked body. He had been gagged with a thin leather strap about his head, an ugly ball of black rubber crammed firmly into his mouth. His eyes registered mild confusion when Lucy came into view, but he was probably having difficulty recognising her until she spoke.

'Are you all right, slave?' she asked, and his eyes seemed to smile. Lucy didn't.

Against the far wall was the selection of tools available to her: whips of varying lengths and thicknesses, some wooden, most leather, and all well-used; handcuffs with varying lengths of chain; tethers and thongs; a surgical table bearing various clamps, probes, lengths of tubing and bottles for enema purposes. Lucy was by no means a prude, but the weaponry on display was astonishing in its variety and vicious potential. The dildos arranged on the lower tier of the movable table were arranged precisely, and bare patches of the white linen liner betrayed the absence of those tools which were already in use.

She looked long and hard at the implements available on the wall before selecting a thick-handled whip with a bush of leather thongs. It was surprisingly heavy.

Drawing the tool slowly through her left palm as she returned to face the kneeling girls, Lucy spoke to Naomi. The girl's arse was raised, the fullness of her figure quite striking compared to the other girls, and wonderfully accentuated by the rubber skirt, her buttocks shaped into an inviting pear-shape which begged to be flogged.

'I will order you, Naomi, and you will translate immediately and accurately,' Lucy said slowly, giving the girl a fair chance.

But there was no answer. Lucy stepped between the three uniformed girls and Naomi's behind, and stood staring at the raised bottom below her before bringing the lash across the head girl's buttocks. Naomi jerked forward, then touched her head to the floor and gushed the apology, first in rapid Japanese, then stuttering English.

'I'm so sorry, Miss Lucy. Yes, I understand. I will do everything you wish,' she said, her voice high with shock and submission.

'Very well,' said Lucy as she paced back towards Ryan, 'get your girls up. Up!'

Naomi rose first, ushering her staff to do likewise, and they did, scurrying pathetically, clearly fearful of Lucy's presence. Whatever they had been told, it was clear that they were more than eager to please – they had to be under orders to follow her bidding. Lucy's insides seemed to be rejoicing, the freedom and power coursing through her like some fantastic drug as she went to examine the plastic-bound figure.

She was aware of all looking, waiting, as she stood directly in front of the cruelly bound figure. He was a massive man, his height exaggerated by the brutal stretching he had endured, and Lucy could see now that he was coloured. His eyes, red-rimmed and weary, stared from the carefully-cut slits with an expression of tired fear.

'Why is this man wrapped like this?' she asked, and Naomi shuffled nearer, whispering the explanation.

'He is a special man,' Naomi said, 'and we have been keeping him like this for you to arrive.'

Naomi scanned the hanging body. At his feet, a pool of sweat had gathered, and the stench of him was caustic.

A sudden whimper from behind made Lucy turn. The small dark-haired girl was sobbing into folded arms, still on the floor.

'This is his woman?' Lucy asked, and Naomi nodded.

'Scissors,' Lucy said, and Naomi instructed the School-girl to retrieve a pair from the steel table.

The Schoolgirl was unsure who to give the scissors to, but when Lucy indicated the sobbing girl, it was Naomi who roughly brought the girl to her feet, pulling on her short hair until she was upright, squealing in protest.

'You understand English?' Lucy asked, and the girl nodded, her eyes pleading, as if escape might be possible now.

'I want to see his cock,' Lucy said, deadpan and stony-eyed. The girl's expression displayed a sudden anger. Lucy drew back her arm, eyes still locked on the girl, and brought the lash across her bare thighs with a resounding crack.

The girl knelt before her boyfriend and, still sobbing, carefully punctured the tight film shield before cutting up and across. The oily, shimmering plastic coating began to warp and shift and, before the girl had managed to complete the rough triangle, the man's penis had sprung forward, bringing an audible gasp from Lucy.

It was a bestial cock, unlike anything Lucy had ever seen. It was, in its semi-flaccid state, almost a foot long. The cockhead was surprisingly light in colour, almost pink, and the ridges of his foreskin were, if anything, even lighter. But it was the sheer length and girth of him which astonished – it was like the cock of an animal, a beast. Lucy gulped, struggling to maintain the icy exterior as she stepped closer to the bound figure and gestured the kneeling girl aside.

190

His eyes had not shifted from Lucy the whole time. He obviously knew that his fate was in her hands.

She drew the lash through her palm once again, and stared down at the obscene length of flesh, then back at the eyes. He was more awake now. No wonder.

She stepped back and to the left, brought the lash behind her, then drew it across his midriff in a hard, full swoop which made him buckle his torso, his cock jumping with the suddenness of the movement.

Lucy then stepped forward and, as his body settled, his eyes screwed shut, she gripped the monster cock with her right hand and squeezed hard, forcing blood down towards the pink, plum-sized bulb. It was like milking a cow – she released her grip, moved her hand back to the root of his dick, then repeated the motion. The smell of him was pungent, sweet. She looked down to see a silvery thread of pre-come snaking, like a spider, towards the floor. He was full, of that there was no doubt, and she briefly allowed her gloved hand to delve inside the plastic film to assess his testes. They were swollen and hard, tight within the sweaty scrotum. Her handiwork had barely affected his stiffness, although the length had visibly increased.

But that was enough for him. For now.

Lucy knew now how she wanted to proceed, and she barked the orders quickly, Naomi struggling to keep up with the flow of instructions as the Schoolgirl was commanded to once again enter the dark-haired student with the fleshy dildo, this time on the floor in front of the chained man, so close that he could, if he had been able to, have touched his feet to the point where his girlfriend was being penetrated from behind, her well-slackened arse now easily accommodating the short, sharp stabs of the little dildo.

And the Mistress, so stern in manner and expression, didn't have to be told twice to start sucking Ryan's rubber-bound cock, eagerly mouthing him as the Nurse resumed her creaming of his face.

That left only Naomi. Lucy made sure everyone was doing as they were told before she could turn her attention to the senior girl, and the lash had to be used more than once; across the belly of the groaning Ryan, his torso already straining with the exertion of the two girls; across the buttocks of the Schoolgirl fucking the redhead, urging her deeper and faster as the bound boyfriend groaned and swayed, his cock starting to thicken and bob gently towards a semi-erection.

And when Lucy commanded Naomi to kneel, it was done instantly, as if reward would surely come. Lucy lashed the rubber-bound arse with a fury she would never have dreamed herself capable of, and the girl stayed perfectly still throughout, never once whimpering as the thick leather thongs cracked into her sheathed flesh.

'Raise the skirt,' Lucy ordered, and Naomi did so with some difficulty, drawing the thick rubber up and over her knees, then over her thighs to reveal the smooth, stocky legs in their rubber-enclosed fullness, and the lash was at her again then, another five strokes, the skirt higher so that the full, rosy buttocks were exposed, and now her flesh was free, quivering under the strokes as Lucy counted twenty and decided that the woman had had enough.

A sudden series of loud grunts made Lucy turn, and the Mistress had Ryan's balls in her fist, pulling them down towards his arse as if trying to remove them altogether, and her mouth was still open above his pink-rubbered cock as orgasm peaked and the bulb of the condom swelled and shifted to accommodate the erupting sperm. The Mistress waited until he had stopped jerking, then carefully nipped the teat of the condom between her teeth and tore it off him. As the reservoir of creamy whiteness spilled, the rubber snapped and shrank down his stiffness, allowing his constricted member to fill with blood, and it was still spurting the final vestiges of his fluid when the Mistress gripped him tightly at the base, his rubber-encased balls between her fingers, and lowered her face to take him completely into her throat.

Lucy returned her gaze to Naomi, who had now raised her head from the floor. Her arse was still motionless and high, her lightly haired pubis barely visible below her pouting anus, but glistening white foam at the ridges of her sex betrayed the pitch of her arousal. The heaving of her shoulders gave some clue as to the extent of her desperation, but the angle of her face led Lucy's eyes to it's cause – the black man was now almost erect, his penis pointing, swaying at ninety degrees to his body, like some devilish compass.

Lucy, her shoulders and arms already tired, brought the lash behind her right shoulder for one last swipe, her legs spasming against the unnatural elevation of the high heels as she brought the leather thongs across the openness of Naomi's sex.

The direct hit on the swollen labia was more than even the stoic head girl could manage, and she slumped forward, shrieking, drawing a gloved palm to her sex by way of comfort as Lucy stepped forward, nearer the hanging man, and drew the bunch of thongs beneath the groaning girl's jaw.

'Get over there and suck that cock,' she said, and it was with some effort, but with new groans of relief and gratitude that Naomi raised herself, drew down the rubber skirt about her thighs, and moved towards the object of her lust.

The man seemed to know what was about to happen, for he froze, only his hips carrying any movement at all as he raised himself on to tiptoes and thrust his erect member further towards the advancing Naomi.

Lucy brought her own hand down to her thighs as the girl first ran her palms up the sheathed thighs of the giant, then clasped them about his dick, both palms gripping hard, inches of cock still to spare.

It didn't seem possible that any throat could take the hugeness of it, but Lucy stared in amazement as Naomi feverishly fed the gigantic dick into her mouth, not even licking or sucking, simply swallowing the whole thing as far and as deep and as fast as she possibly could, eventually palming his groin by way of resistance when she had taken almost three quarters of it.

The nagging reluctance to touch herself with other people present was suddenly absurd, almost comical, and

Lucy brought her own gloved hand down to her clitoris with a wave of relief which almost threatened to overwhelm her. Her bud was hard and prominent enough to feel clearly, even through the warm rubber, and she had a fleeting recollection of Phillipa's pussy as she drew her own fingers up her wetness, her eyes straining not to blink as she savoured the sight of the huge man's penis being expertly gobbled by the kneeling woman.

Naomi shifted and started to stand, forced to raise herself as the man's erection became fuller, and now, with both hands working along his shaft as she fed the first third of him in and out of her face, Lucy had to move to the side to see what was happening.

It was almost painful to stop them, but it was clear from the spasmodic thrusting of the man's pelvis that he was due to come imminently.

Naomi jumped back when the lash struck her yet again, and Lucy followed up the strike with another to the man's chest.

'That's enough!' Lucy shouted, and Naomi backed off, drooling heavily, her eyes dark with tears and desire.

Lucy directed Naomi to unfasten Ryan. He was spent, glassy-eyed and soaked in his own sweat as the Mistress helped Naomi to turn him over, then bound his arms firmly once again beneath the bench.

Lucy was dripping, her pussy already clamping with myriad mini-orgasms as she supervised the final binding of Ryan, his gagged head protesting wearily as the Mistress emptied the tube of cream between his parted arse cheeks and worked the fluid viciously into his anus with stabbing, unmerciful fingers.

'Right, get him off,' said Lucy, and Naomi quickly undid the straps and released the hoist which had been restraining the coloured giant for so long.

When he was released, he seemed somehow to grow in stature yet again, as if the torture had simply added to his power, and he needed little direction. His girlfriend was swift with the scissors, and the other girls helped haul the greasy plastic from him, revealing his splendid physique.

Ryan was squealing into the ball of leather, aware that he was about to be buggered, but there seemed to be an acceptance, even with the coloured man's girlfriend, that this would have to happen.

Lucy used the lash to make the girls back off as the man neared Ryan, his cock pointing towards the ceiling, its huge thickness coated with the saliva of three women, his balls hanging heavy and full below the solidity of his shaft.

Lucy instructed Naomi once more. The coloured man stayed standing, his cock full and ready, shards of plastic still clinging to him, a mere six feet behind the strained and open arse of Ryan.

Upon Naomi's order, the Schoolgirl advanced first, the dildo in her hand, and she twisted the instrument only once at Ryan's opening before roughly plunging it into him. Ryan protested as the tool was worked into his behind, his arse cheeks instinctively spasming as it was fed in and out. Lucy timed the attention, allowing a count of thirty before urging Naomi to summon the Nurse, with her black strap-on, and she too was brutal and took advantage of the man's restriction, plunging the hard plastic into him with deliberate strokes which had him banging his head on the bench-end. Then it was, as it had to be, the black man's girlfriend, with the largest toy of all, the black rubber one which she'd previously been using on the Mistress, and she seemed to enjoy hurting him with it, burying it to the shielded hilt with vicious thrusts as if she somehow held Ryan personally responsible for all that she and her man had endured.

When the student withdrew, the Nurse advanced to apply more cream, and Lucy stepped forward to once again feel the full length of the black man in her hand.

The look in his eyes was one that Lucy would never ever forget – he looked ready to die, ready to kill. Poor Ryan.

It was impossible to close her fingers about the thing, until the upper five or six inches. He closed his eyes as Lucy firmly stroked the peak of his shaft, twisting her rubber-bound fingers cruelly about his helmet. He didn't even wince.

'You must be ready, dear,' she said, smiling, 'go on then, it's all yours.'

And he stepped forward and pushed his cockhead against Ryan's arse, testing it, then stroked it further down to nudge the strapped man's balls, but when he brought his tool up again, he simply stuck it straight into the distended hole, grasped Ryan's hips, then thrust himself into his arse with a movement which made a couple of the girls intake sharply in sympathy.

Ryan made no sound at all, but dropped his head to the bench's end and breathed out as the man started to fuck him.

Lucy was almost ready to expire with lust. She instructed Naomi quickly, while language was still at her command, and the girls were about her then: the Schoolgirl at her behind, nibbling Lucy's arse cheeks, teasing her cleft with her tongue; and the Nurse sucking at her left breast while working two fingers into her arse; the Mistress was sucking at the right breast while feeding the black dildo of the redhead against Lucy's pussy lips, and Naomi, dear Naomi, had lost control completely, and was frantically licking at the heavy balls of the black man as they slapped against the besieged arse of Ryan Villiers.

When Lucy finally allowed herself to come fully, all had changed again, but the combination of jet-lag, pure lust and abandonment of responsibility gave the experience the quality of a hallucination: she was on her back, on the bench, with the huge black man's cock being worked in and out of her pussy, but there was another dick in her behind, and it had to be Ryan's. Naomi's pussy was hovering above her head, the fully parted lips shimmering pinkly as they were brought down to her face in a slow, grinding sway which allowed only the swollen clitoris of the head girl to graze Lucy's nose. Hands, so many hands, were all over her body, several grasped about the black man by way of protective restraint as he powered his potentially damaging thrusts, others kneading her buttocks as Ryan's rubbery length pumped at her behind. She could do little more than gasp her relief as the orgasm sparked

196

in her belly, shooting down her jerking thighs as the black man was pulled from her and there was just the faintest recollection of the head of the massive black cock, almost completely sheathed in the fingers of the girls, as its eye opened and a thick, soupy jet of semen was fired towards her. Her come peaked. Her anus closed tight about Ryan's cock, sparking another come for him, and as his dick thickened and juddered in her back passage, she lay fully back, body opened, and felt the warmth of the fresh semen being massaged into her face under Naomi's pussy as Ryan's offering was received in her arse.

Ten

Don felt fantastic. The highland air seemed to have seeped into his skin, his bones, and he was ready to return to face the mess at home. With Julie on his arm as they returned to the hotel from the thirty-minute walk alongside the old canal, he was enjoying imagining himself as part of a honeymooning couple.

Julie had expressed uneasiness at her situation, but Don had placated her, telling her they would soon be back in London. Just another couple of days, then he'd call the office, arrange a helicopter.

It had been difficult not to use the telephone in the room, and he'd eventually disconnected it before bundling it into a cupboard. He'd also insisted that Julie do likewise with her mobile, at least until they were on the way home, but she'd muttered something about her mum not being well, so it would have to be left on, just in case.

The three days had flown by, even though they'd barely left the room. The cold wind sent them scurrying back inside the couple of times they had ventured outside for a walk, and even when the wind did die, the rain seemed to take its place. But today it was fine, if bitterly cold.

And now that the peak of anxiety had passed, he realised it was folly to involve Julie. The girl was barely twenty, had no idea who he was, and had clearly become infatuated with him. He felt for her, perhaps even loved her in a curiously juvenile way, but it was a doomed affair, and he prayed that she knew it as well as he did, otherwise there would be hurt in the days ahead, and he truly wanted to spare her that.

But it was idyllic while it lasted, and as they entered the low stone doorway of the hotel's ancient façade, he wondered if the little old owner would be open to offers for the house and grounds.

As if on cue, the man appeared as they passed the reception desk, and he was smiling broadly.

'Mr and Mrs Whalley. It's a fine day for a walk right enough,' he said cheerfully, and Don nodded agreement.

As they started up the stairs, Don was aware of the man still smiling, looking at them.

'I've left your breakfast by the window,' he called after them.

Don didn't even notice the neatly folded newspapers on the chair by the table, and busied himself pouring tea while Julie removed her coat and boots. It was when she moved the papers to take her seat that he noticed his face on the front page. It was a badly lit, grainy photo of him, and he looked to be in pain. TYCOON PERV FLEES! blared the banner. Don knocked over the half-full cup as he jerked his hand across to snatch the newspaper away from her view, but she hadn't even noticed it.

'Are you all right?' she asked, already using napkins to soak up the spillage.

'Fine,' he replied as he headed for the toilet with the tabloid.

Lucy couldn't help laughing. At first, the shock of seeing Don's face splashed across the front pages of half a dozen European newspapers in the airport had been numbing, but now that it had worn off, she was enjoying the details in the feature articles. He'd fucked up spectacularly.

The flight had been delayed, but only because Lucy had insisted that she wanted a whole first-class cabin reserved for her, Ryan, Naomi and her girls. And there was also Georgie and Ken. The captives had already been well-paid for their suffering but were only too glad to take an all-expenses paid trip to Europe to exact revenge on the person who'd caused it all.

But now, halfway back to London, a full seven hours into the flight, the plan was almost complete, and Ryan had been most useful in ironing out the nigglier details.

According to the press, Don had vanished after an altercation with Major Bowden. She could imagine Dad's fury, his features contorted with righteous rage. Thierry must have filled him in. And as for all the council scandal relating to the Farmfresh developments, it was clear that there were others apart from Thierry who had used their influence to train various spotlights in unison, and in some ways it seemed that Don was simply in the wrong place at the wrong time – he had been caught in a whirlpool of intrigue, greed and revenge which was not entirely of his own making, but his skull would make a spectacular trophy for more than one party, and the reports were almost gleeful in their condemnation of him, his business, and his private life.

Ryan had already called ahead to his office, recruited the services of the best people he knew. They were more than happy to abandon all other current work and supply their expertise. Ryan was assured that Don would be traced before the entourage arrived in London.

'When you get to him,' said Lucy, 'make sure he doesn't know it's anything to do with me. Just hold him, do what you want with him, let the girls play with him. But my name is not to be mentioned.'

Ryan nodded, smiling, and Lucy could see that he was relishing the challenge. For her own part, Lucy had other plans: she wanted to get back to the Fulham apartment and have her belongings removed before even clapping eyes on Don. Then, if the meeting was not satisfactory, she would never have to see him again. It was down to him. She wasn't quite sure what to expect, but she knew exactly what she wanted, and this time, there would be, could be, only one answer that would satisfy.

She made one last call before catching up on her sleep. Phillipa was delighted to hear from her, but was being prepared for the midday bulletin and couldn't chat. But yes, she'd be available that evening, and yes, of course she'd bring some of her Hellhole outfits.

'I don't care how much it costs,' said Don, 'I want it here first thing in the morning. And for God's sake make sure you remember my passport.'

Martin had been curiously truculent, almost dismissive of Don's predicament, but he was perhaps mindful that the cheque could still be stopped, and so had agreed to prepare for Don's escape.

For escape it had to be. The editorials were baying for Don's blood; to read the rags one would think that he alone was responsible for the destruction of the country-side, wholesale prostitution, and a myriad of other sins, the severity of which shifted adultery almost to the bottom of the list. One of the more popular tabloids had even promised to launch a crusade against the moral panic which Don's behaviour had instilled. It was most definitely time to scarper.

If Martin got his finger out and did as he was told, a helicopter should be on its way before dawn.

He emptied another double into the ice-filled glass and looked at Julie. She was asleep, the duvet drawn over her shoulders, her hair partly obscuring her face. Perhaps she would come with him. She knew nothing of the reports, still didn't know who he really was. But now, Don wasn't even so sure himself. It had all gone. As if by magic, it had all disappeared. The empire his father had devoted a lifetime to had been slashed and snaffled by profiteers, and the family name was now mud. Life in London would be unbearable. Lucy was still gone, presumably with Levant, and even his own father had issued a terse statement that he was looking forward to 'having a chat' with his only son. Don knew that 'having a chat' was the quaint euphemism the old man used whenever he was about to fire, humiliate or otherwise destroy someone. It was all over.

The States? A few of the uni old boys had gone over there and made a decent fist of things. There might be a place for him there. Or Australia, if they would have him. The investigations being launched by the Fraud and Vice Squads would take months, but there was every chance that his leaving the country would not be appreciated until they had been completed. Best that he take a very quick holiday, then prolong it as long as necessary. Ireland seemed the best bet.

He took a long cool swallow of watered whisky, and looked at Julie's reflection in the darkened bay window. She was so like his wife, so like Lucy had been just five, six short years ago. Then he focussed on himself in the glass and saw a tired, cynical failure who the Lucy of then would not have looked at twice. Something had left him, something was lost, and he hadn't a clue what it was, or how to get it back. The self-pity made him nauseous, but there was no denying it – all was lost and it was now time to flee.

He looked up at the sky, at the dim pinpricks of stars over the ocean, and wondered what direction the helicopter would approach from in the morning.

With Ryan and the rest of the gang *en route* to the hotel to await further instructions, Lucy had the cab-driver drop by Phillipa's place first. She was there, smartly dressed in her work clothes, and assaulted Lucy with questions on the way to the car.

'I've been trying to get you for days!' she exclaimed. 'Where the hell have you been? It's Don, isn't it? I've seen the papers.'

'I'll tell you all about it later. Just help me do this first,' Lucy replied, but she was aware of a change between them – her friend was looking at her differently, with an admiration she'd never noticed before.

The drive to Fulham was mercifully swift. Lucy left a fifty-pound note with the driver along with the promise of another if he was still waiting in half an hour.

'Lucy, please, what the fuck is happening?' asked Phillipa as she followed Lucy out of the cab.

Lucy had remained tight-lipped on the short journey. Conversation seemed difficult – there was so much to think about, so much to plan.

'I just want to get some bits and pieces, and there's a little bit of business I have to attend to,' said Lucy 'but I might need your help.'

'This is all brilliantly mysterious.' Phillipa frowned. 'Is it some sort of a game?'

Lucy smiled. 'Yes, I suppose it is.'

The apartment was pretty much as she'd left it on that last night with him, but now she knew that she could smell other women in the place, that it had never ever been just a suspicion. She could imagine them sprawled over the sofa, kneeling on the carpet – the carpet she had picked. Phillipa watched, arms crossed, frowning as Lucy knelt in front of the fireplace and lowered her head to the thick black marble support of the right-hand base.

'Lucy, dear, are you feeling all right?' Phillipa asked, but Lucy answered only with a beckoning hand.

'Look, down there,' Lucy commanded, and Phillipa also had to kneel to see what Lucy was on about.

A tiny, cleanly drilled hole in the stone was what Lucy had been looking for, and found. It had taken a while to work out, from Don's footage, exactly where he had placed the cameras, but this one was the most obvious.

'I'll show you what it's for sometime,' said Lucy, 'and on the subject of which, what have you got in that bag?'

Phillipa meekly handed over the bulging carrier holding the costumes.

It didn't take long for Lucy to select a tight pencil skirt. She had heels that would match, and Phillipa had a brand-new pair of stockings with her. Phillipa waited as Lucy changed, flounced her hair and applied some make-up.

'I've learned a trick or two in the past few days,' Lucy said, and Phillipa, eyes wide, nodded, 'and now, if you don't mind, I'd like to put some of them into practice with one of the neighbours. Fancy keeping an eye out for me?'

Phillipa, dumbfounded, could only follow as Lucy led her to the elevator. They descended but one floor, and when Lucy emerged, she was breathing heavily, standing tall in the heels, her pupils dilated. She looked ready to fight.

The door was answered almost immediately by a tall, thin girl wearing a bra and a thick towel about her waist. She had obviously just showered, and was expecting someone else.

'Sorry to disturb you dear,' asked Lucy sarcastically, 'is Kelly in?'

'No, eh, she's down in the laundry room. Want to wait for her?' the girl asked pleasantly.

Lucy smiled.

'No, it's all right. I'll see her down there. We're just leaving anyway.'

Two minutes later, Phillipa was guarding the door in the basement corridor as Lucy slowly pushed it open. The girl had just started loading one of the large dryers which were arranged along the far wall of the low-ceilinged, dim, dank room, and Lucy's entrance clearly alarmed her.

'Jesus, you gave me a fright,' Kelly said.

'So sorry. Kelly isn't it?' said Lucy, and she was aware of a slight tremble in her voice as the girl nodded, arms crossed, seemingly more intent on chewing her gum than engaging in any conversation.

Lucy mentally checked herself. She felt good, strong, clean and ready to do some nasty work on this bitch. No qualms. No wobbles, tremors or nerves. It had to be completely and utterly convincing, or else nothing.

'Kelly?' said Lucy as she stepped closer.

'Yeah?' responded the girl, crouching, loading her clothes into the open porthole of the tall machine.

'I believe you owe me an apology,' said Lucy.

Kelly stood up and frowned, then smiled, intrigued. Lucy swiftly scanned her. Shorter than her, but not by much, strong legs under the micro-skirt, shapely but powerful, broadish hips complemented by a tight narrow waist and quite exceptionally attractive breasts, beautifully arranged beneath the thin, pink, woollen, short-sleeved sweater. And Lucy could see now what Don saw in her: sure, she had the pigtails and the blue teddy clasps holding the strawberry-blonde locks together, the glittery girlie eye-shadow and the luscious pink lip gloss, but there was a defiance about her eyes and jutting chin which seemed to arouse something male in Lucy. She could see how this one would be trouble back in boarding school, and she might very well be trouble here. But Phillipa was outside the door, and would be delighted to help placate this lovely little thing if need be.

'It's as well we meet now. Get this over with. I was actually going to make a point of seeing you somewhere dark and quiet, but this is just as good,' Lucy said, and the voice now was firm, direct. By the shift in the girl's expression Lucy could tell that the authoritative tone had registered.

'Yeah?' Kelly replied, and her chin seemed to raise as she resumed chewing languidly on the gum.

Lucy looked down at her skirt, smoothed a speck of fluff off her hip, then took a couple of steps nearer the girl.

'Yeah,' said Lucy with a similarly sarcastic tone, 'the thing is, I want a little bit more than an apology.'

'Yeah? Well you can't always get what you want,' replied the girl almost immediately, and with a ring of confidence that made Lucy cringe. This wasn't going to be easy.

Lucy stepped forward another couple of paces. Kelly had her hands on her hips, her head tilted in insolent challenge.

Lucy was no more than five feet from the girl now, and she could feel herself blanche. No need to act now. Her anger had suddenly become very real, and the sparkle of defiance in the girl's eyes seemed to intensify the rage.

'What age are you?' Lucy asked.

The girl didn't answer but, still chewing her gum, looked at Lucy's shoes, her ankles, her legs, and carried the stare up until she once again met her eyes. And then, to Lucy's astonishment, the girl stopped chewing, parted her lips, and, with eyes fully focussed on Lucy's, ran the tip of her gum-reddened tongue along the rim of her upper lip, before blowing a small gum bubble.

'Old enough,' she said.

Lucy swallowed in an effort to contain the growing anger and excitement. Perhaps Phillipa was watching, perhaps not. It didn't matter any more.

'I know you're nineteen,' said Lucy.

Lucy was aware that her tone was certainly strict, perhaps an undercurrent of genuine anger in there too, but she wasn't prepared for the apparent submission which followed.

'I won't be naughty any more, Miss,' said Kelly, glancing down at Lucy's chest, then further down, at the floor between them, but there was a suggestion of a smirk about the glazed pink lips which bolstered Lucy's anger.

Lucy felt strangely removed from herself. It all seemed to slow and mute, like some freeze-frame of someone else's memory. The dull whirr and thump of the lone tumble dryer in the background seemed to pulse and drum in tandem with Lucy's heartbeat as she quickly stepped forward, raised her hand and lightly grasped one of Kelly's pigtails. The girl inhaled sharply and raised her face, but her eyes were now shut and any hint of a smirk had definitely gone, replaced with static fear. And even Lucy's voice seemed to be coming from someone else, such was the note of menace as she tightened her grip, drew the girl's face closer to hers, and whispered.

'You're fucking right you won't be naughty. I'll make sure of it.' Lucy traced a finger down the girl's smooth cheek as the words emerged through clenched teeth.

'Please Miss, I promise,' Kelly whimpered, and Lucy could feel the tremble in the girl's voice vibrating throughout her whole body.

And their bodies were closer now, as Lucy, still grasping the tight blonde pigtail, drew her other hand down the girl's neck, then lightly but slowly over the fine thin wool which concealed her torso. Lucy could feel the edging of the girl's bra through the wool, and the sudden cramps between her legs made the seduction inevitable.

'I'm going to spank you,' said Lucy, and now it was her turn to suppress the smile, because Kelly was well and truly scared, and her eyes popped open in disbelief, pupils wide and staring, mouth open.

Lucy stood back, let go of Kelly's hair, turned her shoulder and shoved her towards the humming dryer.

'Bend over it,' she commanded.

The girl whirled, anger overriding her fear.

'Who the hell do you think you're –' she protested, but the slap stopped her mid-flow.

It was a loud slap, precise and hard and undoubtedly painful. Kelly raised a palm to the reddening cheek, her eyes already filling.

'I'm the wife of the upstairs neighbour you've been fucking, that's who I am,' said Lucy, pointing at the dryer. 'Now get yourself bent over that fucking machine and stand still.'

There was just a fraction of a second, the smallest imaginable space where it might have fallen apart, when the girl stared into Lucy's eyes with potent rage, but in that moment, shared, the excitement tripped over from the possible to the actual, and Lucy detected an audible gasp of resignation and surrender as Kelly turned, sniffed pathetically a couple of times, then stepped over to the vibrating box and placed a trembling hand on each corner.

The dull tap of Lucy's heels on the thick linoleum as she slowly stepped nearer the girl was strangely sinister, as if holding the tangible promise of punishment. Lucy scanned the girl from her canvas sneakers up. The shortness of the skirt, the creaminess of her skin, the firm pertness of the prominent, full buttocks, the arch of her neck and the slightly careless pigtails, the sheer girliness of her, made Lucy want to tear off her own staid, womanly suit and blouse, to release her own locks from the restricting clasps, and feel like Kelly looked now; like a young girl.

'You know why I'm doing this, don't you?' said Lucy as she placed her hand on the small of Kelly's back, rubbing gently as if the punishment had already been administered.

'Because . . . because I've been bad,' replied Kelly in a broken, barely audible sniffle.

'Yes, you have been. Tell me what you did,' said Lucy as she allowed her hand to slide a little further down on to the girl's skirt where the coccyx could be felt moving ever so slightly up and down because of, or perhaps in accompaniment to, the insistently throbbing dryer.

'Please Miss, I can't,' cried Kelly, her head bowing, her whole body racked with juddering sobs.

'I won't ask you again,' hissed Lucy, her left fist reclaiming the pigtail as her other hand swept down to the hemline of the skirt and raised it up easily. A quick twist and the hem was safely tucked into the waistband, and Kelly's magnificently tight young arse was free, with only the thin band of white cotton keeping her sex from view. Lucy placed her open palm on the downy warmth of the plump, tight cheeks, and sized up where to administer the first of the slaps as the confession began.

'Please Miss, it was him. He made me do it,' cried Kelly.

Lucy raised her palm to shoulder height, aimed carefully, and brought it down on the girl's left buttock with an echoing crack which frightened them both.

'That's what they all say!' Lucy shouted as she landed a second, and marginally less alarming, slap on the other cheek.

Kelly writhed, twisting her arse away, but Lucy tightened her fingers about the pigtail, drew the girl closer, and crudely thrust her hand between the girl's legs. Lucy felt herself twinge in sympathy, but some deep, dark part of her quelled the charitable urge, redoubling her determination to make sure the punishment was authentic.

'Wider,' she said quietly, and when Kelly moaned but did not accede, Lucy slipped her palm between the clasped thighs and jerked firmly upwards to feel her index finger instantly coated with liquid warmth. Lucy pulled the taut, smooth thigh towards her and, after a token resistance, Kelly stepped to the side, leaned forward on the dryer and raised her buttocks.

A quick glance down: Lucy could see the wisps of hair, still fair despite their dampness, curling about the band of cotton.

'You were saying?' said Lucy impatiently.

'It was that guy Don. He made me do it,' Kelly cried, and Lucy's curiosity was now also getting aroused as she delivered another cracking slap across Kelly's glowing cheek.

'He made me give him a blow job. I was only trying to get some studying done. He came in asking for a screwdriver or something, then I asked him if he wanted a coffee and he stayed for a while. I didn't start it. It was him. He asked me to go upstairs with him but I said no. He told me, told me straight out he wanted to screw me but I told him I was on my period so he just took it out and told me to do it. I was scared he might get angry if I didn't. It was horrible,' wailed the wretched Kelly.

'Did he come in your mouth?' asked Lucy.

The girl remained silent. Another crack across the right cheek. Kelly, for the first time, squealed with pain, and Lucy could see the girl's knuckles whitening on the corners of the dryer, her arms shaking as the machine spun faster.

Lucy glanced at Kelly's cheeks, now glowing scarlet, and with actual fingermarks visible on the tender arse flesh. She brought a third blow down on the left cheek which made Kelly drop her head on to the dryer's surface and release a short, sharp scream. Lucy knew she was hitting the mark now.

'Yeah, he did. And all over my best top too,' said Kelly, but Lucy could hear now the desire in the girl's voice as she brought her hands from the front corners of the machine and grasped on to those at the rear of the juddering white box. The spin intensified.

'And you loved that cock, didn't you?' said Lucy.

With both hands now free, and with Kelly so obviously in pursuit of a come, Lucy concentrated on the girl's pussy.

'It was all right, Miss. I've seen bigger ones, but it's dead thick,' said Kelly, and she started to jerk her buttocks up more obviously now to meet Lucy's flicking fingertips.

'Keep talking. Don't stop until I tell you,' said Lucy as she grasped the panties tightly upwards into a narrow, thicker band, and slowly worked the wet material across Kelly's now visibly pouting pussy lips.

'I was sitting down, so he just sort of stood in front of me and pulled his zip down,' said Kelly, as if under hypnosis, 'and he started pulling it out but he was getting too excited so I did it for him, and I just sort of rubbed it for a bit and he was asking me if I'd done it before and all that but I said no, like making out I was little Miss Innocent, then he got really hard so I started licking it underneath.'

Kelly stopped and released a series of loud gasps as Lucy eased the material away from her cleft, the better to flick at the girl's swelling clitoris with her middle finger.

A thick creaminess coated Kelly's swollen lips, and Lucy smoothed the liquid over the peak of the girl's mound, now bucking urgently upwards in search of Lucy's fingers, crying out for entry.

'I told you not to stop, bitch! Keep talking!' Lucy snarled, and the girl was sobbing, but she breathed in deeply and continued her narrative as Lucy intensified the massage of the hardening bud.

'He was rubbing his cock all over my face, trying to put his balls in my mouth, but he's ever so hairy, so I just rubbed him, put the end in my mouth and did it faster and faster until he came. That was it Miss, honest . . . ah!' Kelly screamed into her arm as the spin on the machine reached the peak of its cycle just as Lucy slipped two fingers fully into Kelly's tight pussy, her thumb arched over the little arsehole.

'Did you like it?' demanded Lucy as she held the girl's back down with her left and finger-fucked with her right, 'Did you?'

'I fucking loved it, Miss, yeah, I . . .' Kelly released a cry which became a juddering moan, her whole body vibrating and quivering as the orgasm ripped through her from toe to pigtail, Lucy's fingers hammering harder into her as she peaked.

Lucy drew her hand away from between the girl's spasming buttocks and kneaded the reddened flesh with her moistened fingers, savouring the tightness, the smoothness of Kelly's juice about her fingers. The girl was spent, back heaving up and down as she remained slumped over the machine.

Kelly, face still semi-buried in her own arm, released a satisfied whine. Lucy pulled the hem of the skirt from the waistband and flicked it back down to cover the girl's exposure, but as she did so she cupped a hand about Kelly's face and felt the heat from the girl's cheek as she detailed the next stage of the punishment.

'Seems like you enjoyed that,' Lucy said menacingly, but Kelly's low groans suggested that she wasn't taking the prospect of further humiliation too seriously. 'Thing is dear, you're not meant to enjoy it. It's time you realised I mean business with you.'

Lucy moved behind the girl, her own crotch already jerking slowly as her hips neared the raised and still parted buttocks, now sheathed once more beneath the thin flannel skirt. Once again, the sound of Lucy's heels on the floor signalled intent, and Lucy was pleased to hear Kelly's breathing stop in anticipation.

The older woman smoothed both palms over the chastised buttocks, eliciting a further whimper from the sniffing girl, then cupped along the curve of her hips, the narrow part of her waist, lingering at the waistband where the material of the thin cardigan had parted to allow a delicious glimpse of the tanned flesh beneath. Lucy stepped closer again and, despite the restriction imposed by her rather tight skirt, she was now close enough to be able to force her crotch against the cleft of Kelly's arse while simultaneously leaning forward and seeking the girl's breasts with her hands.

Instinctively, Kelly raised herself to allow Lucy access, and also raised her head as if expecting a mouth upon her neck. But it didn't come. Instead, Lucy quickly located the full, heaving breasts, cupped them gently in both hands, and delicately traced their fullness within the brassiere as she gingerly nibbled the upper rim of the girl's ear.

Lucy couldn't believe that she was doing this. It was as if she had parted company with herself and had adopted a completely new persona. The thoughts, the impulses, had to be coming from somewhere else. This wasn't her. Perhaps it was the possibility that she was being watched that had inspired such madness, but she was so far gone now she might as well carry on with it. And whether she wanted to admit it or not, there was a part of her that was

211

certainly enjoying this. More than enjoyment perhaps – a part of her that needed this, wanted it, and could actually manage to make it happen. The thought, fleeting as it was, was enough to terrify Lucy, but the need was greater and overrode the fear. She concentrated on enjoying the full firmess of the fantastic breasts in her hands. She would have these at her leisure. But the nagging pulse between her own legs was more deserving of attention right now, and Lucy could think of no better way of relieving herself than to have this wretched beauty make it happen.

Lucy held Kelly's breasts high within the cups of her bra, moved her body down and closer, and tried to imagine herself now a man. She started slowly, clenching the breasts hard, pushing herself up on to the tips of her toes so that her crotch was aiming at Kelly's arse, but as she quickened her thrusts, taking Kelly's ear fully between her lips and teeth as she did so, the urge to buck and bite started to rise, so she drew her arms from beneath the girl, straightened, and with the pumping action uninterrupted, cupped her fingers about the girl's hip bones to gain a better grip on the object of her thrusts.

Kelly jerked and bucked in response, obviously eager to please now that she knew Lucy was serious about this chastisement, but Lucy knew that the action, frantic and pleasurable as it was, would never achieve anything more than a heightening of her already maddening frustration. She stepped back, put her hands on her hips, and commanded Kelly to turn around.

'On your knees,' commanded Lucy, and the voice coming from her now was low and deep and dangerous. Kelly glanced up, eyes aflame with fear and desire, and Lucy sensed that the girl knew what was coming next.

'Please Miss, I've never, I mean ...' Kelly gushed, attempting a pathetic sob, but the flush on her cheeks betrayed the true cause of her cries, and Lucy gently drew her fingertips along the girl's trembling cheek and lips before snaking her fingers into the fine blonde hair and suddenly clenching her fist with a ferocity which made the girl wince with genuine shock.

'You've never what exactly?' smiled Lucy as she twisted her fist, forcing Kelly's face upwards, the dim basement light reflected on the lightly perspiring brow. But the girl could not answer, her eyes shut, her lips pursed as if containing some dreadful secret.

'You've never licked a woman before? Is that it?' Lucy asked, gentler now, and if she hadn't had the girl's hair in her hands she wouldn't have noticed the slightest of nods.

'Well, my dear,' whispered Lucy, her face closer now as she released her grip and drew the girl towards her, 'there's a first time for everything, isn't there?'

Lucy released the girl's hair from her grasp, moved around the frozen figure, and leaned her bottom against the gently throbbing machine, now tumbling in a slow, rhythmic beat which seemed to echo Lucy's own heart; steady, strong, almost audible.

The tiniest of creaks from across the room confirmed what Lucy suspected – Phillipa was peeking through the door, her curiosity getting the better of her. But it didn't matter who might be watching now. Lucy knew she was going to do this, and not for effect. She wanted it. She wanted to feel the dominance she'd felt in Japan, wanted to taste the submission of another completely, and now was the chance. If anything, the knowledge that Phillipa was witnessing the assault was further reason to do it properly.

Kelly moved, as if awakening from a coma, unsure what to do, where to go. She lowered her head, moved in front of Lucy, and clasped her trembling hands at her chest.

Lucy cupped a corner of the machine in each hand, moved her feet apart several inches and, once again, it was the soft click of her heels on the thick linoleum which seemed to act as a signal, a warning shot. Kelly glanced up, catching Lucy's steady gaze for just an instant, but long enough for Lucy to know that further orders were required. She took in a deep, slow breath, and adopted a lighter, matter-of-fact tone, as a teacher might in the classroom.

'You are going to get down on your knees and pleasure me. I don't care that you haven't done it before, and

213

believe me young lady, if you don't do it properly, you will get the thrashing of your life.'

'But please, I don't want to, I can't. Please, I want to go –' Kelly sobbed.

'Well, what was it you said? That's right – you can't always get what you want. Your words, Kelly dear. I know you don't want to do it, but you are going to do it whether you like it or not, and I will not tell you again. Now do it bitch, and do it properly,' Lucy growled.

And then it was happening, so quickly, so damned quickly Lucy could not bring her memory to bear on what was happening. There would be no chance of engaging anything so rational, so logical as memory. It was as if time stopped making sense.

Kelly dropped to her knees as commanded, her hands already palming eagerly down Lucy's skirt, cupping her calves, fingertips smoothing across her stockinged ankles as Lucy gripped the machine, arched her head back and let the girl do what she would.

And she had done it before. She had to have done it before. The skirt moved slowly, so terribly slowly up Lucy's legs, tightening as the material gathered about her parted thighs. Kelly's hands were everywhere, now stroking up as far as her stocking-tops, lingering momentarily to savour the delicacy of the embroidered hem; now sinking fingers into the back of her knees as her head moved between her legs. Lucy felt the brief pain of teeth about her arched foot, a tongue flicking at her shins, a sudden lunge with both hands forcing the skirt an inch higher, and another.

Lucy fought the urge to grasp the girl's head and direct it to her sex. Let her do it, let her do it her own way, the way she knows.

And she did. Lucy, eyes closed, was aware of Kelly's breath on her thighs as the girl tried to force her head further. As if acting on a shared knowledge of what had to happen next, Lucy drew her feet together for an instant, and in that very instant Kelly had the skirt up about Lucy's waist. Lucy made a smart side-step to allow the access they both craved and Kelly was there, palms exploring Lucy's bare hips and belly as she sunk her face into the denuded pubis with a ferocious intensity which made Lucy breathless.

There was no delicacy now, no restraint. Lucy moved her bottom away from the machine to allow Kelly's palms to grasp her arse cheeks, and the girl did so instantly, using the tautening globes to better force Lucy's sex against her face.

Lucy moved against the tongue which had now found her inner lips and was probing, searching, fucking her as keenly as any man's cock ever could, and the girl was only leaving the object of her attention to take huge breaths, allowing her longer periods of uninterrupted tongue-fucking as Lucy increased the tempo and strength of her thrusts against the girl's mouth.

Kelly's buried mouth groaned, a deep, almost pained groan which Lucy heard herself accompany as the orgasm sparked and started to grow.

All control gone, and barely managing to hold her balance, Lucy bent forward, and the sight below her made the orgasm irreversible. The blonde wisps framing her reddened, bulging clitoris and labia, the closed sparkly-pink eyes, the button nose bobbing above her pulsing bud. Lucy grabbed Kelly's head with both hands and rode the girl's face as the climax started to peak, and it was then that Kelly magnified her experience by moving her lips up that vital extra inch, covering Lucy's engorged bud with her open mouth and pressing her tongue against it. The spot had been found, and it was then that the grinding, bucking completion of the come arrived, Lucy suppressing the urge to scream as it washed over her, knocking her final balance away and leaving her slumped against the purring tumble-dryer.

When the waves of colour and light had ebbed away, Lucy, drained to a state of almost unbelievable exhaustion, remembered the role she was meant to be playing, and it was with a start that she stood up and pushed her skirt down. But her dishevelment had probably gone unnoticed.

Kelly was flat on her back between Lucy's feet, eyes closed, one finger toying with her reddened mouth and tongue as the other hand teased her own come from her.

Lucy could only watch as Kelly gasped her final ecstasy and then flopped, spent, but when the girl's eyes opened and met hers, it was as if the script had already been written for her, and she knew the part perfectly.

'I hope you've learned your lesson,' Lucy said, with only the faintest quaver in her voice to indicate just how shaken she really was.

'Yes, Miss,' the girl replied, her eyes hazy with submission and spent lust.

Lucy smoothed her skirt, stepped over the prostrate student, and walked smartly to the door without so much as another word or glance, leaving Kelly where she lay.

When she opened the door, there was Phillipa, blouse ruffled, skirt racked, her hand at her pussy, eyes dark with passion.

'She's all yours,' said Lucy quietly, and Phillipa tottered into the room, struggling to compose herself as Kelly looked up, alarmed.

The door closed, Lucy checked her earrings, then leaned against the wall and smiled to herself as the first muffled cries and slaps echoed in the room behind her.

Eleven

Don had tried to explain, even showed her the newspapers, but Julie didn't seem to care.

'I can come and join you later,' she'd said, 'if you want me to.'

He'd almost given in. It would be easy to take advantage of her myopic devotion, but he was trying, for once, to do the right thing, to think of someone before himself.

'You can't just leave,' he'd consoled as she sobbed, 'I've got reasons to leave. I'm running away. You've done nothing wrong, and you've nothing to run away from. You have to go home. I'm sorry I took you here. I should have just left you alone,' he said, fighting back his own tears of regret and guilt.

It was still pitch-black over the sea, but the royal blue above confirmed that dawn was breaking over the mountains behind the hotel, and when the dim throb of an approaching helicopter started to grow clearer, Don stood and donned his overcoat.

'I'll try to stay in touch,' he said, but she had collapsed, weeping, on to the bed, and wouldn't even look at him as he left.

The old man was at his post, still smiling. It was as if he was there permanently, waiting for visitors to enter.

'Up early Mr Whalley,' he said cheerfully.

'I'm actually leaving,' Don replied, and both men looked to the front door as the helicopter's pumping passed directly overhead, then maintained a steady, even beat some distance from the house. It was landing.

'My . . . my wife is staying on,' Don explained as he scribbled a cheque for two thousand, 'and I'd be very grateful if you could forget that we were here, if you know what I mean.'

'Oh yes, that's not a problem Mr Langford, I mean –'

Don's angry glance was pointless – the man simply smiled ever broader as he saw the amount on the cheque.

'Have a safe trip now,' he called out as Don left and headed for the brilliant red flashes coming from the now-landed aircraft.

Don resisted the urge to look back, to see if she was watching his departure. It reminded him of an old film, a black-and-white tear-jerker.

But as he neared the craft, he realised that the man who had emerged was not Martin. He held his coat tight about him and screwed his eyes shut as the fierce blast of the rotor blades threw a whirlwind of grass and dust against him, and when he next managed to focus on the figure waiting at the opened door, it was a man he didn't know.

With his headset on, the straps secured as the pilot brought the helicopter slowly off the ground, it was the other passenger who extended a hand to welcome Don.

'Nice to meet you Mr Langford,' he said, smiling, and Don accepted the firm, short shake.

'Where's Martin?' Don shouted, and had to repeat the question as he arranged the mouthpiece a little nearer.

'It's all right. I've spoken to Martin and he explained everything. It's all arranged,' the man replied, and Don felt relief override the regret as the hotel grew smaller beneath them.

'We haven't met before,' said Don as he scanned the man's face.

'Sorry. I should have introduced myself there. I'm Ryan. Ryan Villiers.'

The name meant nothing, and Don didn't even register the Irish accent. But what he did notice was the scent of women in the craft. He glanced back to the empty seats behind. The helicopter was unusually large. Perhaps it was the only one Martin could secure at such short notice. But there was a definite female scent in the air, and Don savoured it, closing his eyes as the craft tilted slightly, then picked up speed and headed over the sea.

Naomi was freezing, and couldn't wait to get indoors. The directions from Ryan were clear enough, but still she felt confused and disorientated, and the helicopter flight had been terrifying. The girls had remained quiet and pensive throughout the whole trip, but now, as Ken manoeuvred the minibus down the single-track leading towards the hotel, she sensed that they would have the chance to – What was it again? – yes, let off their steam.

The little old man at the reception area of the beautiful old building looked pleasantly shocked when they entered, and seemed delighted that they were friends of Mr Langford.

'It's a surprise party we've arranged,' explained Ken, 'Don's birthday. He always tries to escape, but we always find him in the end.'

The old man laughed as he stared up in awe at the huge black American, 'Aye, he's away up there in the helicopter, said he wouldn't be back. Won't he be the surprised one!'

'Oh yeah,' laughed the huge black man, 'he'll be surprised all right!'

And then the party made its way up to the room where Julie lay crying. The girl shrieked when the door opened and it wasn't Don who appeared. Although she was wearing the towelling robe, she drew the duvet up to her neck as the strange group made its way into the suite.

At first, Naomi thought the girl was Lucy – the physical resemblance was striking: the same hair, the same complexion. This girl was younger than Miss Lucy, but every bit as beautiful.

'What's happening?' the girl asked, her voice trembling.

'Don't worry,' said Ken, 'we're not going to hurt you. You can leave if you want to. We're here to see Don.'

'But he's gone,' the girl said, frowning, 'he's gone to Ireland.'

'Correction,' said the little dark-haired girl who stood by the massive black man, 'he thinks he's going to Ireland.'

* * *

Don had protested when he realised the aircraft was tracing a huge circle, but the gun being held by the Irishman had forced him to moderate his tone. He tried simple questions, hoping for some clue as to what was happening, but the man was resolutely tight-lipped.

Perhaps they were terrorists, and this was the kidnap Don had always feared, but on top of everything else that had happened lately it seemed unlikely. They'd probably been sent by Dad, or possibly Major Bowden. Whoever they were, they clearly intended to prevent Don leaving the country, and he could only wonder what else they had in store for him as the hotel came into view again, now clearer in the rising sun, and the helicopter made its slow, careful descent to the spot it had occupied only a short while earlier.

The old man laughed uproariously when Don entered the hotel again, this time with Ryan at his back.

'Aye, you thought you were away, and now you're back!' He smiled. 'That's some friends you have there will chase you about the place to have a party!'

Don managed a weak smile as he made his way up the stairs, but when he opened the door of the suite, already trying to form an explanation for Julie, all sense and logic drained from him.

Julie had been gagged, tied to the bed, and was being fucked slowly with a dildo by an oriental girl wearing a white nurse's outfit.

Ryan prodded Don to enter, and then the door was closed. Another woman appeared, this one dressed in what appeared to be a naval uniform, pigtails and white socks, and behind her came a taller woman walking carefully in thigh-high patent leather boots.

It had to be some grotesque hallucination. Had he somehow been drugged? Was he still asleep?

When the bathroom door opened and a gigantic black man walked out, Don felt his guts melt – it was a nightmare.

'You must be Don,' said the giant, and Don could only nod dumbly.

There was a girl behind the man, a small dark-haired girl, beautiful but very angry, and it was she who approached Don swiftly, bringing her fist into his midriff with shocking power. Don slumped to the carpet, winded.

'Georgie here got fucked up the arse,' said the man as he walked around Don, 'and she didn't like it, Mister, didn't like it one bit.'

Don looked up. The mattress was heaving up and down. He couldn't see what was happening, but the Schoolgirl was perched at the bedside and was leaning across, pushing at something as Julie's muffled shrieks quickened.

'This man here got fucked in the arse,' said the black man, and Don glanced up to see that he was pointing to Ryan. The gun was nowhere to be seen, and Ryan was undressing.

'In fact, I'd say that just about everybody in this room has been arse-fucked. How about you, Mister?' the man asked, smiling.

There was a gap in the man's front teeth, and Don shivered to think that it may have been lost in a fight. Who in their right mind would take on someone that size?

But a question had been asked, and Don couldn't answer it. He couldn't frame a single sentence let alone voice one, and the punch to his stomach made anything but groaning impossible.

'Looks like we got you, Mr Langford,' the man continued, now behind Don, and when the hands slipped under his armpits and started to raise him from the ground, he instinctively ducked his head and tensed every muscle in readiness for the next blow, this time from Ryan.

'We got you good and proper, and we're going to have some fun with you,' said the Irishman as he brought his open palm across Don's left cheek.

'What do you want?' Don managed to stammer, but he had a feeling that cash was not the motive for these people.

'What do we want?' repeated the small brunette. 'We want some payback. That's what we want.'

And then they stripped Don, tearing at his clothes, ripping the arms off the coat, ravaging the shirt off his

221

back. He closed his eyes and felt the fear solidify him. They were going to kill him, no doubt about it. He could hear it in their voices, see it in their eyes. And he could smell it in the air about him. He was about to die.

Naomi directed the girls carefully, and although they were tired after the journey, they seemed glad to exercise their skills, to have some familiar work to do in this strange new place.

So they'd bound Don tightly, the ropework intricate but utterly secure. Elbows were bound to knees, his backside fully exposed. He'd resisted at first, but Ryan had persuaded him not to. They'd placed him in the shower and used the cold water to cleanse him. He'd whimpered and moaned, but Naomi had kept him at a pitch of awareness with the lash as the girls inserted the tube into his behind and poured the first of a half-dozen jugs of iced water into the funnel. He would be clean for the black man, and the rest of them.

The girl who looked like Lucy had also been cleaned and groomed by the Schoolgirl and Mistress, and she was huddled in the corner by the window, shaking, as Don was brought in by Ryan and Ken. They threw him, still trussed, on his back on top of the bed and turned their attentions to her as the girls tortured Don.

Ryan took Julie first, from behind as she crouched on all fours, and she needed no persuasion to give oral attention to Ken as he reclined in the old-style wicker chair.

The Nurse smothered Don with her pussy. He was already suffocating beneath a thick leather hood that the girls had applied, but that wasn't fearful enough – he had to be brought to the edge, and as the Mistress used the strap-on to ream him, Naomi could detect the fear in the tension of his bound limbs.

The shrieks from the corner confirmed that Ken had entered the Lucy lookalike, and Naomi moved across to use her lash on the girl's back as the man worked his hugeness in and out of her pussy, preparing himself for Don.

But Ryan took him first, and it was a brutal fucking which elicited panicky cries from inside the hood.

'Bastard!' cried Ryan as he came, and he had barely withdrawn from Don before the Mistress took his place, her favoured black tool secure and greased.

Lucy breathed in deeply. She was wide awake now, as awake as she had ever been. Naomi and the girls would surely have followed the instructions to the letter, and the time had come to face the truth – he would have to answer correctly, first time, or it was over.

Phillipa placed a calming palm on Lucy's arm.

'You look great, dear,' she said as Lucy zipped up the catsuit which was just a little tight for her. 'He won't ever guess it's you.'

The mouthpiece and eye-slits were the only openings in the tight latex suit apart from a coin-sized hole at Lucy's right nipple. She'd coated the sensitive bud with the same gel the girls had used on her in Osaka, and it had already hardened into a cool, rubbery skin.

The knock on the door made Lucy jump. Phillipa opened it to let Naomi enter. The Japanese girl looked flushed, her red gloves gleaming with oil, and she was slightly out of breath.

'He is ready, Miss Lucy,' said the girl, and Lucy nodded before clapping her sheathed hands lightly together.

'He has no idea I'm here?' Lucy asked, and Naomi nodded.

'He knows nothing about anything,' confirmed the girl. 'He is so terrified, maybe he cannot think any more.'

'Fine. Let's do it then,' said Lucy, and Naomi led the way.

Lucy's pussy spasmed when she saw Ken again, his taut buttocks bucking in between her husband's thighs as the girls urged him on, screaming at him to go faster, fuck harder.

If there was any pity, Lucy managed to quell it. Phillipa advanced, as directed, and lowered her head to where the Nurse was still squatting on the hooded face.

The uniformed girl moved aside to let Phillipa speak, and joined her colleagues, slapping Don's raised and open arse as Ken deepened his strokes at the behest of his fiancée.

'Can you hear me?' asked Phillipa, and the hood nodded in tandem with the pained sobs within.

'I'm going to kill you, Don,' Phillipa said then, and her tone was low and calm, 'I'm going to kill you for what you've done. You deserve nothing less. But you can have one last call. You can speak to one last person. Who will it be?'

Phillipa backed off and Lucy took her place. He had to do it now, or it was all over. Of course, they wouldn't kill him, but he didn't know that. The fear had to be as complete, as intense as they could make it, and with Ken now starting to grunt as Naomi pulled on his testicles, the fear was bolstered with pain.

Don said something, but it was inaudible. Lucy's ears were sheathed in rubber, his mouth was full of leather. Lucy directed the Nurse to remove the hood. Don's face was as Lucy had never seen it; contorted so fiercely that he looked like someone else, coated with his own saliva and tears.

Lucy unbuckled the strap which held the leather gag between his teeth, and Don barely had the strength to push it from his mouth. The girls had blindfolded him beneath the hood. It had shifted as the hood was removed, but his eyes were closed tightly anyway.

'One call only,' shouted Phillipa as Ken finished, emptying himself into Don in a series of buttock-bruising thrusts.

'Lucy!' screamed Don once, and then again as Ken withdrew himself, to leave Don's arse red and gaping.

Lucy leaned forward and carefully placed her exposed nipple at Don's lips. He seemed not to notice the flesh at first. Then, as the girls moved away, his lips closed gently about the strawberry-scented nipple.

'Have you learned your lesson, you dirty bastard?' Lucy asked. She removed her hood and watched, smiling, as his eyes slowly opened.

'Well?' Lucy said then, but he was frowning, his eyes scanning her features slowly, uncertainly, as if he was experiencing a vision. And then, as she straightened herself to let him see her fully, she saw the recognition and relief wash over him in the brief moments before he passed out.

Epilogue

Minami scanned the garden. The leaves had dropped from the trees and the shrubs were shrinking, preparing for the cold. She scattered the last of the breadcrumbs on the water and watched the fish speed up in excitement.

The girls had enjoyed their little trip to Europe, and had talked of little else since they returned. And now that the business with the foreigners had been concluded, the visions had stopped. Minami could still remember the name of the girl, but the face had already started to pale and fade.

Only one face remained clear and strong. It was the face of an older man, also a foreigner. His face was thin, his eyes grey. Minami knew why she was still seeing the face so clearly. She took the little green bottle from her pocket and stared at the drying finger inside.

The man was sad, wherever he was. He had lost his love forever, and Minami suspected that it was Loo-see who had been lost to him. But no matter – the business was over. As usual, some people had found happiness, sorted out some problems, but others had found sadness and regret. It was always the same, and always would be.

She clasped the phial in her palm and closed her eyes as she gently tossed it into the pool. When she opened her eyes, the ripples had been lost in the swirling of the fish, but she caught a last glance of sparkling green as the little bottle sank to the bed of the pool, shifting and settling before finally finding its place among all the others.

NEW BOOKS

Coming up from Nexus, Sapphire and Black Lace

Tight White Cotton by Penny Birch
October 2000   Price £5.99   ISBN 0 352 33537 8
Thirteen girls relate their experiences with the depraved spanking fanatic Percy Ottershaw, from his headmaster's daughter to Penny herself. From 1950 to 2000, his life has been dedicated to getting his girlfriends across his knee, pulling down their tight white cotton knickers and spanking their bare bottoms. Otherwise, he is polite, considerate, and always willing to indulge the girls' fantasies – from wetting their knickers in the street to being tarred and feathered.

Peeping at Pamela by Yolanda Celbridge
October 2000   Price £5.99   ISBN 0 352 33538 6
When four cheeky girls are recruited to live, rent-free, in a large house near Cambridge, it doesn't take them long to realise that their benefactor has more in mind than their welfare. Every room in the house is filled with hidden video cameras, which are all linked up to a number of voyeur websites. They also realise that their weekly stipend varies according to how much spanking they receive – which leads to increasingly exhibitionist behaviour. By the author of *The Discipline of Nurse Riding*.

Lingering Lessons by Sarah Veitch
October 2000   Price £5.99   ISBN 0 352 33539 4
When Leanne Dell inherits a former boarding school, now an advertising agency, part of the deal is that she has to share it with an unknown partner. Arriving at the grand house, she finds herself a voyeur to a scene of bizarre chastisement. Her co-partner, Adam Howard, is administering a sound spanking to his pretty young assistant. In the weeks that follow, Leanne learns some lessons of her own; that her handsome new partner in business is a devotee of corporal punishment, and that arousal and shame are two sides of the same coin.

BLACK *lace*

Lured by Lust by Tania Picarda
October 2000   Price £5.99   ISBN 0 352 33533 5

Clara Fox works at an exclusive art gallery. One day she gets an email from someone calling himself Mr X, and very soon she's exploring the dark side of her sexuality with this enigmatic stranger. The attraction of bondage, fetish clothes and SM is becoming stronger with each communication, and Clara is encouraged to act out adventurous sex games. But can she juggle her secret involvement with Mr X along with her other, increasingly intense, relationships?

On the Edge by Laura Hamilton
October 2000   Price £5.99   ISBN 0 352 33534 3

Julie Gibson lands a job a a crime reporter for a newspaper. The English seaside town to which she's been assigned has seen better days, but she finds plenty of action hanging out with the macho cops at the local police station. She starts dating a detective inspector, but cannot resist the rough charms of biker Johnny Drew when she's asked to investigate the murder of his friend. Trying to juggle hot sex action with two very different but dominant men means things get wild and dangerous.

Learning to Love it by Alison Tyler
November 2000   Price £5.99   ISBN 0 352 33535 1

Art historian Lissa and doctor Colin meet at the Frankfurt Book Fair, where they are both promoting their latest books. At the fair, and then through Europe, the two lovers embark on an exploration of their sexual fantasies, playing dirty games of bondage and dressing up. Lissa loves humiliation, and Colin is just the man to provide her with the pleasure she craves. Unbeknown to Lissa, their meeting was not accidental, but planned ahead by a mysterious patron of the erotic arts.

The Hottest Place by Tabitha Flyte
November 2000   Price £5.99   ISBN 0 352 33536 X
Abigail is having a great time relaxing on a hot and steamy tropical island in Thailand. She tries to stay faithful to her boyfriend back in England, but it isn't easy when a variety of attractive, fun-loving young people want to get into her pants. When Abby's boyfriend, Roger, finds out what's going on, he's on the first plane over there, determined to dish out some punishment. And that's when the fun really starts hotting up.

NEXUS BACKLIST

All books are priced £5.99 unless another price is given. If a date is supplied, the book in question will not be available until that month in 2000.

CONTEMPORARY EROTICA

THE BLACK MASQUE	Lisette Ashton	
THE BLACK WIDOW	Lisette Ashton	
THE BOND	Lindsay Gordon	
BRAT	Penny Birch	
BROUGHT TO HEEL	Arabella Knight	July
DANCE OF SUBMISSION	Lisette Ashton	
DISCIPLES OF SHAME	Stephanie Calvin	
DISCIPLINE OF THE PRIVATE HOUSE	Esme Ombreux	
DISCIPLINED SKIN	Wendy Swanscombe	Nov
DISPLAYS OF EXPERIENCE	Lucy Golden	
AN EDUCATION IN THE PRIVATE HOUSE	Esme Ombreux	Aug
EMMA'S SECRET DOMINATION	Hilary James	
GISELLE	Jean Aveline	
GROOMING LUCY	Yvonne Marshall	Sept
HEART OF DESIRE	Maria del Rey	
HOUSE RULES	G.C. Scott	
IN FOR A PENNY	Penny Birch	
LESSONS OF OBEDIENCE	Lucy Golden	Dec
ONE WEEK IN THE PRIVATE HOUSE	Esme Ombreux	
THE ORDER	Nadine Somers	
THE PALACE OF EROS	Delver Maddingley	
PEEPING AT PAMELA	Yolanda Celbridge	Oct
PLAYTHING	Penny Birch	

SAMPLERS & COLLECTIONS

NEW EROTICA 3		
NEW EROTICA 5		Nov
A DOZEN STROKES	Various	

NEXUS CLASSICS

A new imprint dedicated to putting the finest works of erotic fiction back in print

AGONY AUNT	G. C. Scott	
THE HANDMAIDENS	Aran Ashe	
OBSESSION	Maria del Rey	
HIS MISTRESS'S VOICE	G.C. Scott	
CITADEL OF SERVITUDE	Aran Ashe	
BOUND TO SERVE	Amanda Ware	
SISTERHOOD OF THE INSTITUTE	Maria del Rey	
A MATTER OF POSSESSION	G.C. Scott	
THE PLEASURE PRINCIPLE	Maria del Rey	
CONDUCT UNBECOMING	Arabella Knight	
CANDY IN CAPTIVITY	Arabella Knight	
THE SLAVE OF LIDIR	Aran Ashe	
THE DUNGEONS OF LIDIR	Aran Ashe	
SERVING TIME	Sarah Veitch	July
THE TRAINING GROUNDS	Sarah Veitch	Aug
DIFFERENT STROKES	Sarah Veitch	Sept
LINGERING LESSONS	Sarah Veitch	Oct
EDEN UNVEILED	Maria del Rey	Nov
UNDERWORLD	Maria del Rey	Dec

Please send me the books I have ticked above.

Name ....

Address ....

....

....

.... Post code........................

Send to: Cash Sales, Nexus Books, Thames Wharf Studios, Rainville Road, London W6 9HA

US customers: for prices and details of how to order books for delivery by mail, call 1-800-805-1083.

Please enclose a cheque or postal order, made payable to **Nexus Books**, to the value of the books you have ordered plus postage and packing costs as follows:

UK and BFPO – £1.00 for the first book, 50p for the second book and 30p for each subsequent book to a maximum of £3.00;

Overseas (including Republic of Ireland) – £2.00 for the first book, £1.00 for the second book and 50p for each subsequent book.

We accept all major credit cards, including VISA, ACCESS/ MASTERCARD, AMEX, DINERS CLUB, SWITCH, SOLO, and DELTA. Please write your card number and expiry date here:

....

Please allow up to 28 days for delivery.

Signature ....